# DEDICATION

To Tyler, Stacy and Nick...although the road
in your lives may have taken a detour, your
journey continues. Your strength and courage
in the face of adversity has been incredible!
Always stay #tylerstrong.

# ACKNOWLEDGMENTS

With each book I write, I like acknowledge those who've helped in some way. It's a small token of my gratitude.

To Ivette and Dennis, thank you for your medical expertise.

To Karrie P., Mary T., Danielle B. and Elaine D., thank you for beta reading the story. I'm so lucky to have you all!

To the readers who send me messages and stay connected, to the bloggers who share my work, to my fellow authors who offer writing suggestions, thank you! Your words of encouragement mean so much!

To Cassy, Jessica and Juliana, thank you for your creativity and graphic design talent.

To L Woods PR, thank you for getting this book in readers' hands.

To my #roadtrip girls, Kerry and Helene, thank you for being Adam's Girlfriends. Va Pwe!

Most of all, thank you to my husband and kids for once again supporting me. You people are my world!

# FROM
# A
# DISTANCE

# ONE

"**D**O YOU REALLY HAVE TO GO already?" I lower my voice to a seductive whisper, casting a longing gaze up at my husband as my fingers circle the light sprinkling of dark brown and white hair on his chest. With a roguish smile on his handsome face, he sighs then sets his iPhone down on the bedside table and stares pensively down at me.

"Yeah, Tyler qualified for a race so we're heading back down. We don't want to drive through the night. I've got my guys covering everything until I get back in a couple of days. This race is big deal for me and Tyler."

I refrain from rolling my eyes at the mention of his best friend's name.

"Are you sure I can't convince you to stay home this weekend?" I straddle his hips and crawl down the length of his hard body, peeking up through my long lashes when my lips reach their destination. My tongue slides back and forth against the tip of his erection. Opening my mouth, I welcome the feel of him as he hardens and releases a deep groan.

"As much as I would love for you to continue, I really do need to jump in the shower and get the bikes loaded up." He shifts his body and pulls out of my mouth, leaving my lips in the shape of an O and a dumbfounded look on my face. "Be ready for that raincheck when I get back."

I blink rapidly to ward off the tears that threaten to fall while I suppress the sting of rejection once again.

"Besides," he says, sensing my sullen state, "Ty will be here soon."

I mentally curse Tyler Strong's name as I watch my husband stand and reach for his phone then stride across our bedroom into the bathroom. His tight bare ass is the last thing I see before he closes the door.

I hate Tyler Strong.

I hate that he's one of my husband's closest friends. I hate that he lives in an apartment above his motorcycle shop on the other side of town. I hate that he asks my husband to go there all the time to help him fix bikes. I hate that he manipulates my husband to go to these races all the time. I hate that he's an up and coming drag racer whom my husband sponsors financially. I hate that he prefers to sit in his truck and wait for my husband rather than come inside our home and be cordial. I hate the way he looks at me whenever I watch the race from the stands. I hate the way he stares at me with such contempt when I meet my husband at the trailer. I hate that I have to practically shoo away all his "Bike Bitches" who surround and hang around the race team. I hate that he's a man-whore who screws every female who looks his way. And I hate that my husband feels the need to share the details of Tyler's sexcapades with me.

I hate Tyler Strong.

I close the lid on the cooler, walk to the living room window and pull the curtain back slightly, looking out after hearing the obnoxious roar of the diesel truck as it pulls in. I huff, pinch my lips together and shake my head when I see him step out wearing a plain black T-shirt. He pulls off his ball cap and looks around quickly before grabbing the shirt and yanking it over his head. I swallow hard as my eyes scan the length of him from his short hair to his boots and immediately I hate myself for it. There's no denying the fact that Tyler Strong has a gorgeous face and an incredible body to match. His chest is hard, his abs taut. Within seconds, he slips on a black T-shirt with the team's logo and covers his nakedness. Bending down, his dark jeans hug his ass as he opens a side compartment and pulls out a spray bottle and a rag. The ball cap is returned to his head backwards as he runs the white cloth in circles over the large black and orange decal that boasts their team's name. He continues the tedious task as he walks around to the other side. He focuses on the constant circling motion, never once looking up. Stretching to reach the hood, his arms extend to their full length and I can't help but notice how muscular they are.

How strong they are.

"What are you doing?"

I startle and let the curtain go when my husband breezes into the room.

"Nothing," I stutter before asking the question I already know the answer to. "Why doesn't Tyler ever come in?"

"Who the hell knows? Why do you care?"

"I don't! I think it's rude. *He's* rude!"

I ignore the niggling feeling in my stomach I get whenever I think about my husband's best friend and release a quiet, annoyed sigh.

Alex bends down and picks up the cooler I've packed for their trip down south. "Is this all set?"

"Of course it is!" I smile as I walk over and smooth down the cotton of his T-shirt that matches Tyler's.

"We'll be back late Sunday night. I'll try to call you once we get there, but you know I don't have good reception down there." He kisses my forehead softly as I wrap my arms around his waist.

"I don't know why you race in the middle of Hicksville. Do they even have running water there? Don't go falling in love with some toothless trailer park chick!" I tease, knowing that all the country's best drag racers love the southern tracks and most of the women there could be in magazines.

"Funny." He slaps my backside playfully. "You could always come with us and see for yourself."

I scrunch my face in mock disgust, shaking my head adamantly while puckering my lips for a kiss.

"No thanks. You go be big boys and play with your toys. I'll stay here and save lives one patient at a time." He knows I won't go anyway.

Alex steps out of my embrace and heads for the door.

"Hey! Give me a kiss! A good one!"

My husband sighs quietly before lowering his lips to mine and kissing me. I sense a flicker of annoyance when he doesn't slide his tongue in as he usually does. His agitation has become even more pronounced every time they leave for a race.

He doesn't like to lose.

My hands snake around and squeeze his ass. To look at my husband, no one would ever guess he's almost fifteen years older than me. He's tall and handsome with a hint of grey peppered in his dark hair. Between his mesmerizing eyes, that boyish smile and his charm, all my friends at the hospital call him a "silver fox."

"I love you," I sigh.

"What's not to love?" he quips.

With a final and very quick peck to my lips, Alex slips his Aviators over his eyes and slings his backpack over his shoulder. He walks quickly through the front door to where Tyler leans against the chrome bumper, waiting patiently.

"Have fun! Be safe!" I call out my usual mantra.

I find myself back at the window, peering out like a peeping Tom, watching my husband bump shoulders with his protégé as he raises his cell phone to answer a call. Tyler watches Alex talk animatedly to the person on the other end of the line as he climbs into the driver's seat— always needing to exert control. Tyler moves slowly toward the passenger's side, glancing up in my direction.

Our eyes meet.

His bluish- green to my brown. Keeping his eyes on me, he removes his cap, scratches the back of his head and places it back on, pulling the bill low over his eyes. I hate the quick shake of his head and the deep exhale I see. Who the hell does he think he is? He's arrogant and rude. He opens the passenger door and clicks his seatbelt in place. As my husband maneuvers the truck and trailer onto the street, Tyler looks at me with a hard glare and shakes his head. Even from a distance it's obvious he hates me. That's perfectly fine with me because…

I hate Tyler Strong.

# TWO

ROUNDING THE CORNER AS I walk into the nurses' lounge area, I hear the unmistakable cackle of my colleague Odessa, a beautiful Guyanese physician's assistant who calls everyone by their last name and uses humor to hide the fact she simply has no filter. She's one of those people whom you either love or hate. I happen to love her even though she has on more than one occasion told me I look like a Teletubbie in blue scrubs. She says I should wear darker colors to hide the junk in my trunk. I remind her that my husband adores the junk in my trunk.

"Parker, what are you doing here today? she asks with a deep raspy voice then continues, "I thought you had the weekend off."

"I switched my weekends because Alex is racing. He won't be back until Sunday night."

She rolls her eyes, and her face grimaces with a hard scowl.

"When is he going to grow up? Flying down the road on two wheels at one hundred fifty miles an hour is dangerous. It's not like he's a young guy. He needs to act his age."

I laugh. "First of all, one fifty is slow. He usually goes one sixty-five and secondly, he's only forty-four. He's not eighty!"

"Knowing him, he'll want to race wheelchairs when he's in a nursing home."

I carefully pull my leftovers from the microwave and drop the scalding container on the countertop. "Yeah, you're probably right. I don't think he'll ever grow up." I feed myself a scoop of macaroni.

"How's that friend of his? The young one. Tyson? He's hot! If I weren't married, I'd take a spin on his bike."

My eyes slam shut from the combination of hot food burning my tongue and the thought of anyone having sex with Tyler. He's a walking STD who screws any woman, anytime, anywhere.

"His name is Tyler and he's disgusting."

"That's harsh! You really don't like him, do you?"

"Would you like a person who is a bad influence on your husband? Would you like Greg to tell you how he had to disinfect the backseat of the truck because his buddy screwed some random chick? I don't think so!"

"How's your sex life?" She raises a suspicious brow. "Maybe he's living vicariously through Tyson."

"Ew, forget Tyler! *You're* disgusting! My sex life…*our* sex life is just fine. I can't help that I have endometriosis and sex freaking hurts. Believe me, I take care of him in other ways. Just sayin'," I toss in her direction as I leave the room when my pager buzzes.

"I'm just saying you gotta keep your man happy or else he'll stray."

I pop my head back into the room and stick my tongue out.

"Sounds like you're speaking from personal experience."

A plastic fork followed by an empty water bottle flies in my direction as I duck out of the way.

"Code Blue to ICU. Code Blue to ICU."

One would think working the twelve-hour night shift at the hospital would be a quiet one, but no, it isn't. We get all walks of life coming in at ungodly hours of the night. Druggies faking back aches for painkillers, mothers demanding to be seen by a doctor for their child who has been complaining for days of an ear ache, the old woman carrying an oxygen tank around who can't breathe but refuses to give up cigarettes and the barely legal kids who are nearly comatose after drinking themselves into oblivion.

Occasionally we get a few more serious and critical cases. A car accident. Drunk drivers. Heart attacks. Child birth. Broken arms. Battered wife.

Being married to Alex, who runs a successful electrical company, allows me the freedom to work only part-time. Four twelve-hour shifts a month is just enough to keep me busy outside of our home and keeps my nursing skills up to par.

I sleep for most of the morning when I get home from work. After checking my phone countless times in hopes that Alex called, I send him a text and pull on my bathing suit and cover up. I swim a few laps in the pool then relax in the chaise lounge and call my mom.

"Karrie! Hi doll! Long time no talk." She laughs, panting into the phone. It's her usual joke since we talk every day, several times a day. I usually call to ask for the ingredients to one of her recipes.

"Hi Mom!" I reply. "Why are you out of breath?" As soon as the words escape, I cringe. "Oh God! Call me back, Ma."

Her laughter fills my ears. "Stop that! I'm on the elliptical not having sex with your father."

I chuckle quietly as I palm my forehead. With a quick shake of my head, I contemplate the idea that I may have been switched at birth.

"How was work last night?"

"Same as usual. Odessa's back from her trip."

"Oh nice! I'll have to have her and Greg over for dinner soon. They're such a nice couple."

I nod and feel my chest tighten at her unspoken words.

"Do you and Alex want to come over for dinner? Dad is throwing on steaks and I wanted to show you some of the new designs that just came out. I want to play with the colors and schemes a bit more."

I applaud my mother's ability to say Alex's name without contempt or derision. She's never been his biggest fan. Even on my wedding day as she buttoned my beautiful gown, she told me I didn't have to marry him if I wasn't a hundred percent sure. She nodded to her sleek Audi and told me the keys were in the ignition. I assured her that I loved Alex and was happy to become his wife even though he was so many years older.

"Thanks for the offer, but I have to work tonight and Alex is racing this weekend. I can't wait to see what you've come up with. Why don't you email me what you've got?"

"No, that's okay. You know how I feel about email."

I roll my eyes at her conspiracy theories.

"I'll put it on a flash drive."

"Ma, I have like thirty," I chuckle mockingly, "and Alex has some in his office."

I hear the disappointment she fails to suppress while we chat about the few babies she's recently delivered now that she's semi-retired. The hope of delivering her own grandchild has yet to come to fruition.

She sighs quietly. "Alright, sweetheart. Well, if you get lonely in that big house of yours, come on over. Just make sure you call or text first."

I smile as warmth floods my heart. After thirty years of marriage, my parents are still as in love as the day they exchanged their vows. My grandmother didn't need to offer an out to my mom; she had no doubt whatsoever that my mother and father belonged together.

"Love you."

"Love you more." My mom blows a kiss into the phone.

After lounging for several hours, soaking up the sun's rays, I wander over to my vegetable garden, clip some basil and pluck tomatoes to use in my sauce later. Hot and sweaty, I head inside, pour a large glass of lemonade and peruse yesterday's mail. Feeling bored, I text a few of my friends to say hello even though most of them are busy chasing after their children or bringing them to school. Sometimes I miss the single life.

I reach for my phone and swipe immediately when I see Alex's name flash across the screen along with a picture of the two of us. My heart flutters with anticipation of hearing his voice.

I very much miss the man I fell in love with.

"Hey, you sexy beast! How's my husband?" I grin and wait for his reply, calling me his little seductress. It was the nickname he'd given me shortly after we started dating because he claims I seduced him twice without realizing it. I did no such thing. How can you seduce someone who was rushed to the Emergency Department by an ambulance with a bad case of road rash and a badly bruised ego after being sideswiped by an old lady? I can't remember who screamed more— Alex or the old woman. He bellowed that her license should be taken away and she retorted, saying he shouldn't have been driving like a bat out of hell.

"Hello?" I sing-song playfully into the phone once again when I hear the muffled sounds of people's raised voices. "Alex? Hello?" For nearly a minute I listen, trying to decipher the strained conversation until the line goes dead.

I tap his name and call back, but it rings incessantly until his voicemail picks up.

"Hey, babe. I think you pocket-dialed me. Call me back. Love you."

My shift at work begins and ends in the same mundane way. Nothing exciting ever happens around here. When I arrive home early Monday morning, Alex is sound asleep in our bed. I know he's going to be getting up soon for work even though he's probably not gotten much rest over the weekend. Between the hours racing at the track and the eight-hour drive, exhausted is an understatement.

I shower quickly and crawl into bed next to him. His body, kept fit and firm from Crossfit, is spread out, inviting my fingers to touch it. He stirs at my gentle touch.

"Good morning!" I whisper, leaning in and nestling into his neck. I inhale his masculine scent mingled with a hint of cologne. "I missed you." My hand travels lower, trailing lightly along his abdomen.

"Hey, babe. Good morning yourself." He cocks one eye open and then the other. "How was your weekend?" His arms reach upward and cross behind his head as if he's enjoying the feel of my touch.

"Same as always. Odessa's back."

"That's nice."

"How was the race?"

"Awesome! I went pretty fast, but Ty went 6.60 in the quarter mile."

I plaster on a fake smile at the mention of Tyler's name as

I try to give my husband a hand job. I should've waited until he was done rambling on and on about the race and how they're going back down in two weeks because his morning erection wanes in my hand.

"Two weeks?" I shriek, squeezing him hard.

His hand covers mine and pries my curled fingers, wordlessly asking I release him. "Whoa, easy. What's the big deal?"

I jump to my knees, my eyes now huge circles of shock. "You're going racing in two weeks?"

"Yeah, why?"

Throwing my hands up into the air, I yell, "Oh I don't know. Maybe it's just our anniversary or something. No big deal!"

I spring from the bed, stomp into the bathroom and slam the door shut, locking it quickly. I lean over the vanity and stare at myself in the mirror. The woman staring back at me is not happy.

"Open the door, Karrie."

"No!"

"Karrie," he enunciates my name slowly, "I said open the door."

Like a sullen child, I drag my feet and unlock the door. He's standing there naked with his arms outstretched on the door frame. He tips his head to the side and gives me a sympathetic look. "I didn't realize the date."

I exhale a deep sigh of relief and step into his arms. "Thank you."

He kisses the top of my head. "I'll make it up to you when I get back."

"What?" I gasp loudly as my palms flatten against his chest and I shove him away. "You're still going? It's our anniversary for God's sake!"

"Babe, I have to go. Ty's already qualified. People are coming from all over the country for this race. The grand prize is twenty-five thousand."

I stare in disbelief at my husband. Brushing past him, I yank open a drawer and slip on a pair of cotton underwear then trudge over to the closet, pulling on a green sundress sans bra and a pair of sandals. I head back over to the drawer, find a pair of matching blue scrubs and shove them along with black Crocs into my backpack.

"Where are you going? It's seven-thirty in the morning?"

I think quickly and spit out a lie. "I'm meeting my parents for breakfast."

"It's Monday morning. Your parents are at the country club for their early morning tee time," he deadpans as he moves about the room getting dressed for work, pulling on a pair of work pants.

"Well," I stammer as my voice cracks, "I have some errands to run and then I'm meeting them."

Alex strides across the room and wraps his arms around me, pulling me close to his chest. He smooths my long hair back away from my face and searches my eyes.

"What's the matter with you?" he asks as a grin appears. "Are you getting your period? You've been acting like a real bitch lately."

I sniffle and wipe my nose as my lips spread into a small smile at his use of the teasing yet vulgar sentiment. I exhale a deep breath. "No. I just feel like you're never home. I hate that you travel all the time for motorcycle racing. It's a hobby not a job!"

"Come with me then."

I smirk. "You know I don't like going to the track anymore. All I do is stand around all day and watch you go down the track for less than ten seconds. That's not exactly fun."

"Ten seconds?" he quips. "I go way faster than 10-0."

I slap his bare chest. "You know what I mean."

"You should come and meet some of the other girls."

"If by 'girls' you mean 'Bike Bitches', no thanks. I'm all set."

He laughs.

"They're not so bad."

"Whatever." I narrow my eyes at his attempted humor.

"I'll make it up to you. We'll go away for a weekend. Pick an island—any island and we'll go."

"Really? It's been so long since we've had a real vacation."

"I know it. I think the last real one was in the Bahamas when we rented a scooter and drove all around the island." We had just started dating when he surprised me with the trip.

I nod in remembrance.

"And if I remember correctly, it was you who suggested I

get a bike for us to ride on Sunday afternoons."

I nod again, mentally chastising myself for opening that can of worms.

"I've got to get going, but I won't be home too late tonight. I've got to help Ty unload the bikes and change the oil."

"I have a painting class tonight with Pam."

"What's she been up to?"

I detect the change of tone in his voice even though he tries to hide it.

"I don't know." I shrug. "I haven't seen her in a while."

Pam Cooke has been my friend for the longest time and she, like my mother, wasn't convinced I should've married Alex. Not only was she concerned about our age difference, but she didn't like the way he wanted to control my life from what I could wear right down to the friends I should have. I chalked it up to being young and naïve, but I've since reacquainted with most of my friends and wear what I want.

Alex pulls on his work shirt and laces up his boots before answering his ringing phone.

"Good morning," he whispers into the phone before glancing back quickly and smiling tightly. Continuing his quiet conversation, he trots down the stairs and out of the house. I can't imagine why Tyler is calling so early; he'll see him shortly at work.

I hate Tyler Strong.

After meeting my parents for a late breakfast, I drive over to the local clinic where I volunteer a few times a month. It's a sad place in which most people who receive free health care and free medications come. Most of the doctors and nurses are pretty good, but we do get the occasional self-righteous doctor who thinks he's better than everyone else even if he graduated at the bottom of the class. We usually send the patients with really bad hygiene to him.

Turning the knob on the door with one hand as I reach for the medical chart, I walk into the small room, laughing sarcastically at Owen's off-colored attempt at humor. Owen is the resident jerk doctor for the next six months.

I freeze when I notice a small woman sitting on the table with Tyler standing by her side.

"Tyler!" My eyes widen, revealing my surprise and shock. "What are you doing here?" I look at the woman who has red, puffy eyes. A small hiccup escapes from her throat.

"Karrie," he starts nervously, "um…she," he stammers, "she needs to see a doctor."

I clear my throat and pull my gaze away from his bluish-green eyes. I've never really been in this close proximity to him before except for at my wedding reception. I don't understand the emotion running through my veins.

"I see." I glance away as my cheeks flush pink. "So why don't you start by telling me what's going on." I smile kindly at the woman who now has her face buried in her hands.

"She thinks she's pregnant."

My eyes flash in his direction as a scowl spreads across

my face. Of course, Tyler Strong got someone pregnant. How irresponsible!

"I think *she* can answer for *herself*."

He huffs loudly and shakes his head. I lock eyes with him as I wheel the machine over to check her vitals.

"Your chart has your name as Penelope. Do you go by Penny?"

"Yeah, only my granddad and my sister Rachel call me Penelope. I hate it."

"I understand. People always misspell my name and I hate it."

She lifts her arm, allowing me to slide the cuff around her thin bicep. I smile and apologize for my cold hands even though it's ninety degrees out.

"You know what they say, 'Cold hands, warm heart.'"

"You're fine. Thank you." A sweet southern drawl tinges her words. She offers a crooked grin.

"I love your accent! Where are you from?" I ask with a smile after removing the cuff.

"I'm from Kentucky originally, but I moved to Virginia last year."

"Oh wow! My husband races motorcycles down there."

"Can we get a doctor to see her now? She needs a *doctor*," Tyler interjects. His body is rigid as if he wants to be anywhere but here.

I stare at him, noticing that he swallows hard and shakes his head briefly as he shifts his weight from side to side

"Please," he adds.

*I am a nurse. Be professional. Set aside personal feelings.* I repeat the words continuously in my head to calm down.

"Let's have you give me a urine sample. We can do the pregnancy test and then you can see a doctor." I open the cabinet door and take out a plastic cup before looking back at Tyler with malice in my eyes. "That's how we do things around here."

"Thank you." Penny hops down and stands. Her cami is tight around her thin body, her plump boobs displaying ample cleavage. Denim cut off shorts and flip flops make her look as young as a college kid. I remember Alex got so much flack for dating me. His friends liked to tease that I was still in diapers when he was in high school. I guess Tyler likes them young, too.

"The bathroom is around the corner to the right." I hold the door open for her just as Tyler calls my name. I turn slowly to address him.

"What?"

"If she is pregnant, please don't say anything to anyone. Especially not Alex."

I narrow my eyes. "Don't worry Tyler. Your little secret is safe with me."

"What—"

I close the door behind me and wait for Penny. After confirming her pregnancy, I send Owen in to talk to the less than happy couple. From behind the sliding glass window, I sit and watch Tyler wrap his arms around her shoulders and lead her to his truck. Poor girl! If Penny is smart, she'll leave and put as much distance between them as she possibly can.

When my shift ends at the clinic, I send Alex a text, letting him know I'm going to be stopping by his job site. Getting the contract for one hundred twenty-five homes in an assisted living complex was huge and is proving to be quite profitable. He's been so busy, working late into the night and even some weekends. Just to ensure he'd be finished by the anticipated completion date, Alex has even hired a few new electricians.

A.P. Electric is my husband's baby; it's the company he built from the ground up.

I drive slowly over the broken road which has yet to be paved and spot Alex's work truck and two other vans parked haphazardly in the dirt. I squeeze my car into a small space beneath a large tree. Carrying a large, brown paper bag inside a plastic one, I carefully step over the piles of rubble and enter the dwelling through the garage. I follow the sound of music playing.

Tyler, standing on the top rung of a ladder, is the first person I see. His arms reach high above his head as he installs electrical wires in the ceiling. My eyes follow the length of his body from his dexterous fingers down to his tanned neck before lingering on the hem of his T-shirt that is now riding up, showing the hard planes of his abs.

"Karrie!" he calls. "What are you doing here?"

My traitorous eyes snap up to his face and my voice cracks.

"What?"

"What are you doing here?" he asks as he descends the ladder. "Does Alex know you're here?"

I drop my eyes to my painted toenails for a second before speaking. "I texted him and told him I was stopping by." I glance around the room. "Where is he? Is he working upstairs?" My feet turn and begin to move toward the unfinished, natural wood staircase, ready to bolt away from the uneasy feeling settling in the pit of my belly.

Tyler blinks rapidly. "Um," he mumbles as he scratches the back of his head. "He had to go look at another job." Rushed words fly out of his mouth.

"Another job? That's odd. I thought he said he'd be on this one job site for months."

With an unknown look filling his eyes, Tyler shrugs and says that Alex shouldn't be much longer. He looks around and finds an empty five-gallon bucket. Flipping it over, he brushes off the sand and white dusty residue and sets it down. "Here you go. Best seat in the house."

I can't help but smile as I look around the skeleton of someone's home. Wood beams, unpainted sheetrock, scraps of wood and rolls of electrical wires fill the vast room.

"That's okay. I'll wait outside."

If I weren't speaking to Tyler Strong, I might actually appreciate the kindness, the tenderness in his voice, but I can't. Just because he offers a seat doesn't negate how rude and standoffish he's been to me throughout the years.

"You sure?" He cocks his head to the side, narrows his eyes and then grins. In that moment, I see the appeal he has

with women. I can see why they fall at his feet and worship…
whatever it is they worship.

"I'm sure." I set the bag on the bucket, balancing it
carefully. "There are sandwiches and cold drinks in here."

Tyler nods and utters a word of thanks.

As I set out to leave, I hear him call my name softly. I
stop and turn to face him.

"Thank you for today. She's young and scared. I don't
think she knows what she's gotten herself into," he mumbles
quietly.

I sigh at the man staring at me and am suddenly
overcome with raw emotion. I blink quickly to ward off the
threatening tears. The regret etched on his face is clear; he
doesn't want this child. He isn't ready to become a father.
I've seen this look a thousand times on the faces of young
men and women who've come into the clinic. Many of them
opt to keep their child while others immediately ask about
abortion.

"How old is she?" I ask quietly as my eyes drop to the
floor.

"Who?"

After a quick shake of my head to rid myself of
annoyance, I pinch my lips and look at Tyler.

"Penny…your *girlfriend*."

"She's not my girlfriend."

"Yeah, okay." *Jackass.* "How old is she anyway?"

"Uh…I'm not sure." He shrugs nonchalantly. "Twenty-
three? Twenty-four?"

I suppress the feeling of animosity because he doesn't even have the decency to care about her age. I guess it's not something you ask when you're rolling around under the covers with a different girl every night of the week. "And how old are you?" I don't know why I ask.

"Same as you." A crooked smile tugs on his lips, creating a somewhat boyish appearance.

I nod thoughtfully as an awkward silence fills the room. I always assumed Tyler was older than me because he's so close to Alex. Needing something to do with my hands, I run my fingers through my hair and pull at the long strands, avoiding his gaze. Finally, I release a heavy sigh, raise my chin and face him head on.

"Well, I guess you and Penny have a decision to make."

He looks at me with a combination of confusion and sympathy as he shakes his head and scoffs.

"It's not my decision."

Anger builds within me at his callus words, at his irresponsibility, at his lack of accountability.

Annoyed, I clench my teeth, shake my head and toss him a filthy look before I spin around and start walking to my car.

"Karrie," Tyler whispers, calling me once again.

I stop dead in my tracks but don't turn around this time.

"What, Tyler?"

I can hear him coming closer as he clears his throat. "It was nice talking to you."

*It was nice talking to me? Is he insane?* I hardly think

talking to me about his pregnant girlfriend qualifies as a normal conversation. I don't respond, the words evading me as I take a step further away from my husband's friend.

"And Karrie."

I stop.

"Thanks for lunch. That was really nice of you to do. Very thoughtful."

I want to reply and tell him I didn't do it for him, but I don't.

I continue walking until I reach my car, completely baffled by the man inside. The man who has never been anything but distant and cold to me over the years. The man who chooses to wait in the garage rather than come inside if my husband hasn't gotten home yet. The man who comes to our summer picnics and Christmas parties but always has a poor excuse of why he can't stay very long.

A sigh escapes me just before a small chuckle emerges when a silly thought flits across my mind, wondering if he got hit in the head with a two-by-four or maybe he crossed the wrong wires and got zapped by electricity.

Whatever it was, it was strange. I open the car door and drop myself into the driver's seat and text Alex to let him know that I'll wait for another few minutes. The summer heat beats down on my car, driving the temperature upwards into what feels like the hundreds; not even the slight breeze coming in through the windows offers reprieve. Wiping the sweat from my brow, I blink lazily as I yawn. Once. Twice. Three times. My eyelids close for good.

I awaken a short time later and sit up quickly, disoriented and worried that I missed Alex. I scrub my face with my palms and survey the property around me, scanning the new construction until my sights land on a figure in the window on the second floor. I wipe my eyes then blink quickly, bringing my blurred vision into focus. After glancing around hoping to find Alex's work van, I exhale a deep breath and check my phone for a text message. Nothing. No truck. No message.

Frustration riddles my body at my stupidity. I should've told Alex I was going to come for a visit. A movement causes my eyes sweep upward. Standing there against the window, I see Tyler with his phone to his ear. Our eyes meet. I force my eyes to break away, but they betray me so I continue to look at him as he looks intently at me. Even from this distance, I can see the narrowing of his eyes, the contempt, the hate that is directed toward me before he closes his eyes, shakes his head and steps away from the window.

Once again I confirm the simple fact, I hate Tyler Strong.

"MINE LOOKS LIKE shit compared to yours!" Pam laughs, looking at her painting over the rim of the wine glass. "Oh well!" She tips the glass back and chugs the rest.

"You shouldn't have had that last glass of wine," I tease.

She snorts. "Someone needs to represent the LPDA! And I only had two."

I hand over my debit card and turn to Pam, my forehead wrinkling with curiosity. "The what?"

"The Ladies Professional Drinking Association."

"Are you the president?"

"Not yet. I'm only the vice president." She smirks as we walk through the door and out to our cars.

"I'm not ready to go home yet." I sigh. "Alex is at Tyler's garage working on bikes."

With two raised brows and a single look, she says more than she would if she had uttered a thousand words.

"Don't start!"

She tosses her hands in the air. "I didn't say a thing!"

"You didn't have to." I narrow my eyes as I link our elbows and drag her to her sporty coupe. "Come on, you lush. The next round is on me."

Using the rearview mirror, I keep an eye on Pam as she follows me to The Black Horse, the best hole in the wall bar around.

We find a small booth and each order a glass of wine from the over-friendly waitress. Perusing the bar, I notice a few people playing pool while others play darts. It's relatively busy considering it's a Monday night. Lots of construction workers like to stop in for a beer or two before heading home to the wives or girlfriends.

I enjoy Pam's company as she tells me her plans to move to Florida some day when she hits the lottery. We lift our glasses and clink them together, toasting to her improbable dream.

By the night's end, I'm slightly buzzed and eager to get home. As we step outside, Pam's humorous antics force me to wipe away the tears of laughter running down my face. I giggle and stop… then giggle again.

"Stop! I'm going to pee myself!" I demand without an ounce of conviction.

"Well, at least you'll finally be wet."

"Pam! I can't believe you said that!"

"Whatever!" She rolls her eyes and grins.

I pull my keys out of my purse and once again snake my arm around her, linking elbows with the one friend who can cheer me up like no one else can. Although we don't see each other often, we manage to pick up right where we left off. We walk silently across the crushed stone parking lot as crickets chirp and the sound of muffled country music floats through the warm night air. We stop immediately when a woman's high-pitched squeals and moans break the otherwise quiet, moonless night. Pam and I turn to see a man scrambling to lower his pants just enough to expose his bare ass.

Pam whistles then whispers, "Now *that* is a nice ass!"

Leaning forward still wedged in between the open door and the front seat, the tall man thrusts relentlessly while a pair of thin legs wrap around his waist. Pam breaks free of my hold and cups her mouth, hooting and hollering, telling him to "get a room and give it to her really good!"

I slap her hands away from her mouth. "Shut up!" I whisper through clenched teeth.

As if my eyes have a mind of their own, my gaze shifts

back to the couple. I stare in their direction, completely mesmerized by this very private moment. A longing, a desire fills me and an expected throb between my legs commences.

"Right?"

I snap out of the erotic trance and turn to look at her. "What?"

"I said, 'If you're going to get it on, it might as well be with that fine piece of ass, right?'"

My teeth come down hard on my bottom lip to suppress the sensation building in my core.

"Alex has a great ass."

"For an older man, maybe."

I laugh. "No way! He's in great shape."

"If those two don't finish soon I might have to get some popcorn and enjoy the show from the privacy of my car."

"Oh, God!" I slap my forehead. "And that's my cue! Bye, Pamela." I stick my tongue out as I use her full name which she hates.

I open the car door and get in. I start the engine and my headlights flash in the direction of the half-naked man. Wildly searching across the dashboard of my new car, I feel around for the button to dim the lights. Instead of turning the lights off, the high beams shine brightly into the satisfied face of Penny as she peeks over her lover's shoulder and grasps the man's hair, running her fingers down his neck. I press the gas pedal down and race out of the parking lot as one thought consumes me. I just witnessed Tyler having sex with Penny. In his truck. In the parking lot. Doesn't he have the common decency to get in the truck and close the door? And what's even worse is the fact that I was turned on!

My stomach rolls and I choke back the taste of animosity. The voice inside my head reminds me...

I hate Tyler Strong.

The image of him screwing Penny circles over and over in my head as I drive across to my side of town. The part where huge homes are set on sprawling acres of land, the part where teenage kids have birthday bashes fit for a king and receive shiny luxurious German cars as gifts.

The garage door rises at the touch of a button and I pull into my bay, hoping but not expecting Alex's motorcycle will be parked in its spot. I'm happy he has a hobby, something he's passionate about, but it's one that demands a lot of attention. Countless hours are spent working on bikes at Tyler's garage where no one cares how loud the engine revs or how loud the music is.

My hope plummets at the sight of the vacant spot.

I shower quickly, text him and crawl into bed to read. Nights like this have become the norm it seems. A short while later, Alex replies with a text that says he's got about another two hours and I shouldn't wait up. He says things aren't going as planned.

Feeling a combination of hurt and resentment, I text back a snide comment about how he should divorce me and marry his bike.

My husband's name flashes across the screen and I answer his call.

"What's that supposed to mean?" He doesn't even say hello.

I flinch at his harsh tone. "What? I was just kidding!"

"You know what race season is like."

"Yep, I do." My lips form an O and make a loud pop.

"You act like I'm out at a bar or screwing around."

Tyler.

I stare at our wedding picture and sigh, wanting to tell him about what I saw Tyler doing, but I don't. It's none of my business.

"I miss you." I look at my wedding band. "Is that so wrong?" I turn over and pull the cover over my body as I lie alone in our king-size bed.

"It's almost over."

"Ok. Wake me up when you get home." Chastising myself internally, I shiver at the desperation in my voice.

"Gotta go."

Before I can say the words I love you, the line disconnects.

I vaguely remember hearing the shower running at three o'clock in the morning when Alex tiptoed into the room. I think I said hello, but it was late and I hadn't gotten much sleep.

My eyes flutter open as Alex moves about the room getting dressed for work.

"What are you doing up so early?"

"It's not early." He glances up from his phone. "It's almost eight." He pulls his work T-shirt on over his head before dipping his fingertips into the jar of gel. Rubbing his hands together, he runs his fingers through his hair, straightening it in the mirror. I smile in appreciation when he bends down to tie his boots.

"You're very handsome."

He offers a crooked side grin as he saunters over to me, planting a quick kiss on my forehead. "So I've been told."

"You're also arrogant."

"Yep. I've been told that as well."

"Don't forget we have dinner with my parents this weekend."

He freezes mid-stride just as he reaches the door.

"What now?" I ask, unable to hide the annoyance in my voice.

"Ty and I were going to test and tune the bike this weekend."

"Okay," I draw out the obvious.

"In Maryland."

"Oh, c'mon! Are you serious?" I jump out of bed and put my hands on my hips angrily. "This is ridiculous." My foot comes down with a heavy stomp as if I were a spoiled child.

His eyes drag lazily down my stiff naked body until they reach my face.

"I told you it's almost over."

I close my eyes and count backwards from ten, hoping the tension will seep out before I explode. Clenching my jaw, I reopen my eyes, shake my head and trudge into the bathroom, slamming the door hard and pressing the lock.

I fully expect him to knock on the door or demand I

open it, but he doesn't. He just leaves.

By the end of the day, I'm on a nonstop JetBlue flight to my parent's condominium in Florida. I'd give anything to see his reaction when he reads my note.

"It's tanning season. Going to Florida. Not sure when I'll be back."

He calls and texts relentlessly...and I ignore him. His attempts to lure my own mother to his side were in vain. She does argue that I am being childish and immature, insisting I should at least talk to the man since he is, after all, my husband. I agree to call him, but I don't.

I walk along the beach, soaking up the sun's rays as I look for seashells. I nap on the beach after swimming in the blue ocean. I eat a delicious gourmet meal and drink an entire bottle of expensive champagne at a fancy restaurant.

For the most part, I enjoy myself until the voice of sadness creeps in to remind me that I am, in fact, alone.

After nearly two weeks of doing nothing, I'm ready to go home so I say goodbye to the Sunshine State.

# THREE

I'M STARTLED AWAKE BY the sound of heavy footsteps as Alex forces the door open. He looks menacing as he barrels over to my side of the bed. His hot, alcohol-laced breath bellows in my face.

"Who the fuck do you think you are?"

My husband reaches around and yanks me up by my long hair into a sitting position, his snarled face mere inches away from mine.

"You think you can just take off and leave me?"

I swallow hard as tears fill my eyes at both his tight grip on my head and his harsh tone.

"Alex, let me go! You're hurting me!" I scream, hoping my voice will snap him out of his animalistic rage. "Stop!" I scream louder when he tells me to shut up.

"You're nothing but a spoiled little bitch." A spray of

saliva shoots out of his mouth and lands on my cheeks.

My eyes search wildly and hopelessly for the man I married. For my Alex.

"What are you talking about?" I manage through sobs. My fingers slide across his unshaven face, caressing gently, anticipating the return of my husband. "I just needed a few days to myself." I stammer, trying to assuage him. "Alex, please. Let me go."

"I gave you everything. *Everything!* And for what? For you to leave me and take everything I've worked so hard for?"

Confusion blurs my mind. "Alex, I'm not going anywhere. I'm not leaving you." I cry harder.

The hold on my hair loosens as he falls to his knees, his face resting on my lap while his lips move slowly. "All I ever wanted to do was to make you happy."

I run my hands over his head, his hair slipping through my fingers.

"I am happy." I am most of the time.

He shakes his head and mumbles a quick "no."

"I'm lonely, Alex. I'm just lonely."

He doesn't reply.

With my husband passed out on my lap, I lie awake for hours and wonder how we got here. How did my seemingly happy marriage become so unhappy? When did his love for everything else replace his love for me?

I CRUMPLE THE NOTE he left on the island and hurl it across the room before I break down into a fit of sobs.

"Happy fucking Anniversary to you too, Alex."

My eyes are still red and puffy when I arrive at the hospital for my weekend shift. I lie and tell everyone I had a reaction to a new sunscreen.

"Isn't today your anniversary?" Odessa strides into the lounge area to warm up her curry rice dish.

"Yep, sure is." I reply nonchalantly.

Her big brown eyes open wide. "So what are you doing here? Why are you working?"

"I traded last weekend when I was in Florida."

"Still doesn't explain why you're working on your anniversary."

"Alex is racing."

She tightens her lips into a hard line as if she's trying to refrain from speaking. I know what she's going to say and I don't really need to hear it especially after the earful I got from my parents.

"How many years now?"

"Five."

Odessa sits beside me. "You know, in some cultures, five is considered to be a lucky number."

"I thought thirteen was the lucky number." I stab my fork into the greens of my salad.

"When's your birthday?"

"July 7th."

"What year?"

"87."

"See! You're a five."

"A five?"

"Your numbers 7, 7, 87."

I toss a confused look in her direction as I take a sip of water.

"What's seven plus seven?"

"Fourteen," I answer skeptically.

"Okay and what's eight plus seven?"

"Fifteen," I sigh with annoyance.

"Drop the one and you have your number!"

Utterly bewildered, I ask, "What are you talking about?"

"See! You're a five. Just like I said! This is going to be your lucky year. Good things await you. Mark my words... good things will happen."

I chuckle and roll my eyes, trying to understand her rationale, but I can't because it doesn't make sense.

"Did you learn that in your Guyanese school?"

"No! I learned it in an astrology class in college."

I laugh at my absurd friend. "Thank you."

"For what?" She smiles knowingly.

"For taking my mind off the fact that I'm here on my wedding anniversary."

"Awww! That's what friends are for!"

"You are a good friend even though you tried to trick me into eating goat meat that one time. I still haven't forgiven you!"

After sleeping for a few hours when I get home, I lounge

by the pool, tend to my garden, tidy up the house and try my hand at a new recipe. I wave to the group of young fit stay at home moms who push their baby strollers and chat about reality television. I peruse the mail and leave it on the counter, separating Alex's from mine. There's an envelope with a return address label from an out of state attorney. I wonder who's trying to sue A.P. Electrical now. Or maybe Alex has had to put a lien on a property for nonpayment.

I arrive at work early, carrying a large box of scrumptious pastries from Susie's Sweets, a quaint French patisserie and a box of Joe from Dunkin' Donuts.

"You're going to have more junk in the trunk if you keep eating those cookies!" Odessa laughs as she shoves half an éclair into her mouth. "So good," she moans.

I smirk and toss the other half at her. She gasps at the cream on her scrubs before she proceeds to lift her shirt and lick it off.

My mouth falls open in shock and it's my turn to gasp.

"You know I can't let it go to waste! Back in my country when I was just a little girl, I had to…"

Her voice trails off as Anita, a few other nurses and I make a mass exodus out of the room. We've all heard the stories about her childhood in Guyana.

I've still not heard from my husband. Truth be told, I've made no attempt to contact him either. Maybe we both need a few days apart.

Finding the second break room empty, I collapse onto the faux leather sofa to finish my "lunch" hour at two o'clock in the morning. I stare at the clock and listen to its rhythmic pattern. Tick tock. Tick tock. Tick tock. The deliberate movement of the second hand is comforting. It reminds me that life continues on every second of every day.

My neck tips to the side as his soft lips nip and kiss a small trail, his hands run up and down my arms gently and them with more force. His deep voice whispers sweet nothings into my ear and a shy smile tugs at my lips. "Say it again," I plead quietly, turning my head to consider his bluish-green orbs. "I need you," he repeats the words I love to hear.

"Karrie, wake up. C'mon! We need you." Anita wakes me up with firm rubs to my arms. "Karrie, we need all hands on deck."

I toss the small blanket onto the chair and stand as I wipe the sleep from my eyes. My legs feel weak and I'm slightly disoriented. My cheeks flush pink when I yawn, my dream still fresh on my mind. After shaking my head quickly, I comb my fingers through my hair, securing it back into a ponytail and follow her out. While the warmth of the blanket subsides, I notice the warmth and moisture between my legs remains.

Anita and I walk with hurried steps, following Odessa out through the sliding glass doors into the cool night air to wait for the arrival of the ambulance. I can hear the sirens blaring in the distance and when it arrives, the bright red and white lights flash brightly, reflecting off the doors and windows, casting a red glow on our faces.

"John Doe number one. Caucasian male. Mid-thirties. Severe head trauma. Single vehicle rollover. Ejected from vehicle. Found unresponsive upon arrival. BP is seventy over forty. Intubation started."

Sam, one of the EMTs, barks out the status of the patient as the gurney is lowered and wheeled through the door. I hurry to his side and begin an analysis as Odessa and Anita attend to the second patient, John Doe number two, who is being brought in by another ambulance.

In that split second, all my personal feelings are set aside. I don't think of this man as a man. I don't think of the wife and children who might be worried about him. I don't think about how horrible he must feel if he can feel anything at all. All I can think about is what I need to do to save his life. I'm a nurse; it's what I've been trained to do.

There's a flurry of controlled chaos in the usually quiet Emergency Department of St. Luke's Hospital. Rooms are emptied, wheelchairs rolled into the hallway so our team has space to work. I lift the bar and use it to rush the gurney into the first available room. As I press the brake, securing the bed, my hand slips and grazes the man's fingers. I glance down at the blood stains covering his left hand.

A single thought about how strong his hands are races to the forefront of my mind before my eyes follow the trail of his torn clothes and fall to his head completely covered in bloody gauze. I can only see a sliver of his eyes as he blinks slowly. When I feel movement against my hand once again, I look down and notice that he's trying to reach for my fingers.

Compassion wins as I take his hand in mine, squeezing it gently, reassuring him that he's in good hands and we'll do everything in our power to take care of him.

Dr. Stephens, the E.D. surgeon, makes another quick analysis of the situation and looks over at the heart monitor when the beeping decreases in frequency.

"Parker! What are you doing? Let's go!"

I realize in that moment I'm stroking the man's hand gently while everyone is rushing around me, each fulfilling their specific role in an attempt to save his life.

"We've got internal bleeding. We need to get him to the OR, stat."

"What's wrong with you?" Paula asks, glancing at me quickly with a pointed look. "You okay?"

I shake my head then nod, snapping myself out of a daze. "Yeah. I," I stammer, "I don't know what happened."

When John Doe number one is wheeled out of the room and into surgery, Odessa orders me to help with John Doe number two who has sustained equally serious injuries.

"What's the status?" I ask, stepping in closer to understand the situation.

"Single vehicle. Severe head trauma. Looks like he may have been wearing a restraint, but the force upon impact must've ripped it off. Look," Dr. Lopez says and shakes his head as he points the man's bruised chest. "They had to have been going at least a hundred to do this amount of damage."

My eyes crawl upward until I reach the dirty, bloodied gauze covering his face. There is a clear indication of trauma and brain swelling based on the sheer size of this man's head.

Minutes tick by as Dr. Lopez and our team work to save his life and stabilize him. Like John Doe number one, his blood pressure drops then his heart stills. After attempts to use the defibrillator and all other measures fail, Dr. Lopez forced his chest open with a deep incision. I hold my breath and cringe at the sound of the oscillating saw as it cuts through the breastbone.

"Karrie, come here."

I look into the eyes of the doctor whom I respect and admire. A cold shiver runs through me because I don't like what I see reflecting back at me.

"Give me your hand," he orders.

I do as I am told.

"Just squeeze gently. Keep squeezing. Don't stop until I tell you."

My hand is carefully guided into the open chest cavity of this stranger.

"Do you feel it?" Dr. Lopez's hand covers mine and demonstrates the concise pattern. Squeeze. Squeeze. Squeeze.

Dr. Lopez leans over and begins to search blindly yet skillfully throughout this man's broken torso, attempting to locate the source of internal bleeding.

Never in my life have I been the sole source between life and death. My small hand, with its gentle compressions, preserves this man's life.

As I keep his heart beating, my mouth goes dry. I haven't

got even enough moisture to lick my lips. My eyes stay focused on the task until I hear a single long beep spew from the machine.

"Found it!"

I pull my eyes away and look at the surgeon who now has both hands inside.

I don't know if I quiver because of the long, constant and eerie sound or because Dr. Lopez yells in my ear, "Don't stop the compressions. Get him back."

*Focus, Karrie, focus.*

"Please don't die. Please don't die. C'mon John Doe number two. There's a girl out there who needs you to live. Please don't die." My lips move silently as I whisper, pleading with God, willing the man to live.

I need him to live.

*Beep. Beep. Beep.* Slow but constant sounds resonate throughout the room as we all breathe a sigh of relief.

Dr. Lopez gives the order for immediate surgery, calls are made, the patient prepped quickly. He's in critical condition so time is of the essence.

Once again, I'm left in the room as the second trauma team comes in and wheels the patient away. The unmistakable smell of blood and antiseptic permeates the small space.

I blink away the tears welling up in my eyes. Emotions have no place here. With robotic movements, I make my way over to the sink and rip the gloves from my hands, washing them thoroughly until the water runs from red to clear. When the last remnants of blood are gone, I curl my fingers and cup my palm to scoop lukewarm water into my parched mouth. I splash water onto my face and pat my skin dry with a stiff paper towel.

I lean against the counter with my palms pressed into the edge and stare at the mess on the floor as a maintenance worker comes in, rolling a mop bucket in front of him.

"Pretty bad, huh?" Felix asks, shoving the mop into the water before ringing it damp.

I nod solemnly, unable to find any words. I became a nurse to help people, to save lives, to care for the injured, to comfort them. I've seen the cloak of Death skulk in, entering a room to claim its victim. I've seen the merciful hand of God come down and breathe life into an otherwise lifeless form, sparing it, giving it new purpose. I've seen it all. But this…this was different. I was the angel of God keeping this man alive.

I was the one to breathe new life. I was the one who brought him back from the dead.

I was the fine line between life and death.

A flurry of activity mingled with Odessa's voice beckons me into the hallway, searching for the source of her concern. I come face to face with her just as I hear Dr. Stephens declare the time of death of the first victim to arrive. Her normally dark skin is now ten shades lighter. Her hands fly up and grab my shoulders, effectively holding me back. Searching her wide, shocked eyes, I find my voice.

"What's wrong? What happened?" I screech as my hands cover hers. The slight swaying of her body suggests she needs to be supported. Gone for a moment is the tough as nails, blunt doctor's assistant I call my friend replaced by a vulnerable woman.

Odessa's hands cup my face, her thumbs moving across my cheeks slowly. My heart begins to pound in my chest at the sight of her. I plead for her to tell me what's wrong.

"Karrie. Oh, Karrie my love." Fat tears fill her brown eyes. "I'm sorry."

*Sorry?* I'm confused by her words. "Sorry for what?"

With her hands on my face, she guides me until my back hits the wall.

"Odessa, please. What's wrong?" Again I beg her to reveal the reason for her current state.

Worry and fear seep through her dark eyes. "John Doe number one."

Still not having a clear understanding I respond, "Okay? What about him?"

"It's Alex." Her lip quivers as she speaks my husband's name.

"What? What about him?" My veins turn to ice, pumping frozen liquid through my stiff body.

Odessa shakes her head quickly for several seconds as she fights the emotion threatening to erupt.

"He's dead." She bursts into tears.

I freeze. Her words desperately try to register in my brain but fail miserably.

"I don't understand," I mumble.

Odessa wraps her arms around my body tightly and

pulls me close. "Honey, John Doe number one. It's Alex. Your Alex."

My husband. John Doe number one. A million thoughts compete with one another as I struggle to comprehend her words.

My Alex. My husband is John Doe number one. John Doe number one is dead. My Alex is dead. My heart plummets as my knees buckle. Supported only by Odessa's arms, I muster the strength as I inhale sharply. My back stiffens and I pull out of her hold, my feet moving effortlessly and quickly to the room where Alex is. I know she's wrong. It's not Alex. He isn't due home until later in the morning. It's not him. It can't be him.

"Karrie, don't! Don't go in there!" Her voice fades into nothing as I force the door open and stop, coming face to face with the deceased man.

The room is still, every machine now quiet, only the lingering stench of death remains.

"You shouldn't be in here." A faceless person whispers, the compassion in her voice clear.

I sweep my eyes from the top of this man's head to his bare feet. His naked body left broken on the table, a clear indication of the futile attempts to save his life. Death declared victorious. The sparing hand of God was nowhere in sight.

"I'm so sorry." A gentle hand rubs against my shoulder. "I'll give you a minute."

I smile. I don't know why I smile as I pull my eyes away

from my husband to look at her, but I do.

I turn back to look at the man lying still and lifeless.

This can't be happening. This can't be him.

Stepping closer, I raise my hands and allow them to hover over his covered face. I scan the familiar body, the tight planes of his abdomen, the strong biceps, the long muscular legs. He could be anyone, anyone at all, but he's not.

I carefully lift his heavy right arm and look, praying fervently not to see what I know will be there.

At the sight of the etched vicious snake wrapped around the American flag, my stomach flips and rolls. I lean over and dry heave, but nothing comes out.

I am empty.

Completely empty.

I clamber across his body and press my cheek onto his forearm, wishing, needing to draw strength. An uncontrollable fit of sobs and hot tears flood my face as I curse at God. I demand that He return Alex to me. I grovel and beg mercifully that He take someone else instead.

God does not listen.

I hear nothing.

I feel nothing.

I see nothing.

After what feels like an eternity, I sense someone else has entered the room, invading my private time with my dead husband. The strength to lift my head is nowhere to be found. This person walks closer and stops behind me.

"Karrie, my love," Odessa breathes quietly. She leans

forward and angles her chest against my back, cradling me in her arms, whispering softly what I already know.

"He's gone."

I know this.

"We did everything we could to save him." Her thumb glides back and forth over my hand.

I know this, too.

"I'm so sorry."

This I also know.

Yet knowing that these medical professionals worked tirelessly to save my husband does not diminish the indescribable ache piercing my heart, searing it straight down the middle with a hot, fiery blade from hell.

"Alex, come back to me," I cry softly, burying my head, resting my forehead against the ink on his skin. "Please come back to me."

Odessa's hold on my shoulder tightens and she draws me upward, away from the man I married five years earlier. The man who swept me off my feet in a whirlwind romance. The man who pledged his love and fidelity until death do us part.

Death has parted us.

"Come on. Let's get you cleaned up." My friend guides me toward the door, my feet become cinder blocks, too heavy to even drag. "I've got you." With her left arm around my back and the other tossed around her neck, Odessa carries me away from my husband.

The last of my tears have fallen. The ache in my chest

has vanished. The tremor in my body has ceased.

I collapse onto the soft leather chair in Dr. Stephens' office.

Completely numb.

Completely hopeless.

Completely alone.

Completely incomplete.

Staring out the window as the morning sun breaks through the purple sky, making promises of the day to come, I try to feel something. Anything at all, but I feel nothing.

My husband, Alexander Parker, is dead.

# FOUR

"KARE BEAR," MY MOTHER CALLS, wrapping her arm around my slumped shoulder. "You should try to eat something." She hands me a package of salted square crackers. "Or drink something. Alex would've insisted."

I blink slowly, letting her words register.

*Insisted.* Past tense.

I lift my eyes to meet her gaze, silently asking if this is all real. Did my husband really die? The endless amount of sympathy combined with such pity shines through her eyes as she nods once and then brushes the hair away from my face.

"He did. I'm so sorry, sweetheart."

A constant stream of people flock to the room where I've been sitting for the past two hours. Each comes and goes, offering quiet, awkward words of condolence. I nod and thank them, returning the gentle hugs.

"Sweetheart, let's get you home and cleaned up."

My gaze travels from a speck on the linoleum floor and follows the sound of my mother's voice as she places her hand under my arm in an attempt to lift me to my feet.

Our eyes connect and I can see my pain reflected in hers. The dam of emotions breaks free. My face crumples in agony as I throw my arms around my mother's back and wail. Deep, painful, sorrowful wails. She doesn't tell me to stop. She doesn't tell me to be quiet. She doesn't say a single word. She just holds me and allows me to experience the grief that consumes me.

The circling of her hand on my back finally comes to a rest. I hiccup and wipe my face with my blood-stained scrubs.

"Let's get you home."

Feeling helpless and weak, I am once again supported and led out to the hallway. I keep my head down as we pass patients and their worried families.

"Daddy will be here any minute."

As if he were an angel appearing before me, my father, the man whom I loved first, strides in through the double sliding doors and rushes toward me.

"Kare Bear." He wraps his arms around me and tucks my head beneath his chin. I feel his chest shudder against my cheek.

"Thanks for coming," I say as I link my fingers together behind his back. I can feel the perspiration moistening his button down shirt.

"I came as soon as I heard," he mumbles quietly before speaking to my mother.

"Code Blue to ICU. Code Blue to ICU."

Untangling myself from my father's hold, I watch the team of medical experts rush in the direction of John Doe number two.

"I should go help." I turn, ready to follow them.

Strong hands take hold of me. "Oh, no you don't."

"Dad, I have to. I have to save him. I told him I would save him."

"Sweetheart, let them do their jobs." He lowers himself to look directly at me. "Please."

I pull my gaze away from him and look down at my trembling hands.

"I brought him back to life. With my own hands, I brought him back to life."

Guilt surges at the thought that if I had stayed with Alex, I could've saved his life, too. I could've done something. I could've helped in some way.

AFTER TAKING A LONG hot shower, I wrap myself in my mother's long white silk bathrobe and lie quietly in the bed of my childhood. I pull the quilt up, tuck it under my chin and close my eyes, praying that when I awake, this will all have just been a horrible nightmare.

A light knock on the door jars me, forcing my eyelids to part and focus on the figure moving closer.

"Alex?" I call.

After slow, quiet steps bring my mother closer, she sets down a black mug which has silver letters, etching the words Lake George, NY on its side. My mother's proclivity for collecting tourist mugs has become somewhat of an obsession. And it was the last place Alex and I vacationed.

She smiles kindly as she sweeps a hand across my forehead then slides it down to caress my cheek. Her soft touch is warm and comforting.

"I brought you something to eat."

My lips tighten into a hard line at the sight of the dry toast alongside the cup of freshly brewed tea. While I appreciate the kind gesture, my throat is raw from constant crying and screaming. My stomach muscles ache from vomiting as hard as I did when I insisted that my father pull his SUV over. Even my back muscles hurt.

"Thanks, Mom." I motion with my chin to the sustenance but decline the offer.

I see her move the picture frame and alarm clock to make more room for the small dish and tea cup before I close my eyes again. My mother doesn't like to see me like this; it makes her nervous.

"Do you want to talk?" she whispers. I feel the dip in the bed as she sits beside me, smoothing my long hair back.

"What," I start, clearing my raspy throat before continuing. "What is there to talk about?" My eyes fill with tears and stare at her pointedly. "My husband died today."

"Yes, he did, sweetheart. Alex is gone, but you're still here."

I mop my eyes with my fingertips, suppress the sob waiting to emerge, and shake my head in disbelief.

"I have so many questions. I don't even know where to begin."

My eyes glance around the room and land on the shelf where my cheerleading and gymnastics trophies still stand all these years later.

I had my life planned out. Go to college. Perhaps marry John. Become a nurse. Have babies. Live happily ever after.

Then Alex Parker came along and swept me off my feet.

Thoughts about the first day we met flood my mind and I smile as my index finger rubs back and forth against my thumb. Then my mother's words cut through the memory and my fingers still.

"We need to start thinking about arrangements."

I close my eyes and exhale quietly.

I don't want to make arrangements. I want to go home, pick fresh basil for the pot of sauce and make chicken parmesan with a side of angel hair pasta. My husband's favorite.

"Can you call for me?"

My mom looks down sheepishly and says that she could, but she thinks I need to do it. "A way to begin closure," she continues with a small voice.

I nod, knowing she's right. Somehow, my mother is

always right.

Struggling to sit up, I reach for the cup of tea and take a quick sip, but it's hot, causing me to flinch when the liquid burns my lips and the tip of my tongue.

"Easy," my mom reprimands as if I'm a child.

Needing something to replace the tremendous ache in my heart, I bring the mug back to my lips, and tip my head back, forcing down a huge gulp of the liquid, its heat burning my throat as it travels down to my stomach.

The tightening of my face and the clenching of my teeth do little to erase the fire in me.

My mother attempts to take the cup of tea away from me while tossing me a dirty look. "You're an adult, Karrie. Act like one."

I snatch it back and cock my arm back, hurling the cup and its contents across the room, the brown liquid splashing against the closet door.

"I'll leave these right here for you."

My mother, my best friend, turns and leaves the room. I know she's not intentionally being callous; it's just the way she is. She's one tough lady who deals with things head on. I usually take after her but...not today.

Glancing at the printed papers, I swipe my hand across the nightstand, sending the toast and paper flying in every direction.

By mid-afternoon of the following day when the arrangements have been finalized, I've chosen the funeral home, selected a beautiful casket, spoken to the priest at our church and even picked out a suit for my dead husband to wear. I've taken care of every last detail even down to his socks and shoes. I don't understand why he has to wear them, no one will see them anyway. I begged everyone at the hospital to search for his wedding band. I didn't want to bury him with the ring; I wanted to keep it.

Three days later on a drizzly and humid morning, I scan the scores of people who've come to pay their last respects and say goodbye to my husband before he's lowered into the ground. I've run out of tears as they simply won't fall anymore. My eyes slide across from my friends and colleagues to the stay at home moms who came to visit as soon as they heard, offering to make food for me and finally to the people, mostly men, who knew a different Alex. Each of them wears a black T-shirt with Alex's race team logo. I wish I could say I know their names, but I can't. I've only ever met a handful of them at our wedding.

Racing was Alex's thing, not mine. Although we'd met at the race track, I quickly lost interest when it dominated our time together and transformed him into another person.

Each one of them gave me another "last hug" after commenting that he was such a "great guy." I nodded and agreed because he really was...in the beginning.

While their faces morph into masks of sorrow, my mind wonders about the petite blonde named Penny who stands solemnly amongst racing friends, waiting to pay her respects to my husband and then mostly likely return to the hospital to sit with Tyler. I hadn't given him much thought; every thought preoccupied with my own grief and I was unable to see beyond it. But for a brief moment, I thought about him.

Tyler Strong.

I thought about the child growing in Penny's womb who might never have the opportunity to meet his or her father. The child who might possibly be raised by another man in his or her father's absence. I wonder what Penny would tell her child. How would she raise the baby on her own?

I close my eyes, silently and, quite selfishly I suppose, thank God for not giving me a child with Alex. As awful as that sounds, I wouldn't want a constant reminder of him living and breathing while he lies still, forever dead, beneath the earth.

Taking small steps in a short black lace dress which seems more appropriate for a bar than a funeral, Penny walks over to me.

"Karrie," she says with a sympathetic half smile.

"Penny," I reply in greeting. "Thanks for coming today. I'm sure Alex would've been happy to know you made the trip up."

I don't know why I say that. This woman is one of the many women featured in the never-ending tales of Tyler's love fests.

"I'm sorry. I'm really so sorry." Penny leans in and embraces me, squeezing almost too hard. For God's sake,

I've only met her once at the clinic and we hardly spoke at all. It's not like we know each other well or would even have anything in common.

Patting her back gently, I offer comfort even though I have very little left to give. After several moments, I release her and step back.

"How's Tyler? Any change?"

She pulls a balled-up tissue from her purse and wipes her eyes then her nose.

"No, he's the same. I hope he makes it."

I pinch my lips and nod in agreement as she turns to walk in the opposite direction where a small crowd remains gathered.

Tyler Strong was John Doe number two and he remains in a coma. His brain is swollen, the cuts on his face stitched up from going head first through the windshield and his right leg is severely fractured. Apparently, he was the sole passenger seated next to my husband in the truck when Alex suddenly swerved and hit the tree.

My father and I drove by the scene of the accident and saw the skid marks on the black pavement. Not too far from where people had created a makeshift memorial, I had vomited once again.

I searched for the spot where the police say both men were ejected from the vehicle. Supposedly the imprint appeared as if only one person had lain there bloody and broken. Somehow and quite inexplicably, Tyler landed on top of Alex; it's the only reason he is still breathing, even if it is with the assistance of a ventilator. The multitudes of doctors were skeptical to offer a prognosis, but the fact that he survived at all was a miracle.

At least that's what Odessa told me they had said.

I haven't been to the hospital to see him.

Why would I? Why would I become a hypocrite, sitting by his bed, reassuring him he's going to be okay? Why would I suddenly change how I feel about him just because he's on the verge of death? Why would I want to look at him and wish he died instead of Alex?

I can't go there.

I can't see him because...

I hate Tyler Strong.

"You ready to go?" my father asks with a strong and steady voice as he drapes his arm over my shoulder.

I clear my throat.

"Just another minute."

With solemn steps, I walk over to the floral arrangement and remove a single red rose, bringing it to my nose as I inhale the sweet scent. My heart quickens and I smile in remembrance of the good times we had, yet I don't cry. My lips offer a deliberate kiss on the soft petals before I set it down amongst the many others. My husband's beautiful and exquisitely-crafted casket is covered in a blanket of red and white flowers.

I bow my head, pray quietly, and then whisper, hoping he can hear me.

"Thank you for all the red roses and for sweeping me off

my feet. Thank you for making me feel sexy and loved. Thank you for choosing me. Thank you for giving me a beautiful life. Thank you for the good memories, for the good times we shared. I love you, Alex Parker." *Despite who you became and what you did.*

When I open my eyes and find my father wiping his, my chin quivers and my heart sinks. *Please Daddy, be strong for me.*

After making sure my grandmother is safely secured in her car, my mother joins us. The fingers on each of my hands are laced and squeezed gently, reassuringly.

I slide into the open door of the black limousine, taking the proffered hand of the driver as I lower myself.

"Thank you," I mumble.

"Again Mrs. Parker, we at Chase Memorial are very sorry for your loss. Please accept our sincerest condolences."

I look into his eyes and wonder how sincere he really is.

My parents sit alongside me in silence. I can feel the weight of their stare on my face.

I wipe the tears that found their way into my eyes and hiccup.

"Here." My mother offers another tissue.

Nodding slowly, I wordlessly thank her.

The quiet engine comes to life as we begin our long procession, exiting us from the cemetery, up the winding small crescents of hills then down to the low valleys near an opulent mausoleum.

My eyes remained fixed as everything begins to blur and

they close. I lean against the window and reminisce about the man I married, not the one I buried.

# FIVE

*Six years earlier…*

ALEXANDER PARKER AND I HAD a whirlwind love affair, one to rival any contemporary romance novel.

John, my on-again-off-again boyfriend of almost a year, was heading south to Tennessee, advancing his degree to become a physical therapist. He'd asked me to go with him, but I knew his heart wasn't fully committed yet so I said no, arguing that I wanted to finish nursing school here. There was no point in uprooting myself and applying to a new program for one year.

It was a hot day in July, the temperatures soared into the high nineties, the heat index well above one hundred. Working as an EMT, John often picked up extra shifts a few cities away at the race track. Two or three medical units were often, I was told, on hand in case someone crashed their car or motorcycle.

I thought the whole thing was ridiculous. Grown men and some women, flying down a straight quarter-mile track at incredible speeds. I often joked that I was surprised more ambulances weren't on hand.

I drove my little white mini-cooper there with the top down and the music on high. I didn't care that John was working, I just wanted to be wherever he was. I'd spent the day in the blistering heat. The skin of my shoulders had become bright red, incensed by the sun. I'd forgotten my sunscreen and received a lecture from John. Even the straps of my cami which dug into my shoulders as the weight of my boobs descended by nature's pull hurt to the touch. I kept adjusting my bra and wiping the beads of sweat from the small space between them.

John and I leaned against the chain link fence that separated the participants from the spectators. He stood behind me with his chin resting on my head, careful not to touch my sunburn, but I was hot and I wanted him to give me some space. The heat emanating from his body felt like a thermal blanket. All afternoon, we watched the cars drive up to the line as the announcer's voice ripped through the stagnant summer air, calling out the opponents in the next race.

I watched with rapt attention as two beastly looking motorcycles moved forward, lining up on each side of the track with their engines revving loudly. The starting line was submerged in a plume of white smoke as the tires were spun and heated up.

The driver on the right side shook his head and motioned for assistance. A young man with light brown hair, clad in the same black leather racing suit, emerged from the crowd and walked right up to the rider, spoke to him and proceeded to inspect the motorcycle. He dropped to a squat and made adjustments before standing to his full height and stepping back. With a heavy pat to the rider's back, they bantered back and forth and smiled until the rider snapped his visor down.

The young man's attention was drawn upward toward the cheering crowd. Scanning the faces of people waiting for the race to begin, he looks for something or someone until his gaze comes down in the direction where I stood against the fence.

His light eyes narrowed when our eyes locked.

For a few seconds that seem to stretch on for days, we stared at one another.

There was something about the connection, something innately profound as he commanded my full attention.

With the slow and deliberate slide of his tongue, he moistened his lips. Absentmindedly, I mimicked the motion as his tanned cheek pulled back in a side smile. He looked away, denying me his eyes when he turned and walked away behind the line. My eyes fell to the letters on his upper back, stretching from shoulder to shoulder.

STRONG.

Just before disappearing into the crowd, the sexy racer glanced back.

My teeth clenched down on my bottom lip, suppressing my mouth from displaying a full smile.

AT LUNCH TIME, in a desperate search for shade, I walked briskly over to the concession stand. I needed a respite from the blistering sun and I was hungry. I told John I'd grab some food and cold drinks while he tended to an obese man who was suffering from heat exhaustion or dehydration.

The line moved so slowly and I was anxious to get a drink since I was beginning to feel light-headed from the sun's brutal beating. I wasn't sure if it was the smell of the black asphalt, the fumes from race fuel, the soaring temperatures or the sudden disappearance of Strong, but I wasn't having a good time anymore. In fact, if it hadn't been for my infatuation with my boyfriend, I would never have come to a place like this. Ever.

It was stupid and childish.

I thought these grown men were just big boys who might be just as content racing remote controlled cars instead. Why subject yourself to this craziness?

I ordered my food and moved down the line to where the sign indicated I should wait for pick up. The sharp and distinct sound of a slap turned my head as a woman giggled and leaned into the tall man walking beside her. The playful banter between them told me she didn't mind the red spot that was sure to be across her backside. I rolled my eyes.

Who does that in public anyway?

Again my attention is drawn back to them when she moaned about needing him desperately. Thankful for the dark glasses now covering my eyes, I finally allowed myself to look at him. I didn't really notice his face; my eyes were fixated on the black leather that covered his enormous body. My head, along with my gaze, traveled up and down from his neck to his black boots.

"What the hell are you looking at?"

My eyes snapped up and I flushed red. I quickly turned away, embarrassed at having been caught checking out her man. Well, I wasn't really "checking *him* out," I was merely making an observation of his attire. His "leathers" as I'd heard them called.

"What?" she huffs.

"Knock it off," he hissed.

A full-blown pout mars her face.

"I hate all these bike bitches."

*Bike bitches?* What the hell does that mean?

I heard him ask her what she wanted to eat, but she replied she was only hungry for him.

He told her to go wait in the trailer. Then he added, "Be wet and ready."

I didn't even want to imagine what he was going to do. What a jerk! A disgusting jerk!

"Sixty-nine. Number sixty-nine?"

I looked down at my receipt and realized they were calling my number just as my phone rang. Stepping up to the counter, I carefully balanced the cardboard boxes filled with curly fries and cheeseburgers as I swiped my phone to take the call. My dad had gotten the test results for his most recent MRI.

"Hi, Mom. What's going on?" I asked, keeping my eyes down as I wedged the two fountain drinks between my forearm and chest before turning to leave.

Bam! I collided with a brick wall. Actually, that's what it felt like. Who knew Mr. Leathers had such a hard body beneath the material.

My phone dropped to the ground, my mother's voice fading away. The thin cotton of my shirt soaked with pink lemonade, my boobs a sticky mess.

"Shit! I'm so sorry. I wasn't looking where I was going," I mumbled as I bent down to retrieve my phone while setting the cup on the ground. I pushed my glasses to the top of my head away from my face. Mr. Leathers squatted, too, and reached for my phone. His fingers overlapped mine and I looked up, meeting his gaze. I could hear my mother calling my name, probably wondering why I've not said a word for the last ten seconds.

"Here you go." He handed me the phone and smiled. Not just any smile, it was a heart-stopping, panty dropping yet incredibly charming smile and not the one he had given his girlfriend moments before.

"Thank you," I replied, standing up, feeling slightly off

balance.

He must've noticed because he reached out and placed gentle hands on my shoulders, steadying me. Even though my skin glowed red, I could feel his fingers burning an imprint onto my skin.

"Are you okay?" he asked huskily.

I blinked slowly and held my breath because for as hot and sweating as he must've been in that leather suit, he smelled divine.

He bent slightly at the waist so we were now at an even level. My eyes landed on his face and I thought for sure I was going to pass out. With dark, almost charcoal black eyes, he stared at me, searching deep into me.

Instantly, fiercely, undeniably, he drew me in.

I appraised him quickly. His messy hair, sprinkled with a hint of grey, was framed by a handsome tanned face. A straight nose, a square jaw and the light shadow of a sexy stubble made him gorgeous.

I blew out a slow breath and said I was fine, forcing myself to look away.

"I don't believe you." He raised an eyebrow and smirked.

"Seriously, I'm fine. Thanks." As much as I didn't want to, I stepped back out of his reach and swiped my finger across the shattered screen, silencing my mother's voice.

"Ouch!" I hissed as I turned my hand upward and noticed the smallest sliver of glass sticking out of my skin.

I looked around for somewhere to set the food down so I could attend to my injured finger.

Without a moment's notice, Mr. Leathers raised my hand to his mouth and tilted his head slightly.

"Allow me."

I swallowed hard when I felt his lips part and his teeth grazed my skin. I was completely mesmerized when he clamped his teeth down on the sharp glass and pulled it out. My tongue darted out to lick my dry lips.

He spat the shard to the broken and cracked concrete. "All better."

I expected him to drop my hand after I thanked him, but he didn't. He again lifted my hand and slid my thumb into his mouth, his warm tongue sucking gently, purposefully, on the pad while his eyes remained fixed on mine.

I sighed like a damn fool.

A rush of adrenaline followed by a sudden surge of heat raced through my body at the simple, yet loaded, touch.

I had no idea what was going on; I'd never felt this before with anyone.

He lowered my hand and smiled. *That* smile again.

"Let's get you some new drinks. Seems you've spilled lemonade all over us."

I looked at his leather suit and noticed the remnants of where the liquid splashed.

"Sorry."

After arguing that he didn't need to replace my drinks especially given the fact it was my fault, I stood quietly and waited at his insistence.

I was handed a sturdy beverage holder along with

another one of his smiles.

In my peripheral vision, I saw John making his way over to us. I nodded my thanks once again and turned, making my way over to my boyfriend.

"Hey. What took you so long?" he asked, detaching a drink from the holder.

"I got into a fight with the lemonade." I spread my arms wide and looked down at my drenched shirt. "Clearly, I lost." I chuckled.

"We're leaving in about an hour. Do you mind sticking around until then?"

I offered a quick shrug, suddenly interested in the motorcycle races that were beginning in less than fifteen minutes.

John took the tray of food and popped a curly fry into his mouth as we walked back toward the ambulance.

I knew I shouldn't have looked back and glanced at Mr. Leathers, but I did. With his head looking over his shoulder, I caught his eye and guilt flooded me when I allowed him to hold my attention for a moment too long. I looked over his shoulder to where Strong was slowly walking over with a deep scowl and furrowed brows. He also held my attention for a moment too long.

The beast of a man in black followed my eyes then looked back at me. His lips tugged into a knowing, sly grin before he turned his head, continuing to stand in line for his order. Silver block letters stitched closely together spelled "PARKER" across the wide expanse of his leather-covered back.

PARKER.

I only made it twenty steps when lust urged me to look back. My eyes grew wide when I noticed the two men, Parker and Strong, standing there, watching me. Feeling guilty, I made myself turn away.

I followed a clueless John back to the bench near the ambulance and ate the barely warm cheeseburger while we waited with anticipation for the races to begin again.

"Up next, ladies and gentleman, we have the race you've all been waiting for. Lined up on the right is Alex Parker and to his left Tyler Strong. These two have been going head to head for some time. Let's see what happens today."

I craned my neck and tiptoed against the chain link fence, hoping to get a better view. Strong was seated on his bike, his hands rested on his thighs, and his head hung low beneath his helmet. Minutes later, the two men revved up their motorcycles and created thick clouds of smoke beneath their rear tires. I could've run up and climbed to the highest level of the aluminum stands, but I didn't. I felt closer to the action on the ground. And I had an even clearer view of the man named Parker.

There was such a feeling of excitement in the air; it was almost tangible.

John leaned over and yelled in my ear, competing with the noise and rumble of the crowd.

"I've got money on this race."

"What?" I chuckled lightly because John was as straight

and narrow as they came.

"It's no big deal. I put a few bucks down on the guy in the left lane."

Strong.

"Why?" I asked. "You don't know a thing about either one of them."

John twisted to face me as he raised an eyebrow and smirked. He was used to my passive way; this contention took him by surprise. With narrowed eyes, he stared at me, probably trying to figure out where Karrie, the girl who always went along with whatever he said, went.

It's the same look that appeared on his face when I told him I wasn't going to Tennessee with him.

His chest rose and fell as he looked at the two motorcycles lined up at the far end of the track. "The guy on the right is a complete douche." His face contorted while his voice dripped with disgust.

Parker.

"How would you know that?" I wondered aloud as I snapped my teeth then proceeded to shake my head, adding in a subtle roll of my eyes.

John gave me another sideways glance. "He's got a reputation around here. He's a D & D."

I laughed dryly, not appreciating his tone. "D & D?"

"Yeah. He's a dick and a douchebag."

What sounded like thunder followed by a freight train drew my attention back to the stretch of asphalt before me. I watched with rapt attention as the two motorcycles barreled down at insane speeds. My head snapped from right to left as they flew past, side by side as if they were one.

The crowd cheered when a light on the right lane illuminated with the numbers seven-five-two, indicating Parker to be the winner.

"Shit!" John roared in my ear, slamming his hand down on the top of the fence. "Son of a bitch!"

I stood there for a moment, completely and utterly baffled by my boyfriend's reaction to some silly bike race. With rounded shoulders and his head hung low, John shuffled back to the ambulance then kicked the back tire.

I realized then he'd bet a whole lot more than just a "few bucks" and lost. Big time.

Enraptured by the thrill in the air, I continued to stare down the track as the two racers slowed their pace and circled around along the side.

A thrill shot threw me the moment Parker rolled past me. It wasn't seeing him on the bike that made me shiver. As if time stood still, Parker and I were alone. He raised a gloved hand and lifted the clear visor of his helmet to look at me. In return, I removed my sunglasses and brought my hand up to my eyebrows, shielding the sun. Even though there had to have been two hundred people in the crowd, I knew the crinkling of his eyes as he smiled and the deliberate wink were for me. I felt it in my bones.

My head fell forward, my eyes looked at the gravel as my cheeks flamed red and a rush of excitement raced through me.

When I looked up, the second racer was now watching me, but he wasn't smiling, he was snarling with narrowed eyes. I thought it might be a good idea to give up racing if he were going to be such a sore loser for having lost. I kept my gaze on him and followed his line of sight to the blonde I'd seen earlier at the concession stand. She didn't look too happy.

The two men were lost to a sea of black leather.

*He smiled at me* I'd thought with a smile of my own. And then I remembered what John called him. "D & D."

And I felt guilty.

I found John sitting on a rock, still pouting like an overindulged brat.

"You ready to go?" I asked, offering a gentle rub of his back.

Air filled his cheeks before he allowed it to release through rounded lips.

"You probably shouldn't bet," I teased. "Stick to saving lives. It's what you're good at." I leaned over and kissed the top of head.

TWO WEEKS LATER, I accompanied John once again to the race track for the final race of the season. I didn't really want to go, but I felt as though I'd been summoned. Someone… something, was calling me, beckoning me to stand amongst all the others in the crowd, subjecting myself to a brutal beating of the late summer sun.

I walked over to the same spot as I had once before, claiming it to be mine and mine alone even though John stood by my side.

Immediately I recognized the two motorcycle drag racers. Parker and Strong were once again lined up side by side, motors revved up, tires spinning, creating a cloud of white. A tiny smile crept on my face, and I silently wished Parker "good luck."

"C'mon, douchebag. Win this race." John mumbled through clenched teeth.

I laughed as I turned and looked at him. "That's not very nice, you know."

As if he were mesmerized by the whole situation, he whispered, "He just needs to win. I *need* him to win."

Again, both racers moved up to the line and stared straight ahead. The intensity on both their faces matched the hard grips of the clutch and throttle. I had no reason to be nervous, but I was. I feared for Parker's safety. A hollow pit developed in my stomach as they both launched and came barreling down the quarter mile track.

My palms grew sweaty and my heart beat faster. Then Parker's rear tire began to fishtail from left to right. He managed to straighten out only to begin the sideways motion again. And then CRASH! In an instant, Parker's body was thrown into the air and tumbled like a leather-clad ragdoll behind his motorcycle until he eventually stopped a few feet from the finish line.

While I panicked and screamed a repeated cry of "Oh my God! Oh my God!", John cursed and moaned about having lost another bet.

"Smith! Let's go!" Gary, the other EMT called John's name.

Strong raised a fist in victory but circled back around immediately after crossing the finish line. He practically threw his bike to the ground before ripping his black helmet off and dropping down to his knees, yelling at his opponent.

Running full speed behind them as they rushed onto the scene, I came to an abrupt halt where Parker laid motionless on the black tar. I couldn't believe this man so full of life now was dead. His days on Earth were done. And for what? The adrenaline rush of racing a motorcycle down a straight strip of road.

Strong was told to move, but he didn't listen.

"Get your ass up so I can beat you fair and square. You hear me?" He lifted Parker's visor and spoke directly to the man who remained seemingly lifeless.

A deep, raspy voice emerged from Parker.

"I let you have that one, kid."

"Asshole!" The younger racer laughed.

When Parker turned his head in my direction, I released a huge sigh of relief at the sound of his voice and that smile. I didn't understand the feelings I was experiencing; this man was nothing to me. Nothing at all.

He couldn't stand on his own two feet without leaning to one side, even with Strong offering support. Despite that fact, it still took serious negotiating from Gary and John to convince Parker to get evaluated.

"I'm alright!" he kept saying. It was more than obvious he didn't like to depend on anyone.

I stepped forward as my traitorous mouth opened and spoke while my eyes softened and beckoned him to listen.

"Just let them check you out. It's better to be safe than sorry."

"You going to be there, angel?" His eyes traveled the length of my body from my hair pulled back in a ponytail to my flip flops. And back up again.

The eyes of all three men snapped at me and I gulped. A wave of heat surged through me and although I was embarrassed, I was flattered at the attention. I loved the way he looked at me. I loved the sound of his voice. I loved feeling desired. I loved it all. But I hated that my boyfriend was staring at me with confusion and hurt on his face.

"Let me help you," I offered when Parker once again lost his footing. So together, Strong and I each took one of Parker's arms, slung it over our shoulders, crossed our other arm across his back and walked him to the ambulance.

With a quick shake of my head, I rebuffed John's attempts to intervene and then offered an apologetic shy smile at Strong when our fingers accidently touched. Instead of a smile in return, I received the same harsh expression he wore weeks earlier. Disgust was back in place on his face. It was a shame because he was a really great looking guy.

One might even call him hot.

I rode in the ambulance with Parker at his insistence. John practically barked at me to leave the patient alone every time Parker tried to talk to me. When John turned to look at the small monitor mounted in the corner, Parker, with his neck firmly secured in a brace, squeezed my hand to get my full attention and then he winked at me.

John and I had the biggest argument we'd ever had in our relationship. Well, he yelled while I remained silent. What could I say to defend myself? I didn't ask to be hit on by Alexander Parker. I didn't ask to be the object of his affections, but clearly I was.

"Karrie," John started before he hesitated. "I think we should see other people. I'm going to Tennessee and since you won't come with me, I don't think it's fair to be tied down. I'm sure you'll find someone else, too."

My boyfriend didn't have to say the words, but I knew he was referring to Alex, the man who started showing up at my job and begging to take me out to lunch as a way to thank me for helping him that day at the track. I declined and declined…until I finally gave in.

It was supposed to be lunch, but we'd spent the afternoon talking and ended up having dinner together. I found him intriguing and knowledgeable. He could talk about anything because he was older and had experienced so much more that I had. He lived a full life and wasn't looking to slow down.

I knew in my heart that John wasn't the one for me, but never did I think Alexander Parker would be. Less than a year later, I became Mrs. Parker.

John texted me several times right before my wedding. He warned me about Alex's philandering ways, but that wasn't who he was anymore. He was no longer the D & D. He was my husband. And together we lived a full life, traveling to tropical destinations, dining at the best restaurants and rubbing elbows with a few A list celebrities he'd met along the way from racing.

Everyone wanted a piece of Alex Parker, but he was mine.

All mine.

# SIX

"HEY, YOU!" ODESSA CALLS AS I walk into the lounge area to warm up my dinner. "What are you doing here?"

I unzip my bag and remove the Tupperware of lasagna my mother packed after last night's dinner and toss it in the microwave. I haven't been in the mood to eat or even cook. Who the hell wants to cook for *one* anyway? That's almost as bad as going to a restaurant and asking for a "table for one." Pressing the buttons on the flat surface, I watch the food rotate until it dings.

"Karrie! Did you hear me?" Odessa asks pushing the fork away from my mouth. "Don't ignore me!"

I glare at her. "I heard you. What do you think I'm doing? I'm working. I do have a job to do." I proceed to eat my dinner.

"It's only been six days since…" she whispers with a voice filled with sympathy before it trails off.

"I know exactly how many days it's been since my husband died."

The walls start closing in on me, the air too thick to inhale. My chest tightens with anxiety and pain. Rising quickly, I toss my dinner, container and all, into the garbage can and walk out of the room without a single word.

I wander the floors, riding the elevators up and down, stopping to look at the newborn babies and then torture myself by standing outside the morgue. I ignore the stares and whispers.

On the way back to my floor, I walk past the MRI center and freeze. Lying perfectly still on the hospital bed, Tyler is wheeled past me. His face is swollen and his eyes are shut. If it weren't for the machines, one would think he were sleeping peacefully.

"How's he doing?" I ask the transporter whose nametag reads "Curtis."

He raises an eyebrow, indicating either he doesn't know or he can't tell me. Damn HIPPA law.

"He's my husband's best friend."

With a pitiful look on his face, Curtis realizes who I am and offers his condolences.

I thank him and glance at Tyler. My heart fills with remorse for not having been nicer to him. For so long I've hated Tyler Strong and now as he lay motionless and helpless before me, I can't help but feel sorry for him.

The irony of the situation is almost comical.

Almost.

"Is he going to make it?" I ask, running my hand along the bed rail, holding it still.

Curtis looks uncomfortable. "It's hard to say. I'm not a doctor, but I think with each passing day that he remains in this coma, his chances decrease."

I know this, but it's not what I was hoping to hear.

"Has anyone come by to see him?"

His lips narrow into a tight line and he shrugs his shoulders. "I don't know. I just transport."

Sympathy washes over me at the idea that he may have no family. I don't remember Alex ever talking about one. I sigh with sadness. "He's all alone."

"Actually, now that I think about it...I think I've seen a petite blonde hanging around at night."

"A blonde?" *Penny.*

"Yeah, the last time I had to transport she was there crying over him."

Something stirs in me and I lean over to inspect Tyler closely. I caress his unshaven cheek as moisture creeps into my eyes. This man, this broken man, meant so much to my husband. He was his closest friend and confidante.

"Listen here, Strong. Alex wouldn't want to see you like this so pull yourself together alright! You've got a little one on the way who is going to need a daddy so cut the shit and wake up."

With the tips of my fingers, I comb his wayward hair to

the side, his natural part no longer visible.

"I don't know what to do with all of Alex's things so I'm going to need your help."

Curtis walks forward and presses the elevator button. The doors slide open and he wheels Tyler in.

"He's in Room 1034 ICU."

I nod my thanks for the information and walk away in search of the nearest restroom. I step into the stall and lock the door when I'm overcome with emotion and vomit violently. I cradle the toilet and slide to my knees as my body shudders. And I cry. Hard.

I cry for my husband whose life was cut short. I cry for the years I will live without him. I cry for the young man who is in a coma and may never reopen his eyes. I cry for the child who will never have a father.

"Morning!" A surprised voice wakes me and I sit up, pulling the lever to return the chair back to its original position.

I yawn and wipe my eyes, glancing around the room. "Hey. Sorry I stayed so long. I guess I was more tired than I thought."

"No worries. It's nice to see someone finally coming to see him."

My eyes travel across the room and fall on Tyler. I feel an ache in my chest at her words.

"Why hasn't anyone been by? He's been here almost three weeks." I'm sure she can detect the resentment in my voice.

"Well...that's not entirely true. A couple of guys came by to see him, but they didn't stay long."

"No family? No blond woman?"

As she checks Tyler's vitals, she shakes her head and says no, but then adds that she only works the day shift so maybe people come later to visit.

I scrub my face and readjust my ponytail.

"You should talk to him. You know some doctors say they can hear people talking even when they're in a coma." She grabs his hands, one at a time, and massages each palm gently.

I force myself to walk over and stand beside the bed. I search Tyler's face as I had last night during my second break. After apologizing to Odessa and my charge nurse, they told me to go home, but I couldn't leave— not without stopping by to check on him.

"It's been eighteen days." I exhale sharply. "Why won't he wake up?" Hesitantly, I touch the hand closest to me and glide my fingers over the hard callouses on his palm. His hands are the hands of a hard-working man. A man who labors himself to the bone. With a soft touch, I encourage him to wake up. I need to tell him about Alex. I need to find out what happened. I need to know what transpired before Alex veered off the road and hit that tree.

"His brain took a pretty good beating. I think it needs

some time to heal."

Everything she says I already know from a medical stand point, but my emotions don't want to hear any of it. My chin quivers and I swallow the boulder lodged deep in my esophagus.

The weight of a stare prompts me to look up into the face of the curious nurse.

"Is he yours?"

A gasp reveals my shock. My face flushes red as mortification sets in and I drop Tyler's hand which lands on the white blanket with a light thud.

"God no!"

The tight smile combined with the expression on her face suggests a suspicion of my words.

"I'm married." I retort, glaring at her and then correcting myself quickly. "I mean… I was...I was married." Stuttered words emerge from my suddenly parched mouth.

Her bright blue eyes drop to my left hand where my wedding rings still sit.

"I'm sorry." She clears her throat and muddles through an apology. "I didn't realize."

I blink slowly and nod, absorbing her sincerity. She doesn't know my situation. She doesn't know I buried my husband a few weeks earlier. She doesn't know how broken I am or how lost I feel. She has no idea what I've been through or how it's possible in this vast world with its billions and billions of people, I can feel completely and unimaginably alone.

Alex Parker quickly became the center of my universe. My life revolved around his; I would've followed him to the end of the world. He wouldn't have had it any other way. He said we were unbreakable.

I release a deep breath when she leaves the room. Left alone in the sterile and quiet room with Tyler, I'm hyper aware of the ventilator. Its sound is ominous and sobering.

"Um…hey Tyler… it's Karrie. Karrie Parker, Alex's wife."

My eyes flash up to the door when I hear a light knock, but no one enters.

"So I don't know if you can hear me or not, but I'm really sorry you got hurt. You got pretty banged up. The doctors think you need to rest and I guess they're right."

I feel emotion starting to creep up on me, but I force it down.

"I'm sorry you're like this. You must feel pretty shitty right about now. I know I do."

Alex's face appears in my mind and I smile.

"Alex sure did love you. God, he used to talk about you all the time to the point I didn't want to hear it anymore. I guess I didn't want to hear about all the girls you banged in the trailer or how they threw themselves at you. It was disgusting and degrading. That sounds weird, I know, but I guess I was afraid Alex would want the same attention from them. I know what it's like at the race track. After all, that was where Alex and I met, remember?"

I chuckle at the memory of meeting Alex at the concession stand.

"You didn't like me much back then either now that I think about it. I never did anything to you. I welcomed you into our home, but you were always so…rude."

I jab my finger at his waist.

"The truth is Tyler, I don't like you very much, but I would never wish this upon my worst enemy. Maybe we weren't very nice to each other. Maybe when you come out of this we can try to be friends. I think Alex would really have liked that."

The beeping on the monitor accelerates for several seconds before resuming to its normal rhythmic pattern.

I TAKE THE LONG way home, driving the scenic route but not really looking at it. Procrastination has become my middle name. I don't want to press the garage door button and see the empty bay where Alex used to park his truck. I don't want to be in the big house by myself with every wall covered in pictures serving as a reminder of my life with Alex.

After finally convincing myself to drive home because my eyelids were closing, I pull onto our quiet street and narrowly miss colliding with a silver sedan parked near the driveway. I glare at the older man sitting in the front seat, but I don't have the strength to beep my horn. I continue on and park in front of the closed garage doors.

In my peripheral vision, I see the figure approaching, coming closer with each step along the stamped concrete walkway. Wondering who this person is and what he's doing here, I raise my hand to prevent the morning sun from shining in my eyes so I can get a good look at him. He's in his early sixties with thinning white hair. His belly protrudes out and over his belt, a badge of some sort around his neck. The buttons on his shirt seem as though they might pop in all directions if he should so much as sneeze.

"Can I help you?" I have no patience to be cordial and friendly. "Are you lost?"

"No, ma'am." A sheepish expression crosses his rosy cheeks as his eyes find mine.

"What can I do for you then?" I smile, feeling more at ease.

"Are you Karrie Parker?"

I nod. "I am."

He lifts his right hand and presents a bulky envelope. I stare at the official document before drawing my eyes back up to look at him.

"What's this?" I ask, taking the heavy envelope.

"You've been served."

"Excuse me?" My face transforms with confusion. "What are you talking about? I think you have the wrong person."

"I'm sorry, ma'am. I'm just doing my job. I need you to sign and date right here." He points the tip of the pen on the line marked with an X.

"What?" I seethe.

"I need your signature ma'am to verify receipt."

I haphazardly scribble my name and hand the pen back.

"Have a nice day," he forces a tight smile as he turns, walking back in the direction of his car and starting the engine. My line of sight is focused on his car as he drives away until I can no longer see him.

My hand suddenly feels heavy; my fingers grip the folded parcel tightly before I allow my eyes to look at it.

Dropping my workbag and my purse to the concrete beneath my feet, I tear the envelope open and stare at the printed words. Left to right. Left to right. I skim the contents detailed in the letter and my heart begins to beat faster as comprehension hits me.

Divorce.

Alex is asking for a divorce. My husband wants to divorce me.

"What?" I scream, but nothing comes out. "This can't be. But, no!"

My chest hurts. I feel as though a spiked sledgehammer has plunged down onto my heart and carved out a hollow deep hole. I cover my mouth to prevent myself from vomiting as the air in my lungs escapes on a loud gasp. My fingers lose their grip and the papers slip from my grasp.

"Karrie? Where are you?"

I vaguely hear my mother's voice wafting through the air as she climbs the hardwood steps onto the second landing.

"Karrie! What's going on?"

I want to answer. I want to tell her about the papers I'd received hours ago. I want to tell her that my dead husband was going to divorce me and break our marriage apart, but my mouth is frozen, my voice is nowhere to be found, silenced by the decimation of my heart.

The door swings open and my mother bounds into the room, rushing to my aid when she spies me lying on the hardwood floor with my cheek flat against the long wide planks. My eyes focus on one thing and one thing alone.

"Sweetheart, what's going on?" My mother pulls me into her arms and cradles me as her fingers smooth back my hair. I know she's preparing to comfort the sobbing she's sure will come.

*My world is falling apart.*

With tears in her eyes, she looks down at me, the sympathy and perhaps pity is transparent. "Kare Bear, I told you it was too soon to go back to work. You need time." She leans over and kisses my forehead. "You need time to grieve and you need time to heal."

Time.

Time to grieve.

Time to heal.

Those three words seem impossible. How will time help anything? Will time give me back my husband? Will time fix what he thought was so broken he wanted to leave? Will time glue back the pieces of my splintered heart?

The faintest trace of my voice emerges as I draw my eyes to my mother's matching ones. Her normally bright eyes are red-rimmed and weary.

"Ma, I feel like I'm dying. I feel so lost. So alone." I gasp for air and cry out. "I can't do this."

The tears which refused to fall multiply and stream down my face, each one stinging my skin. As if my heart could take any more, the news that my husband wanted to end our marriage tugs at the thin stitching and leaves me wide open, vulnerable and empty.

I am empty.

"Honey, that man loved you. Even after all the times I wished he wouldn't, he was crazy in love with you."

*No, he wasn't.*

Again, her fingers slide across my cheek, pushing the long waves of hair back away from my face.

I attempt to open my mouth and articulate just how wrong she is, but I don't. I can't. I don't want the image of my husband, my dead husband, to be tarnished. Not yet. It's too soon. No one will ever need to know what his intentions were. No one needs to know that our marriage failed. No one will ever know this secret. *Or the others.*

"C'mon, let's get you up. You need to shower, eat and then get into bed." Begrudgingly I sigh and get up after a few more words of encouragement from my mom.

"Do you want to go away for a few days? We could be in Florida by tomorrow afternoon."

I blink lazily, remembering the last time I hopped a plane and went to their condo. I left my husband for a few weeks because he had forgotten our anniversary. Now I understand why. Perhaps he hadn't forgotten; it just wasn't important. Our marriage wasn't important. I wasn't important.

Shaking my head, I decline her offer, wordlessly picking up the picture of Alex and me on our wedding day to arrange it in its place on the bedside table.

My fingertips slide down his face. I remember cupping his jaw and kissing his mouth, telling him how happy I was and that I was the luckiest girl in the world. He couldn't contain the emotion from seeping out of his eyes. His smile was bright, his spirit elated the moment I became his wife.

I turn my hand and cover his face with my thumb, punctuating the fact he's really gone. And I realize if I hadn't lost him to death, I would've lost him anyway. The picture is but a memory of a happier time in my life.

"Go take a shower and I'll make you something to eat. You can't live on Coca Cola alone, you know."

"I don't. I add lemon wedges." I crack a tiny smile in appreciation for her attempts to lighten my mood. My smile grows in remembrance of all my mom has done for me as I head into the bathroom to take a hot shower. She and my dad…they are my rocks. My constant companions. My biggest fans.

"Thanks, Mom."

"Do you mind if I open a window? The room smells like smoke."

My eyes flash across the room to the garbage can.

With a quick shrug of my shoulders, I provide just enough affirmation for her to push the curtains back and open the windows.

As I close the bathroom door, I hear my mother call my name. I open the door and look through the small opening, finding her standing there with a warm smile.

"You're going to be okay, sweetheart. You're going to be okay."

# SEVEN

AFTER USING VACATION TIME, I request an extension of my bereavement days. I need another week off from work to cope with the loss of my husband. I spend each day grieving him, grieving our marriage and grieving myself.

The following Monday morning, I finish my twelve-hour shift and head over to the ICU. I set my workbag down on the chair and walk over to read the cards sitting along the window sill. The once bare walls are now lined with pictures of Tyler racing his motorcycle. Wilting flowers grace the tray table.

I smile at the picture of Tyler, Alex and many others standing around a tall trophy, each with an index finger pointed upward, exemplifying the team's final standing that day. Number one. Always number one.

I lean over the bed rail and look at the man lying still

as if he were sleeping peacefully. The constant beep of the monitor is a reminder of where I am. Where Tyler is.

"Looks like you've had some company."

The lower half of his face is covered with an unkempt scruff. The swelling appears to have gone down, but according to the nurse, nothing else, aside from his physical appearance, has changed.

"So how long do you plan on sleeping? I mean, don't get me wrong. I love to sleep, too, but I think you're taking it to the extreme." I offer a cheeky grin, but he doesn't respond.

Obviously.

He lies there motionless. I wonder what he's thinking about or if he can even think. Who knows what cognitive ability he'll have once he wakes up.

"You need to wake up because I have something really important to tell you and …I have to ask you a few questions. Really important questions…about Alex. "

The erratic sound of the machine catches my attention. I stare at the machine as I watch the red line peak and then fall.

"Can you hear me?"

Again, I look at the monitor and watch for the influx of activity.

Nothing.

"God, I'm so stupid. You don't even like me. Why would you want to talk to me? Me of all people. Maybe I should try to get in touch with Penny."

*Beep, beep. Beep, beep.*

The red line spikes.

"You can hear me, can't you?"

A wave of anticipation flies through me as I glance at the door before lowering the rail to lean over him. I rest my hand on his shoulder.

"Tyler, can you hear me?"

I rub his shoulder.

"You are stronger than this. You have to be. It's your name. You are Tyler Strong and you need to wake up. You have people here who obviously care about you. Some of these people traveled hours to see you and you didn't have the decency to open your eyes for them."

A slight movement of his left hand demands my attention.

"What are you doing?" I mumble to myself.

I watch the slight movement again. My eyes move down the length of his body to the movement under the white blanket.

Left hand. Left foot.

I blink with comprehension and swallow hard.

"You're racing, aren't you? That's what you're doing. Clutch and shift."

I pull my lips in tightly and refrain from laughing out loud.

Silvia, the nurse I'd seen last time breezes into the room.

"How's the handsome devil doing today?" she asks as she reviews his chart then checks the IV bags.

"I think he's waking up. Or at least he's trying to. Watch."

I point to the extremities he moved moments before.

Staring at the unmoving hand, I narrow my eyes and will him to move it.

"C'mon. Do it again."

She looks at me with a mixture of sympathy and pity and I find it rather annoying.

"I know what I saw. He moved his left fingers and raised his left foot."

"Okay. I'll make a note."

"You don't believe me. I'm not crazy and I'm not making this up!"

The irregular sounds coming from the monitor demand our attention immediately and I turn back, looking at her pointedly.

"He can hear me and I'm pretty sure he's thinking about racing."

The countenance on her face transforms into one of an apology. "Maybe you're right. Maybe he is waking up. Keep talking to him."

"What's that look for?" I ask.

"Look, you haven't been around for a few weeks. He took a turn for the worse at one point. His family called the priest and had his last rites read."

"His *family*?"

She nods.

"But he's still alive," I retort, trying to understand what it all means.

"He's alive physically, but there's no guarantee what he'll

be like when or if he wakes up."

An ache fills my heart.

"He's so young." I turn watery eyes on Tyler and sigh, feeling remorseful for having treated him indifferently, and sometimes even unkindly, over the years.

"And handsome," she adds before turning to the door. "I'll be back soon. His sheets need to be changed and he needs a sponge bath. He could use a haircut, too."

I shiver at the thought of this nurse touching him intimately.

My arms cross over my chest in anger when I picture him having sex with Penny that night at the bar. I remember her legs were wrapped around his bare ass and her hands ran wildly through his hair and over his neck. According to the intimate stories Alex had told me, Tyler enjoyed a rather colorful sex life. He doesn't seem like the type of man to depend on anyone, and though I don't know Tyler well at all, I'm pretty sure he'd be mortified at the idea of some stranger caring for him.

It's hard to determine if what I feel is anger or sympathy. Where are all the people who cheered him on? Where are all the people who came to my husband's funeral? Where is Penny? Why isn't she here caring for him? Why isn't she holding his hand, talking to him or bathing him?

And his family? As far as I knew, Tyler had no family. His parents split up when he was a kid and his mom lived out west. I thought that's why he gravitated toward Alex so much. The years between them were plenty, but they were the best of friends. One might even have thought they were brothers.

I run my palms over my face and release a deep breath of exasperation.

So many questions and no answers.

Judging by my internal clock, I realize it's time to go home and get some rest. My body is weary and my lids are heavy. I yawn as I walk over to the chair and toss my bag over my shoulder. A series of pictures grabs my attention.

They all appear to be of Tyler at different ages. Tyler on a dirt bike. Tyler on the pitcher's mound. Tyler at the Grand Canyon. Tyler playing hockey. Tyler smiling with an elderly couple. Tyler holding an infant swaddled in a hospital blanket.

Each photo tells a story of his life, but it's the black and white picture that calls to me. I lift it, inspecting the image captured along a beach. A young Tyler stands alongside a boy who looks just like him. Their white polo shirts and board shorts match the color scheme of the pretty woman and handsome, dark-haired man who stand behind them as each embraces a child lovingly. The joy of this family is apparent in the smiles on their tanned faces. It's obvious how much love is shared amongst them.

"You have a twin." I glance to the side at Tyler. "I didn't know that about you."

I chuckle humorlessly and wonder how I would have known that anyway. The only glimpse into Tyler Strong was through my husband's perspective, through his words, through his eyes.

I yawn again and set the picture back in its place.

"I've got to go Tyler. I worked all night and as much as I don't want to go home, I have to. Can I tell you something?" I roll my eyes at my own stupidity. It's not like he's going to answer anyway.

"It's so quiet at the house. I miss the sound of the trucks. I miss Alex talking about racing. I miss seeing you wait by the truck. I'm surprised you never took off a coat of paint with all the waxing you did while you waited for Alex to come out."

Laughter erupts when I realize how crazy I must look talking to myself.

"I'll be back in a few days. I might even bring something back for you."

From the corner of my eye, I see the fingers of his left hand curl inward.

"Have fun. Be safe," I utter quietly.

I close the door behind me, hoping Tyler has a good ride even if it's only in his dreams.

THE FOLLOWING WEDNESDAY after dodging phone calls from Alex's attorney for several days, I finally slide my finger across the screen and accept his call.

"Hello, Roger. What can I do for you?" My voice is even and stiff. Roger had not only been Alex's attorney and closest confidante for years, but also the one who'd saved his ass so many times in their younger days. I still can't believe how reckless they had once been. The women. The sex. The parties.

"Karrie," he starts then pauses with a raspy timbre. It appears the years of hard alcohol and smoking cigars have finally caught up to him.

"I'm so sorry. I got back from Africa late last night and just heard about Alex. My God, I don't know what to say."

That makes two of us. Words evade me as thoughts scurry away from my brain.

I hear him sigh on the other end of the line. "What happened?"

Taking a deep breath, I tell Roger about the accident. I spare him the horrific details I witnessed at the hospital when he was brought in.

"I am so sorry." It's obvious he's fighting a losing battle with his emotions. "Alex is gone." The resolve in his voice wanes as reality sets in. Alex is gone.

"You were a good friend to him. I know he cared about you very much."

"He was like a brother to me."

I nod even though he can't see me.

"Can I come see you?"

"Why?" I blurt out and then restate my words. "What do you need to see me about? Is this about his will?"

"Karrie, please. I need to see you…in person."

"I'm working all week," I lie. "We can meet next week."

"I'd rather see you sooner than that if you don't mind."

"What's the rush?"

"I need to tell you something before you get ser—"

"Served? Is that what you were going to say?" I spit as a flood of disgust rips through my tense body.

"Oh God." I hear the pity in his voice and the creak of his chair. "You know already, don't you?"

"Know what? That my husband filed for divorce before he died?"

A rush of air releases from his lungs. The silence builds until he utters on simple word, "Yes."

"Does it really matter now? He died! My husband died!" Tears spring to my eyes and release in a torrent.

"I'm coming to see you. Don't leave." The line goes dead instantly.

An hour later, I answer the door and am hauled into Roger's chest. His button-down dress shirt reeks of smoke and stale whiskey. Minutes tick by as he offers and receives comfort for the death of his friend Alex.

I lead him into the living room and we sit adjacent to one another. I sit in the single chair as he takes a seat on the oversized sofa.

"Karrie, I have to tell you how shocked I am by this almost as much as I'm sure you are. I had no idea. He never said a word. He didn't seek advice from me. He didn't file with me. I'm completely dumbfounded by this whole thing. And what makes matters worse is the bastard isn't even here to answer any questions."

I search into his gaze, trying to find a shred of deceit in his eyes, but I find nothing but pure shock and surprise. He really didn't know Alex was going to leave me.

"How did you find out then?" I wonder aloud. "If he didn't file with you, how did you know?"

"I received a certified copy of the letter seeking the divorce with a Post-It note attached that said, 'I'll explain later. I need to do this.'"

I sit there solemnly, absorbing his words, knowing I'll never have the opportunity to ask Alex the millions of questions I have.

"There's more I need to tell you."

Roger rises and sits closer to me, taking my hand in his, preparing me for more bad news. A lump forms in my throat, and I force it down.

"Alex changed the beneficiary of his will."

Goosebumps dot my skin as my blood runs cold.

"He what!? Why?" I scream, pulling my hand away and yanking at my long hair. "Why would he do that? I don't understand!"

"I don't know! He had become distant and…secretive. I thought he was having a mid-life crisis or something."

"Who is it?"

"What?" Roger's eyes widen, rounding like giant orbs and he swallows nervously.

"Who is it? Who's the beneficiary?"

With shagging shoulders, Rogers sighs in what seems like relief.

"Tyler."

"Tyler?" I breathe. "Tyler Strong?"

Roger tightens his lips and he nods a glum confirmation.

"I," I stutter. "I don't understand any of this. We had a good marriage. Was it perfect? No, we had our problems. No one's marriage is perfect, but this—

I race to the bathroom, slam the door shut and vomit what little sustenance I was able to keep down at lunch.

Ignoring the soft knock on the door and Roger's pleas, I kneel over the porcelain bowl and continue to unleash the involuntarily purging of my stomach. It feels as though my soul is being expunged, too.

An eternity seems to stretch as the afternoon sun descends in the sky, its light shining brightly through the window as if taunting me with happiness.

"Call me later. We can talk about your options."

When I'm sure he's gone, I open the bathroom door, go upstairs to shower and drive over to get some answers. I'll wait forever if I have to

# EIGHT

Six days later stiff and stone-faced, I lean forward with my elbows bent, resting on the cushioned arms of the chair. I carefully watch the rise and fall of Tyler's chest. My blinks become few and far between as my eyes focus on his every movement. I don't speak to him today. I can't be responsible for the hateful words I'll spew.

"Do you want a cup of coffee?" An older nurse asks after she checks Tyler's vitals.

I draw my eyes up slowly and meet hers. I shake my head subtly, wordlessly.

"He's not going to be too happy to see you like that when he wakes up again."

Again, my eyes snap upward. "What did you say?"

"He's going to want to see you healthy with a pretty glow on your face."

My lips curl upward. "What are you talking about? When did he wake up?"

She gives me a sympathetic smile. "A few days ago. He opened his eyes and looked directly at the chair you're sitting in. He let out this deep howl and then closed his eyes. Didn't anyone tell you that?"

I blink and return my eyes to Tyler. "No."

"I think he was looking for you."

My breathing quickens as my heart beats harder.

I don't respond.

"I know what all the young people around here think. I'm a nurse. I get the science behind it all, but I also see the connection between people's souls. I feel it in here." She flattens her palm against her heart. "His soul was looking for yours. He's waiting for you to bring him back or let him go."

Tears fill my eyes at the thought of letting go. I've lost so much already.

"He needs to come back," I whisper.

The plump, kind-hearted woman walks over, pats my shoulder and smiles.

"Then tell him that."

Moments later, I'm left alone with Tyler.

Dragging the heavy chair closer to his bed, I rest my chin on the rail and stare at the man who conspired with my husband to take everything from me.

"I hate you," I whisper through gritted teeth as angry tears spring from my eyes.

"I hate you so much. You and Alex...I hate you both so

much. I don't know what I did to deserve this, but you're not going to win. You are not going to take my life away from me. I won't let you."

I swipe my sleeve across my nose as I hiccup through tears.

"I will find out why you guys did this to me and I will never forgive you."

*Beep, beep.* The monitor increases its usual pattern. *Beep, beep, beep.*

"What's the matter? I know you can hear me." I rise to my feet and lean over the bed, my mouth inches from his face. "Open your goddamn eyes and look at me!"

*Beep, beep, beep, beep.*

"C'mon you stupid jerk! Open. Your. Eyes!"

Tyler's eyes, although still closed, move erratically as if he's trying desperately to open them. His lips twitch and purse.

"That's it! Wake up!" I raise my voice, encouraging him. "I need you to wake up."

Again his eyelids flutter but then close.

My voice drops to an ominous tone, my words emerging through gritted teeth. "It's okay, Tyler. I'll be right here waiting for you when you wake up." Little does he know that my wrath also awaits him.

I sit back in the chair and stare at him. He holds the answers to my questions. I've got time. Plenty of time.

A few hours later, after his vitals have been checked for the umpteenth time, Barbara, the grandmotherly nurse looks back and forth between Tyler and me.

"There's a lot of negative energy in the room. I feel it. Why don't you take a walk? Go get some fresh air."

I refrain from rolling my eyes as I shake my head and decline her recommendation.

"What does he like?"

"Excuse me?"

"Tyler. What things make him happy?"

"How should I know?" My forehead wrinkles with disdain.

"Aren't you two together?"

"No! I hate him!"

It's her turn to look confused. "If you hate him, why are you here then?"

"Because…well, because…I…it's complicated. He has something I need."

She smirks. "I'm sure he does." Then she winks.

"He has answers. I need *answers*."

"In God's time, darling. In His time."

I stare at her blankly.

"I'm going on lunch soon. Care to join me?"

"Thanks, but no. I'm going to wait for him to wake up."

"And when he does, be kind. Whatever this animosity is, you can't bombard him with it right away. He's been through enough hell; don't you think?"

My cell phone rings and my mom's name appears on the screen.

I stand, walk to the door, and step into the hallway

toward the waiting area before I answer the call.

"Hey, Mom."

"Hey, love. Where are you?"

I trace the joint line of the linoleum tile with the tip of my shoe. "At the hospital."

"Oh, you're working? I thought you had today off."

"No. I'm here with Tyler," I confess quietly then close my eyes as if that might drown out her next words.

"Why? Why are you torturing yourself? Sweetheart, he can't bring Alex back."

"You think I don't know that?" I open my eyes and exhale through my nose. "I need to talk to him. I need to be here when he wakes up."

"Your dad and I want to take you for dinner before we leave."

"Okay," I agree, knowing my stomach won't be able to retain much anyway.

"Are you sure you're okay with us leaving for a few weeks?"

"I'll be fine, Mom. Go. You've had this trip planned for so long."

"Call me when you get home. Love you."

"Love you, too."

Just as I turn to reenter Tyler's room, a petite woman with shoulder length hair walks in, towing a cute little boy gently behind her. I move closer to the door and watch through the small rectangular window as she lifts the boy onto Tyler's bed.

"Barbara," I call as the nurse heads down for lunch. "Who's that?" I motion with my chin.

"That's Stacy, Tyler's mom." A smile spreads on her face, pulling her full cheeks back, revealing high cheek bones. "And the little guy is Tre."

"His *mom?*"

"Yep."

"Is that his son?"

She shrugs.

"*That* I don't know."

"Thanks."

I stand against the wall, lurking for several more minutes until I hear a child's cry and instinctively, I rush into the room.

"What happened?" I ask, noticing a few blood drops on the floor near Tre's feet.

"Oh, baby. Let me see!" Stacy inspects Tre's fingers and hand, assuring him that it's only a small cut and that he'll be fine. She scoops him up and brings him to the sink to wash his hands off.

I move closer and ask if I can have a look.

She tosses me a suspicious look and asks who I am.

"I'm a nurse. I actually work here."

My words must convince her because she sets Tre on the small counter and allows me to inspect the cut.

"What happened?"

"He accidentally knocked over the vase of flowers. He's an accident waiting to happen."

I set about cleaning the superficial wound with antiseptic, smiling at the adorable boy.

"I'm Karrie, by the way."

"Stacy." She offers her hand and stares at me for a long while. She then smiles warmly and turns her sights on Tyler. "My boy's still not woken up again, huh?"

My eyes follow and land on him as well.

"No, but he will." I clear my throat. "He has to."

"I can't lose another son." Her voice drips with pain.

I gasp. "You lost a son?"

"Four years ago," she mumbles quietly. "Still feels like yesterday."

"I'm so sorry." And I truly am. The death of a loved one is almost unbearable.

An awkward silence permeates the room until Tre asks to get down.

"Let me clean up the glass. We don't need any more injuries, right buddy?"

From my squatted position, I can hear Stacy talking to her son, urging him to wake up if not for her sake, for Tre's.

I deposit the broken pieces of glass into the garbage and wash my hands all before grabbing my bag and heading for the door.

"I'm going home. It was nice meeting you."

Another warm smile beams from her face. "Hope to see you again. Thank you for taking care of my boy. He and Tre are all I've got left."

My legs carry me quickly to her as my arms wrap around

her thin shoulders.

"He's going to make it."

"Thank you," she sniffs.

Walking to the door, I pull it open and step through.

"That's her, isn't it?" I hear Stacy whisper to Tyler just before the door closes.

THREE WEEKS AND four days later, while I sleep soundly in the padded chair beside Tyler's bed, a grunt startles me, causing my eyes to flash wide open and my body to stand on two wobbly feet. I rub my eyes when I realize Tyler Strong has awakened from his coma.

His eyes are glassy as he stares in my direction. He's got a spacy, far-away look as though he's not actually looking at me but rather looking past me.

With a quick lick of my tongue, I moisten my lips, preparing to hit him with a barrage of questions, but not a single word manages to escape.

"W—"

His words cut short and he blinks slowly. "Wat—"

He's thirsty.

I step out of the room and find a Styrofoam cup to fill with ice chips.

"Wa—"

"Here. I pinch an ice chip between my thumb and index finger, sliding the frozen liquid back and forth across his cracked lips. A drip trickles down the crease of his mouth and disappears into his beard. His eyes never stray from mine as I continue the intimate motion.

"Don't move. I'll be right back." I close my eyes and mentally chastise myself. *Of course he isn't going anywhere, you idiot!*

A doctor and a nurse follow me into the room and check his vitals then run a series of quick tests which include flashing a small light into his eyes to assess his condition. His eyes appear to have more of a blue hue than green. When Dr. Bancroft completes his assessment and releases the hold on the skin above each eye, Tyler's eyelids remain shut.

"Did he say anything?"

I nod. "I think he was trying to say 'water.'"

"I'm sure he's parched. Wouldn't you be?" The doctor smiles, widening his eyes as his eyebrows shoot up. "We don't want to push him or expect too much just yet. It may take a few more days for him to be fully conscious and able to speak if he can at all."

Fear mingled with anxiety lance through me at the idea that Tyler may not be able to speak. What if he doesn't remember? What if he's suffered brain damage? What if he can't give me the answers I seek?

"We'll be sure to let his mom know when she comes back."

I look at him curiously. "When was she here?"

"About an hour ago. She didn't want to disturb you."

"Me?" I'm dumbfounded. "What do I have to do with

anything?"

"I don't know. She said you were talking to him. She said something about not interrupting the intimate moment and that she'd come back later."

Intimate moment? She must've seen me leaning over his bed, berating him. I had to restrain from ringing his neck because for every question I asked, I got no reply. It was far from intimate.

Claustrophobia sets in as the walls feel like they're caving in on me. I struggle for each and every little breath.

"I have to go." The words tumble out of my mouth as I grab my bag and race to the door. I can't get out of there fast enough.

"Where are you going?"

"Away from here." A gush of air escapes my lungs as I glance back at Tyler. "Away from him."

Tears blur my vision of the evening sky as grey clouds loom overheard. The sky opens up and buckets of rain fall angrily, pelting the roof of my car. I manage to arrive home although I'm on the verge of a full-blown panic attack.

My heart aches, my chest is tight and my lungs beg for air. Pulling into my spot, I blindly search for the button to close the garage door. Only the sound of the rain and the low idling of my car fill the space.

My arms circle the steering wheel and I cry harder than I have since the day I found out my husband was going to divorce me. Everything hurts. Even the follicles of my hair are sore from being pulled violently. My eyes, swollen and red, are like natural springs, continuing to produce endless streams of water.

I have a million thoughts running rampantly through my mind, a million questions battle to be asked.

With shallow breaths shuddering from within my chest, I look around the interior of my car. The time on the dash morphs into one number, the fuzziness becoming a solid speck of illuminated green. My head feels light, my body weightless.

Fumbling desperately, I find the button and open the garage door. I put the car in reverse, slam my foot down, clip the front quarter panel on the stone wall and back out haphazardly until I am parked in the middle of our upscale suburban cul-de-sac. I stumble out of the car and collapse onto the wet grass. I gasp for air like a fish out of water.

It's here where my parents find me.

"Karrie! Wake up!" I hear my father's deep voice.

"Oh, God. Is she okay?"

The worry tainting their voices is unmistakable.

My eyes flutter open and strain to focus on his face. "Daddy?"

"I'm here, baby girl." I'm lifted up by strong arms, cradled into his chest and carried into my home.

He sets me down on the leather couch and cups my face. "What happened?"

"I'm going to call Paul," my mother says, pressing the screen of her phone. "I want to see what he thinks we should do."

I search my brain, trying to remember exactly what led up to the episode which left me on my front lawn. "I couldn't breathe. I was dizzy."

"Have you eaten anything?"

My silence provides the answer for me.

"You've been under a lot of stress."

I struggle to sit up, but my dad forces me down with one firm word. "Rest."

"Does anything hurt?"

I nod and point to my chest. "It hurts so bad." My attempt to refrain from crying fails miserably. "I can't believe this is my life, Dad. How is this possible?"

My mother comes into view. "Paul thinks we should take her to the hospital…as a precaution."

With careful eyes, my father searches my face, looking for some indication that I need to go.

"I feel like I'm losing my mind, Dad." My voice cracks and my chin quivers. "I think I'm going to die of a broken heart."

He glances to my mother who quickly wipes her eyes.

"Let's get you checked out and then we'll come home. Okay?"

What can I say? My parents have always known what was best for me. If I only I had listened to them about Alex, my life wouldn't be in complete shambles right now.

"I want to shower first."

My mom walks me upstairs and gets me into the shower. Closing the lid on the toilet, she sits and talks to me. I ask about her upcoming trip and she does her best to keep things light. I know what she's thinking.

She thinks I tried to kill myself.

But the truth is my life is trying to kill me.

After pulling on a pair of yoga pants, long-sleeved shirt and my sneakers, I climb into the back of my dad's Audi and stare out the window as the night sky passes by. No one utters a single word.

I'm admitted to a private room for "observation". My vitals are taken every few hours and a line of IV fluid compensates for my dehydration.

The weight of someone's stare rouses me from a tumultuous night of rest.

"Hi, Karrie. I'm Dr. Mancini. I'm sorry to wake you."

My eyes widen and rake over the plainly dressed man standing beside my bed before I glance around the room, looking for my parents who are nowhere to be found. The only evidence of my mother is the black pashmina draped across the plastic chair.

"Hi. It's okay. I was just getting up anyway. Don't want to miss the breakfast buffet." I reply with a smirk while sitting up quickly and running my fingers through the tangles of brown. The aftermath of arriving last night with wet hair must be quite a sight. I pull the wild mane together at the nape of my neck. My fingers work quickly to divide the strands into thirds as I yank through the knots to form a long braid, securing the end with an elastic from around my wrist.

"That looks painful," he grins, teasing me.

"They're extensions. I don't really feel it. In fact, I don't feel much of anything at all." I give him a pointed stare.

He nods once. "So I've been asked to come pay you a visit."

I blink and lick my lips, preparing to ask the question to which I already know the answer. "Are you a shrink?"

He hums in confirmation. "Yes, but I prefer psychologist."

"Did my mother ask you to come?"

"She did," he confirms with a quick nod. "She's worried about you."

I snap my teeth and meet his stare. "I didn't try to kill myself."

"No one said you did." His voice, although pleasant, is patronizing.

I roll my eyes. "You didn't have to."

"Do you mind if I sit?" He points to the chair and when I agree, he sits, setting my mom's wrap on the edge of my bed.

"You've been through a lot in a short amount of time."

"Yep," I answer dryly. "My husband died quite unexpectedly...and he was going to —

He cocks his head to the side, listening intently.

I reach for the Styrofoam cup and sip the tepid water. "Is what I tell you confidential?"

"Of course. While you're not technically a patient of mine, ethics would disagree, so yes." A comforting smile tugs at his lips.

Nodding firmly, I announce, "Good, because I think I'm

going to explode if I don't tell someone soon."

Given the rising of his thick eyebrows, this man must think I am certifiably insane until his face returns to one of coolness. With gentle encouragement, he tells me to go on.

"I'm sure my parents told you what happened to my husband, but they don't know everything."

He tips his head once and confirms the situation.

"Well, a short time after I buried him, I arrived home from work to a strange man waiting for me."

"Go on."

"I was served with divorce papers. *Divorce papers!*" I sneer incredulously. "My husband was going to leave me!"

Even this trained professional can't hide the shock when his stoic face transforms to one of disbelief.

Leaning forward to reiterate my point. "That's not even the worst of it. He changed the beneficiary of his will."

As if robbed of his ability to speak, Dr. Mancini sits there cross-legged, stunned, searching to find appeasing words to offer.

"He named Tyler the sole beneficiary."

Finally, he speaks. "Who's Tyler? His brother or his son?"

I laugh sardonically. "Neither."

"He named a stranger the benefactor of his estate?"

My eyes roll. "Tyler's his best friend. He was in the truck the night Alex died."

The conversation continues for what seems like forever as I tell him about Tyler's condition and about my feelings toward him.

"Hate is a strong word."

"Well, it's true. I do hate him. He conspired to steal everything from me."

"And you're sure about that? Do you have proof or are you speculating?"

I narrow my eyes in thought, realizing I don't have proof and I won't have any answers until I have the chance to talk to Tyler.

Air whooshes from my lungs in a deep exhale.

"Please don't tell anyone, especially my parents." I smooth my hands over the thin white blanket and reach down for the soft black material. I pull gently at the frayed edges of the wrap as I digest his words.

"Karrie, I'm bound by confidentiality not to tell anyone… but I think it's a conversation you might want to have with them when you're ready."

"Let's talk about what happened last night."

I recall the events from the moment I ran away from Tyler's room to the second I entered the garage.

"What was I thinking?" I tip my head back on the pillow and look at the lights on the ceiling.

"You could've died from carbon monoxide poisoning had you not had enough sense to open the garage and back out."

The thought sends shivers down my spine, goosebumps line my arms.

He reaches into the front pocket of his button-down shirt and scribbles effortlessly on a pad, lifts the paper by the edge and then rips it off. "Here."

I reach for it. "What's this?"

"A prescription for Xanax."

"Why?" I ask with reservation.

"What you experienced was an anxiety attack. This should help."

"But I don't typically have anxiety," I retort, setting the paper down.

"That may be true, but what you're going through isn't exactly 'typical.'"

The pad is tucked back into his front pocket. I'm grateful he isn't writing any more prescriptions. I hate to put anything into my body.

The door opens, my breakfast is carried in on a mauve colored tray and set on the table.

I thank the young girl who quickly ushers herself out.

Dr. Mancini stands, reaches into his navy blue dress pants and pulls out his business card. "Here."

Tight lips express my skepticism before releasing a quiet sigh. I stare at the card for some time then accept it.

"Why don't we set up a time for you to come in and talk?"

I want to scream and holler that I don't want to talk to him. I want to tell him that I simply want my old life back, but I don't. I quietly thank him before he turns and leaves.

My cell phone rings with a familiar tune. I see Pam's name on the screen and once again reject the call. It's the fifth time I've rejected her call. I know she wants to help, but

I just need to be left alone.

Wrapping myself in my mother's pashmina, I am comforted as if her arms cradle me. I close my eyes and don't reopen them until my parents come back into the room.

Sympathy and pity spread across their faces.

"Can we go now?" I ask.

"As soon as you're discharged," my mom says, caressing my face softly.

My dad steps forward. "We think you should stay with us for a while."

They're still not convinced about last night's incident.

"Dad, I promise you. I would never do that. Ever. I love you guys too much to be that selfish."

Hours later, I step into the elevator assisted by a parent on each side. My dad presses the button for the lobby, but I reach out and press number five.

He gives me a questioning look.

"I need to see Tyler."

# NINE

AFTER FINALLY CONVINCING MY parents that I was in fact okay, I hug my mom then my dad before stepping out of the elevator with a promise to call them the second I get home.

I walk down the hall and press the button. A monotone voice asks who I'm here to visit.

"Tyler. Tyler Strong."

The door clicks and opens. I raise a hand and wave as I pass the nurse's station.

Peeking into the window I see Stacy resting on the chair; it's the same chair I've sat in over the past few months since the accident. Debating whether I should go in, I eventually knock softly on the door. With a warm smile, she motions for me to enter. I glance around the room and notice more pictures now line the window sill and fresh flowers fill the tall vase.

"Hi," I whisper as I wash my hands at the sink after setting my purse down on the counter. "How's he doing?"

"Okay," she sighs, her eyes drifting back to her son. "He was awake earlier." I detect hope in her voice.

"He was? That's great!" A feeling of euphoria passes through my body.

And I don't understand it.

Not at all.

Stacy stands and offers her seat, but I decline, choosing to move closer to Tyler's bed.

"You look tired. Is everything okay?"

I nod and admit that it's been a rough couple of days, but assure her that I'll be fine. *After all, how much worse could things really get for me?*

"What are the doctors saying?"

She looks at me. "They're hopeful. He hasn't said much. He mumbles incoherently and stares in this direction."

"You can touch him. He won't bite." She smiles after noticing how my fingers are curled around the metal railing.

My eyes drag upward toward Tyler's face. "He could use a haircut. I've never seen his hair this long."

"Oh, that boy would blow a gasket! Did you know he goes to the barber every ten days?" She rolls her eyes playfully.

I smile crookedly. "No, I didn't know that. He sounds kind of high maintenance."

"He had a head full of curls when he was little. He would threaten to use a pair of scissors on himself if I didn't take him for a cut."

Unexpected words slip from my lips.

"I could give him a haircut."

"You're a hair dresser and a nurse?"

I laugh and shake my head.

"No, I used to give Alex a trim when he didn't have time to go to the barber. I could bring the clippers tomorrow."

Blue eyes watch me carefully.

"Oh God! I'm sorry. I didn't mean to overstep." I rub my forehead nervously.

She stands and runs her fingers through her son's hair.

"No, it's fine. I think he'd like that. He'd like that a lot actually."

I tip my chin to the window sill. "What's with all the pictures?"

She looks over her shoulder, smiling at the multitude of snapshots. "The doctor said to talk to him about things he's done, places he's gone. You know… to remind him he's got a great life to come back to. He's always been the kind of person people naturally gravitate toward. So many people love him."

A nasty thought surfaces about the number of women who also love him, but I suppress it, wondering why I care. Tyler Strong is nothing to me. Perhaps it's because if all these women flocked to him, they would've flocked to Alex, too. My husband loved being the center of attention.

"This one," Stacy says, holding a silver framed photo, "is one of my favorites. My mom and dad adored him."

It's the picture of Tyler leaning forward in between an elderly couple. His boyish smile stretches from ear to ear.

"He was so good to them. Went to visit them every Sunday, mowed their lawn, fished with his grandpa and ate whatever my mother made. Needless to say, she wasn't a very good cook. Apparently bland was an ingredient she used often."

I chuckle lightly and smile when I notice she's grinning back at me.

"He really is a good guy with a big heart. He would never hurt a fly."

I want to agree, but I can't. The man she describes is not the man I know.

"May I ask a question?"

Her hand stills on his cheek and she replies with, "Of course."

"Where's Ty's dad? Has he come to visit?"

The color on Stacy's face pales, turning a shade of grey as she turns her eyes on me.

"No. He left when the boys were twelve."

"Oh." I flick my gaze to the picture of the family of four. The years between the photo and when he left weren't many.

"He left me for a woman with four kids of her own." She sighs sadly. "He left his children to raise someone else's."

My heart cracks for Stacy, for Tyler and his brother.

"I'm sorry."

"I should've divorced him years earlier, but I couldn't do that to my boys. Tyler never forgave him. His father was his world."

Again, my eyes land on Tyler, observing every detail of his face as my hand follows, resting on his. I squeeze his warm hand gently, offering my condolence for the pain he went through. No child should have to experience that.

Inhaling deeply with closed eyes, Stacy kisses the photograph.

My fingers squeeze again and for a second, I almost think I feel a squeeze in return.

"He was my wild child." She picks up a picture of the boys at their graduation, complete with caps and gowns.

"Thomas never played by the rules. While Tyler worked through his father's sudden departure, Tommy couldn't deal with it. At sixteen, he started getting into all sorts of trouble. Drinking, girls, partying. He couldn't hold a job and only cared about himself. My heart broke for him." She presses the picture to her heart.

"He never even got to see his son."

My brain struggles to comprehend everything she's just said. Her words reveal a much different Tyler Strong.

"Ty did everything he could to rein his brother back in and when he died, Tyler lost it for a while there. He started to follow in his brother's footsteps with the drinking, women and partying."

*That's the Tyler I know.*

"I'm sorry about Thomas. Losing my husband was hard enough, I can't imagine what it's like to lose a child."

"And to think I almost lost two."

Stacy gives me a pointed look which makes me uneasy.

"You need to bring him back to me. Please."

"Me?" I gasp. "Tyler and I aren't exactly the best of friends. In fact, we're not friends at all."

She drops her eyes to my fingers clamped around her son's. She doesn't say anything; she doesn't have to.

"It's complicated." I pull my fingers away, choosing instead to hold on to the rail as a current of confusion flies from my head to my heart.

*What is going on with me?*

"Did he ever talk about Alex?" I ask hesitantly, tugging on my braid to keep my fingers from returning to touch Tyler's skin.

"Sometimes. He looked up to Alex sort of as a father figure or maybe he was trying to replace the brother he lost. But more recently, Ty talked about you." Her words are uttered so softly I think I've misheard as she looks down to the floor.

"Me? Why would he talk about me? He hates me." *And he conspired with Alex. They thought they could just take everything and leave me in the dark.*

Without lifting her head, Stacy snaps serious eyes upward to meet mine. I don't understand the implication behind her stare. "No." She shakes her head as she swallows quietly. "My son doesn't hate you."

I lick my lips and force myself to swallow, processing her words as a ball of jumbled nerves rolls in the pit of my belly.

"Are you going to be here for a bit?" she asks, reaching

behind her, grabbing her purse from the lone chair.

"Yes." I reply in confirmation, hoping to ease the stress on her pretty face. *I've got nowhere else to be and I still need answers.*

"I'll be back in about an hour. I've got to pick up Tre from school."

"I'll be here." I smile tightly.

Stacy pulls her phone out and asks for my number. "I'll call you so you have my number. Please call me if anything changes."

Sliding her phone back into her purse after securing my number, Stacy walks out of the room, her steps seemingly a bit lighter and somewhat buoyant.

I use the bathroom and check in with my parents. After my mother offers unsolicited advice matched by thousands of questions as to why I'm still at the hospital, I end the call abruptly and then text her an apology.

My feet stop dead in their tracks when I step out of the bathroom and see Tyler. His eyes are open and his head turned in the direction of the chair. He blinks slowly as if trying to focus. The soft material of white covering his chest rises and falls with a heavy sigh.

I creep over quietly, unsure about his coherency, wondering what his reaction will be to seeing me here again. The last time he was so parched; he seemed only concerned about a drink of water to moisten his cotton mouth and dry, cracked lips.

Tyler moves his head and stares at the ceiling for a long

while until his eyes close. He doesn't ask for water, he doesn't utter a single word, but I get the feeling he's disappointed for some reason.

Once he's asleep again, I take full advantage and walk over to the window sill to get a better look at the photographs. Staring at the images captured, I'm overcome with the knowledge that I don't know Tyler at all. Not really.

Minutes pass by, turning the hands of time into hours. I find myself sitting quietly in the chair, reading on my phone. I've answered a few texts from my mom and one from my dad. Guilt washes over me when I decline Pam's call yet again.

When I look up, I'm stunned to find bluish-green eyes staring at me unwaveringly.

I stare back.

"Hi." I smile and rise to my feet, sliding my phone into my back pocket and reaching for the metal rail.

His eyes smile in return as he attempts to move his lips.

"How are you feeling?"

A grunt escapes from his chest.

"Are you thirsty?"

Tyler blinks slowly, his lids displaying a negative response.

Opening his mouth, parting his full lips, he squeaks a single word. "Why?"

*Why?* The utterance is packed with a million questions.

"You were in an accident. Do you remember?" I ask cautiously, reaching down to touch him, running my fingers over his warm skin in preparation for his response. "You got hurt pretty badly."

With each slow blink, Tyler's eyes scan every square inch of the room as if he's trying to process my statement. Then he looks directly at me.

"Al—"

I swallow hard as he waits for my reply.

His eyes widen as he repeats, "Al—"

My heart breaks for the amount of effort it's taking for Tyler to speak my husband's name.

My chin quivers and tears fill my eyes as I shake my head. "I'm so sorry."

A gut-wrenching groan mingled with a deep inhale release, marring Tyler's serene face. His face crumples and his eyes slam shut. The beeping on the monitor shrieks loudly, erratically.

"It's okay." I soothe him. "It's okay."

As if trapped in his own body, Tyler's head thrashes from left to right, but the rest of his long body remains still.

I reach for his hand and squeeze it gently, calming him, reassuring him, comforting him.

Tears slip from the corner of his eyes and race down his cheek. His chest rises quickly with hiccups. It's as if he's struggling for air.

I know the feeling all too well.

I run to the sink, grab a paper towel and wipe his cheeks, feeling off kilter as my fingers touch his face.

"You're going to be okay. You have to be."

Unfocused eyes, light years away, gaze into mine. I think he's gone back into his own little world until he whispers with a raspy voice.

"Y—you," he breathes as if it's taking so much effort. "Kay?"

I moisten my lips with a quick swipe of my tongue.

"You...okay?" he whispers yet again.

I collapse into the chair, burying my face in my palms and sob quietly. My shoulders bounce as emotion rips through my body.

"K—"

I can't stop the deluge from escaping. All the feelings I've experienced since that night in the hospital when they, my husband and his best friend, were brought in as John Doe number one and number two gush out of me.

"K—" Tyler's voice is strained.

"I'm sorry." I lift my head and show my face as hot fat tears continue to fall. I want him to see how much Alex has hurt me.

I want him to see how much *he* has hurt me.

I want him to feel my pain.

Tyler's fingers move to the edge, making their way closer to me. My fingers reach out and link with his, offering something I don't understand. Sympathy. Compassion. Understanding.

In that instant, one moment in time, something changes, something shifts. A bond is formed.

His grasp on my fingers tightens, slowly bringing our

joined hands upward to his mouth. With gentle pressure, he kisses my knuckles. The contact sends an ache through my core and forces my eyes to search his.

*What is this?*

He keeps his eyes focused on mine until they close and his hand goes lax. I wish I could explain what I see in them, but it's something I've never seen before. From anyone.

"Are you crying?" Stacy asks, breezing into the room with Tre and stopping at the foot of the bed. "What's wrong?"

I sniffle and wipe my tears, unsure why I feel disappointed to remove my hand from Tyler's soft hold.

"Nothing's wrong. He woke up and I told him about Alex."

The widening of her eyes reveals her surprise.

"You told him?"

I nod, looking up.

"I did."

"What did he say?" she asks, stepping closer to her son as she runs her fingers through his hair.

"He…he cried…and then asked if I was okay."

Sympathy spreads across her face. "Oh, my poor boy."

"Don't cry, Grandma."

Stacy and I look at the adorable little boy, Thomas' son.

"I'm crying happy tears, Tre," she lies, patting the child on the head.

I watch the interaction carefully and smile.

"Why does he keep doing that?"

My eyebrows furrow. "Why does he keep doing what?"

"Tyler. He waits until he's alone with you. I swear it's like he only wants to talk to you."

I cast a quick glance at Tyler before looking back to his mom. "No, I don't think that's true. I just happen to be here when he wakes up."

"Then you can't ever leave." She chuckles lightly.

Looking at the clock on the wall, the second hand moving quickly, I say, "Actually I do need to get going."

"Are you coming back tomorrow?"

I smile awkwardly. Taking hold of the bar, I lower it carefully and lean over. I place a quick kiss on Tyler's cheek then whisper in his ear.

I don't return for a month.

THERE'S A BRISK CHILL in the morning air which matches how I feel on the inside. It's been thirty-four days since I last sat next to Tyler. Thirty-four days since I last held his hand. Thirty-four days since I last saw his face.

"Why don't you just go there already?" Pam asks, walking quickly, breathlessly beside me on our five-mile trek around town.

I chug water from my bottle and shrug.

"I'm sure he's up now."

"He is." Guilt washes over me. "I had Odessa find out for me."

"Then go see him!"

I exhale a deep breath. "And what exactly am I supposed to say? 'Oh, hey! Sorry I ditched you for a month after I broke the bad news.' I don't think so!"

"You have to see him at some point. Just walk in there and talk to him."

"I can't," I refute. "He's being moved to a rehab center."

"The one on Belleview?"

I shake my head. "No. The one on Fordham."

"Oh." Her eyes widen in disgust. "That place is gross."

"I know." My heart drops a little.

"Well that explains the sudden change in our route!" she laughs, teasing me. "I'd go out of my way to see him, too!"

"Cut it out. That's not why! Have you noticed how fat I am? If I were pregnant, one might think I'm carrying the kid in my ass!"

"Hah!" she laughs. "First of all, you're not fat whatsoever. You have an ass. Do you know how many people would kill for that ass?"

"Not Odessa!" My legs quicken their pace to the point I'm almost jogging. Almost.

Silence becomes the third participant as we pass the Catholic school while young children step out of their parents' cars and walk to meet their teachers. I see Father Greene wave, greeting all the families before he waves to me. With a toss of my hand in the air, I reply swiftly and then redirect my attention to the road ahead of me just to avoid looking at the church where Alex's funeral was held.

"So have you finished yet?" Pam finally asks, giving me a raised brow.

I glance at my friend and nod quickly. "Just about. There's only a little bit left."

Each day for the last month, I've gone through Alex's things, donating most of it to Goodwill or the local shelter. I haven't decided what to do with his motorcycles, work trucks or trailer. His crew has been keeping up with the contract at the assisted living complex and should be there for quite some time.

Since our divorce was never finalized and Alex's will has not yet been read, I'm going about, doing things any wife who's lost her husband would do.

Out of sight. Out of mind.

Pam and I end our walk with a quick stop by Susie's Sweets for coffee and a freshly made lemon scone. Finding an empty bistro-style table for two outside, we sit and wait for the server to come by.

"I like your hair like that," Pam comments, eyeing my slicked back hair.

I run my hand over my short ponytail and tug at the end.

"It feels weird. I had long hair for so long."

"But you didn't like it long." Her lips tip into a smirk.

"I know... but Alex did."

I ignore the look on her face as we chat about nothing until our treats arrive.

Dunking my pastry into my coffee, I scan the street and notice an ambulance at the stop light. In the minivan following close behind, I see a familiar face. My eyes widen at the sight of Stacy who catches my eyes on a double take. The passenger window rolls down slowly and I rise, making my way over to the idling vehicle.

"Hi." I smile.

"I've been trying to call you." She glances ahead at the light and then back to me.

"Sorry. I've been really busy lately," I lie, looking into her vehicle at the empty water bottles on the floor. I feel horrible knowing that I've been ignoring her calls, choosing to decline or send them all to voicemail. In the beginning, I listened to a few of the messages she left, but after a while, I noticed when she called, she chose not to leave a message even though I sent it to voicemail.

"Ty's doing a lot better."

I see her genuine smile and reply, "That's great. I'm happy for him."

"You should come see him."

I sigh quickly and add a shake of my head. "No, that's not a good idea."

"He's been asking for you." Her tone is forceful and carries a hint of reproach.

"He has?" I gasp. "Why?"

"Karrie," she sings my name slowly before glancing at the traffic light.

"Tell him I said hello and that I'm glad he's doing well."

The ambulance moves ahead through the green arrow.

"You should come and tell him yourself." She motions her chin toward the medical vehicle. "He's right there. They're transporting him to the rehab facility on Fordham."

"Yeah, I know." The second the words escape I realize my error. Stacy knows I've been keeping tabs on her son.

The driver of the waiting SUV has lost his patience and honks, earning him a dirty look in Stacy's rearview mirror.

"He'd be really happy to see you."

I'm left alone on the side of the road as she turns left on Cherry and right onto Fordham.

"Hey, are you just going to stand there?"

I turn around and glance at Pam, rolling my eyes playfully when I notice she's now eating my scone.

"I think you're walking back on your own." I snatch the small piece that remains.

"Why?"

After taking a deep breath, I exhale slowly through a small opening of my lips. "I'm going to see Tyler."

"Like that?" Her eyes travel the length of my body and settle on my face.

I narrow my eyes. "What's that supposed to mean?"

"At least shower."

"Why? I'm not trying to impress him." A snapping sound emerges from my teeth.

"No, but you also don't want to send him back into a coma." She pinches her nose and pretends to gag while waving her other hand back and forth, insinuating that I smell badly.

Light laughter fills my belly. "I don't know why I keep you around!"

"Because you love me."

# TEN

I'M GRATEFUL FOR PAM'S advice. Deciding to wait until Tyler's settled in to his new living accommodations, I go home, shower and put on decent clothes. Fitted jeans, a long ivory-colored sweater and tall brown boots replace the tattered yoga pants and T-shirts I've worn for the past month. I spritz a light scented perfume on, air dry my hair, allowing the shorter locks to fall into soft waves. My face is kept natural with only mascara and lip gloss.

I struggle to understand why my nerves are a bundled ball of yarn; each end entwined with the other, creating a tangled mess.

I'm going to see Tyler just as I had for so many weeks when he lay still in ICU.

*Get it together!*

My car is parked in the visitor's lot, and I'm signed in

with my identification recorded. Although this facility isn't the best, its security is top notch. This place is like Fort Knox.

"Room 215. Down the hall, through the double doors. It's the third door on the left."

I thank the kind woman and set off to find answers.

"You can do this," I whisper to myself, finding the courage to enter the room.

With a light knock, I wait for a response, but then I turn abruptly when fear grips me.

The door opens, and I nearly do a complete one-eighty as Stacy stands before me.

"Hi! You came," she sighs, throwing thin arms around my shoulders. With another deep exhale, I can almost feel the tension dissipate from her body.

I wait for her to release me.

"Hi. I'm not sure if I should be here or not, but I need to talk to him."

"Of course! I can't wait to see the look on his face when he sees you!" She drags me by the hand. "Come!"

Here goes nothing.

"Tyler, I have a surp—"

Wide, shocked eyes lock with mine.

"Hi," I squeak.

I am not greeted with a kind welcome. His shocked countenance is replaced by a hard scowl and a gritted question.

"What are you doing here?"

Mortified, I step back, preparing to make a mad dash

from the room.

"I'm sorry. I shouldn't have come."

"Tyler, stop that! What is wrong with you?" Stacy reprimands her grown son as if he were a child.

Unsure about what to do, I stand there awkwardly.

"Do you want me to leave?" I ask Tyler. He responds by turning his head toward the window.

"Why don't I give you two some time to talk?" Stacy reaches for her purse and rushes out the door after giving her son a meaningful look.

I feel awkward and uncomfortable, instantly regretting my decision to come here.

I begin to utter an apology for my presence when he begins to speak.

"I'm sor—"

"Why—"

Tyler snaps his head in my direction. "Go ahead."

I force my eyes to pull away from his face as they drop to the floor. My mind races, struggling to remember how to speak coherently. The flutter in my belly is unexpected and unfamiliar. I'm left speechless.

"Fine," he snaps. "I'll go first." His voice drips with condescension. "Why are you here?"

*Great question. Why am I here?*

My eyes find their way to his. "I wanted to make sure you're okay." The tone in my voice lacks conviction. "How are you?"

A sardonic chuckle releases from his throat. "I was in a

coma for months. How do you think I am?"

I stare into those bluish-green eyes, trying to decipher how to respond.

"You were hurt pretty badly. I'm sorry about that."

"What are you sorry for? Did you cause the accident?"

I feel small and helpless until anger consumes me.

"Look! I don't know what your problem is with me. For years, you've hated me and for no apparent reason. I never did anything to you. I tried so hard to like you and welcome you into our home, but you didn't want to be a part of it. You just wanted to be Alex's friend. God only knows what things you got him into."

I shake my head and look down, whispering.

"I never understood what Alex saw in you."

I can tell my words are being absorbed by the rapid blinking of his eyes. Perhaps he's thinking of the reasons he dislikes me so much.

"Wow!" His eyes widen then fall. "Why don't you tell me how you really feel."

The hurt look on his face makes me want to apologize.

"I'm sorry. I shouldn't have said that." I admit. "I just don't understand this animosity you have toward me. Every time I've ever seen you, you had this scowl on your face."

"That's just my face." A small smile spreads across his face.

I appreciate his efforts to lighten things between us.

"And for the record, I don't hate you, Karrie. It was never about you...and yet it was."

Confusion sweeps across my face and I swallow the boulder of emotion in my throat. "What? What does that mean?"

He inhales sharply and shakes his head. "Nothing."

I should leave and never return, but I still need answers.

"Do you mind if I have a seat?" I motion to the plastic chair beside his bed.

"Sure," he replies with a quick shrug. "But it's probably not as comfortable as the other one."

Tyler looks at me with a slight smirk, followed by roaming eyes which travel the length of my body.

"What other one?" I ask, as I hang my purse on the back of the chair, looking around the room which is so different from the ICU.

"The one you sat in at the hospital." A meaningful stare laces into me.

His words floor me.

"You knew I was there? But—"

"I could hear you talking sometimes. At first it was fragments, just bits and pieces. It didn't make a lot of sense to me most of the times. Obviously."

My gaze falls to the colorful trees outside in the courtyard. My brain trying desperately to remember what I said, what I talked about, what I confessed. There were weeks when days and nights drifted into each other, where one began the other ended. It had become a vicious cycle of waiting for him to wake up. I wanted to tell him about Alex, yet I didn't want to crush his will to live.

Tyler and I sit in silence for a long while, each wandering in our own isolated thoughts.

My phone chirps with a text notification. Reaching back and retrieving it, I read a message from Stacy. I smile and then text back.

"Your mom is really nice. She's very sweet."

"She's a great person."

An appreciative smile graces his face before he continues.

"She's been through a lot. And now this. She's tough as nails. So much stronger than she looks."

Admiration rings straight from his words. There's no question how much he loves his mother.

I pull my eyes away from his and peruse his body until I reach his leg still clad in thick plaster.

"How's your leg?"

He sits up and curls his fingers into fist, knocking on the cast. "Still broken."

I feign a smile, but my eyes lock with his and reveal the truth.

Tyler is a walking miracle.

"The doctors said I'm lucky to be alive. Alex saved my life."

I want to counter his words and argue that it's Alex's fault he's here.

Every time I think about what happened that night, a niggly feeling creeps into my belly. Alex was the safest driver I've ever met. There's no way he lost control of his truck and trailer. It's impossible.

Something happened in the cab of his truck and I'm determined to find out what it was.

"Did a lot of people go to his funeral?" Tyler's voice drops to a sad whisper.

My eyebrows wrinkle with skepticism.

"You really want to know who was there?"

He nods.

"I don't really know. People from work, our friends, neighbors, and a whole group of bikers. It seemed as though a ton of people were there." The emotion I expect to erupt is absent. "You know how Alex was; he was Mr. Popular. Everybody loved him." I chuckle lightly, "Especially the women."

When Tyler doesn't respond, I continue to tell him about the memorial ride that's being set up for next spring in Alex's name.

"Who's organizing it?"

"Two guys I never met. I think they're from down south. And I think they said Penny was going to help, too."

His eyes widen at the mention of his baby mamma's name.

"Has she been up here?" he asks with a scowl.

I find the question particularly odd. Why wouldn't she be here? She is having his baby after all. I would assume either she's moving up here or he's going down there so they can raise the child together. The night I saw them having sex in the parking lot was definitely a couple in love. Or lust.

Shaking my head, I reply with a "no."

He seems satisfied with my answer.

"But she was at the funeral. It was weird. She gave me this really long hard hug and just kept saying how sorry she was."

"And that's it? That's the only time she's been here?"

I shrug. "I guess. I mean, I never saw her at the hospital. And I was there a lot."

My confession surprises both of us. My cheeks flush pink as embarrassment races through me. My eyes find the tip of my boots, avoiding the look of curiosity on his face.

"Why?"

I look up. "Why what?"

"Why did you come to the hospital so much?"

An expression of something resembling hope fills his eyes.

"I wanted to make sure you were going to be okay."

His single-word of "And?" indicates he knows there's more to the story.

I lick my lips before conjuring up the confidence to speak. "I want answers."

"What do you want t—"

The door swings open and a nurse with long red hair spun into a high bun wheels in a cart, greeting us kindly as Mr. and Mrs. before she begins the routine of checking Tyler's vitals.

Tyler and I quickly correct her misconception.

Minutes drift by as she continues her assessment.

"Chin down." She yanks her glasses from the top of her

head and slides them onto her face before grabbing his head and inspecting the jagged line on his skull. "Looks good. You'll have a good story to tell your grandchildren."

"Great," he retorts sarcastically.

"You're a real looker, ya know." She taps his cheek gently.

He blushes and mumbles, "Thanks."

"Oh, c'mon lad. Don't tell me ya don't hear that all the time."

"No, ma'am."

She cocks her head back, looks at me and rolls her eyes. "Does he always tell evil lies?"

Smiling, I raise my hands in the air in defense, removing myself from her line of questioning.

"If it weren't for that leg of yours, you'd be as healthy as a horse. Strong as an ox."

I grin at the woman's frank demeanor whose thick Irish accent is difficult to understand. I find myself laughing quietly as Tyler struggles to decipher her words.

"Name's Sinead. Let me know if you need anything." She tosses a word of farewell as she wheels the cart out of the room.

Tyler and I burst into laughter.

"*Sinead?* Who names their kid *Sinead?*"

"Sinead O'Connor's mother did apparently." I deadpan, suppressing another outburst.

A loud yawn erupts from Tyler as his chest rises and falls.

"You're tired." I glance at him quickly, noting his eyes

have become glassy. "I'll let you get some rest." I stand, but he reaches over and grabs my wrist, letting his fingers slide to mine.

I know the tickle in my belly and the erratic beats of my heart are in direct response to his gentle touch.

"You... don't have to go."

I detect a plea in his soft voice.

A swell of emotion forces my chest to rise and fall. I blow a small puff of air through my lips and sigh heavily.

"It's late."

"Stay with me," he murmurs before his voice trails off and only silence fills the room.

My eyes lock with Tyler's as my brain struggles to grasp the mixed emotions running rampantly through my body, wreaking havoc.

I lick my suddenly dry lips, forcing them to move from their frozen state. "I'm tired and I have to work tomorrow."

The expression on his face falls and his eyes fill with a sense of sadness mingled with compassion.

"I understand."

"I'll come back soon." I squeeze his fingers, releasing them only to lean over and place a slow and gentle kiss on his cheek. "I'm really glad you're okay, Tyler."

With careful eyes, he searches mine, perhaps looking for the truth in my words. "Thanks."

I gather my purse and turn for the door even though I don't want to leave just yet. Every fiber in my being is telling me to stay. *What am I doing? What is wrong with me?* Pulling the door open, I glance back over my shoulder when I hear him call my name.

Gone is the forlorn expression now replaced by a crooked grin. There's a hint of mischief in his eyes which holds my attention before he speaks.

"Don't make me wait for another month."

Inwardly, I'm filled with a sense of elation and excitement. Somehow I manage to simply respond with a small reassuring smile and a quick nod as I pull the door open and step through. Glancing quickly to my right and then my left, I search for the owner of the muffled laughter I hear only to realize it's coming from behind me.

I don't turn around.

*"Don't make me wait for another month."*

His words replay in my mind as my legs carry me away.

I whisper to myself.

"I won't. I can't."

My dad breezes into the kitchen and places a kiss on my forehead just as he always does after kissing my mom. The simple act transports me back to my childhood.

*"Daddy, will I ever meet a Prince Charming? Will he ride in on a white horse and take me to his castle?"*

*My father's brown eyes softened. "Princess, real love isn't like that."*

*"But you sweep Mommy off her feet all the time," I countered,*

*remembering all the times I spied them sharing a moment of intimacy, a stolen kiss or a long embrace.*

*My father smiled at my keen observation for an eight-year-old.*

*"Then maybe you're right. Maybe a handsome prince will sweep you off your feet and ride off into the sunset with you."*

"Karrie?"

My mom's voice pulls me from the memory.

I respond with a hum followed by, "What'd you say?"

"I asked how your visit with Connor went," she asks while standing at the stove sautéing garlic and olive oil.

"Fine." I shrug, not wanting to admit how helpful he's actually been. How much we've worked through everything that's happened over the past few months and my unexpected and inexplicable feelings.

"You know you don't have to see him specifically. There are many other doctors to choose from."

I realize she's misconstrued by indifference so I smile warmly, hoping to clarify.

"No, I like talking to Dr. Mancini. He offers a third party unbiased perspective and he plays Devil's Advocate." I look down to reply to Pam's text.

"He is the best at what he does," she murmurs.

I couldn't agree more. Our conversations would often begin down one road and lead in a totally different direction. When I ask him about it, he would always say the conversation leads naturally, going where it's meant to go.

"When are you going to see him again?"

My head snaps up.

"Who? Tyler? I don't' know," I stammer. "I'm not—"

The furrowing of my mother's eyebrows displays her curiosity laced with whisper of suspicion.

"I was talking about Connor."

"Oh," I mumble. "I have another appointment a week from Tuesday. Dr. Mancini is going on vacation."

"Why don't you call him by his first name?"

Again I shrug a lackluster response, offering all the reasons for wanting to keep it professional. The truth of the matter is it's easier for me to open up when I know I can speak freely and it's confidential.

Only Dr. Mancini and I know what's hidden in my heart.

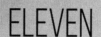

# ELEVEN

"Knock, knock," I say nervously as I tap lightly and peek in through the partially ajar door. My palms are coated with a sheen of sweat and my mouth is dry.

"Come on in," a female's voice calls, prompting me to push the door wide open and enter the room.

The rectangular box nearly slips from my hold when my eyes land on the pretty blonde sitting beside the bed.

A very pregnant blonde.

"Penny," I gasp, whispering breathlessly as my gaze moves to look at Tyler. In that moment, my attempt to decipher what I see reflected back at me is in vain.

"I'll take care of it," he says quietly, giving his girlfriend a pointed look.

A sharp pain lances through my chest when she rises and places a kiss on his cheek, thanking him.

His eyes close at the contact.

"I'll come by tomorrow."

I stand there observing their interaction, feeling very much like a third wheel.

Penny gathers her oversized bag and looks at me, smiling tightly.

I return the smile and ask how she's feeling, noting how great she looks.

"When are you due?"

"Three months." She rubs her protruding belly. "If I'm lucky, he'll look just like his daddy."

"Well, good luck." I say awkwardly.

Penny walks toward the door without so much as another word until she stops and turns around.

"I really am sorry about Alex." Sympathy flows from her eyes.

*Alex.*

I pull my eyes away from hers as I look down and close them, forcing the tears to remain at bay.

Seconds ticks by, forming endless minutes.

"What's in the box?"

The sound of Tyler's voice brings me back to the here and now, reminding my eyes to open.

Swallowing hard, I walk over to his bed and set the box down on the side table.

"I thought you might like some pastry. My friend Susan owns the bakery across town."

I remove the gold sticker holding the lid in place and

open the box, revealing an assortment of scrumptious treats.

"Thanks," he says, picking up a mini éclair, plopping the entire thing into his mouth. He moans his pleasure and I cross my legs, quelling the budding sensation. "Oh my god. So good," he says with a mouthful of a second helping. "So sweet."

I squeeze tighter.

"Aren't you going to have one?"

I chuckle at the playful tone in his voice. With a quick shake of my head and roll of my eyes, I point to the powdered sugar on his T-shirt.

"You're making a mess."

He glances down and then back up with a grin.

"I'm not always a messy eater."

Needing to remove myself from the heat of his stare, I cross the room and grab a few paper towels, offering them while carefully avoiding physical contact.

"Thanks." Tyler wipes his face and crumples the paper towel into a tight ball. "That was delicious! Thank you."

"You're welcome." I stand there, mentally suppressing the bubbling questions about what I am doing here visiting this man.

"Sit." Tyler points to the chair his girlfriend vacated minutes before.

"I'm fine," I retort.

"Do you have anywhere to be for the next few hours?"

His question floors me and I cock an eyebrow with inquisitiveness.

"Why?" I don't attempt to hide the suspicion in my voice.

"We need to talk. I was hoping you would've come by sooner, but three weeks is better than a month."

Embarrassed that he mentioned the length of my most recent absence, I sigh before explaining I've been busy with work, but that his mom has kept me updated with phone calls and text messages.

"You don't always answer your phone."

"What?" I question. "How would you—"

He shrugs. "I tried calling you a few times, but you didn't answer."

"Oh." I blink, trying to think of something better to say. "Sorry. Your mom kind of went overboard with the phone calls."

"I needed to talk to you."

"Needed?" I tease.

"Yes. *Needed*," he reiterates firmly.

I finally concede, sit in the chair and wait for him to begin.

With a soft clearing of his throat, Tyler begins.

"How've you been? How are you dealing with everything?"

I inhale and answer honestly, meeting his serious gaze.

"I've been better. Sometimes I feel like I'm living in a nightmare."

"Me too."

Although sadness tries to overwhelms me, I conjure up the strength to muscle through.

"I can't believe he's really gone."

"I know. I think about him every day. Why me? Why did I survive the wreck, yet he didn't? It's not fair. He had so much to live for."

"And you don't?" I ask, tipping my head to the side, offering a sense of empathy.

"Alex," Tyler utters somberly, "he had *everything*."

I prepare my heart for the words I'm sure are going to follow.

Tyler exhales loudly, pushing the air from his lungs.

"Roger came to see me."

"I know," I admit quietly. My eyes fill with tears that quickly threaten to spill over.

"Alex changed his will. He left —"

"I know, Tyler." I interrupt and reach for his hand. "I know everything." My heart aches for the pain and confusion I see on his face. He genuinely seems to have been unaware of my husband's plans.

Running his hand over his short hair, Tyler exhales sharply and groans his irritation, cursing under his breath.

"I don't understand. Why would he do this to me? Why would he do this to *you*? You of all people."

He focuses on something across the room and sighs, lowering his head as his shoulders sag. A hush of quiet finds its way into the room until Tyler slowly drags his remorseful eyes upward to look at me once again.

"I don't want it," he announces. "I don't want anything of Alex's." His words are laced with an unexpected fierceness.

With the bridge of his nose pinched between his thumb and index finger, Tyler wards off emotion that's brewing just below the surface.

"But it's all yours. Everything that was his is now yours."

"Not everything," he mumbles.

Tyler, taking my hand in his, shakes his head adamantly as if that alone could reject the truth. "I'm so sorry he did this to you."

The sight of his hand enclosed around mine demands my attention. His thumb moves rhythmically in a circular pattern.

"I don't understand it either, but I'm learning to accept it."

"How?" he asks before stammering through questions about why I'm not angry.

"Oh, believe me. I'm angry and devastated, but more that than, I'm confused and I'm hurt. But it's not like I can ask him what he was thinking."

My small effort at light-heartedness does not go unnoticed.

"This isn't really something to joke around about. It affects so much," Tyler chastises me. "So many lives."

I narrow my eyes and purse my lips in response.

"Well, what else can I do?" A broken, weak voice asks, dislodging itself from behind the boulder in my throat.

Tyler leans back on the pillow and looks up toward the ceiling.

"Selfish bastard."

The deluge of questions and accusations that I had prepared for the past few months are nowhere to be found. The anger and betrayal I felt toward this man before me has dissipated.

Alex Parker hurt the ones he claimed to love.

"I wish I could understand. I don't know how things got so…fucked up!"

The sound of Tyler's surprising amusement rings in my ears.

"I don't think I ever heard you swear before."

I release his hand and reach for the balled up paper towel, wiping my nose then eyes.

"You've never seen me mad then."

"No, I guess I haven't." The seriousness of his tone returns.

"Why did you always wait outside? Why didn't you ever come into the house?

His Adam's apple bobs when he swallows hard then shrugs.

"I thought it was best to… keep my distance."

"*Keep your distance?*" I shriek. "Why? Why would you need to keep your distance? And from whom?"

With a hard stare, his eyes gaze into mine.

"I just had to."

I blink rapidly, trying to understand the meaning behind his words.

"That doesn't make sense. You were the best man at our wedding and you helped me find Alex when he disappeared for almost an hour at the reception."

Tyler's eyes close and he clenches his jaw tightly as he swallows hard.

"Karrie, it was best for everyone."

Something in me snaps and I respond harshly. "Well I think that's rude. As a matter of fact, come to think of it you've always been rude. I remember looking at you as I walked down the aisle and even then, even on my wedding day, you had a goddamn scowl on your face."

The grave look on his face softens when he cracks a smile.

"You swore again."

"Because I'm mad!"

I rise to my feet and pace the room, running my fingers through my shoulder length hair.

"Please sit down or I'm going to hobble on my good leg and force you to sit down."

"Can't you see where I'm coming from though? There was never a reason for you to stay away. Why couldn't we have been friends? I wanted to like you. I tried so hard to like you, but then all the stories began." I roll my eyes as disgust mars my face.

"What stories?" He looks at me as if I'm insane.

"Oh, come on! Don't act like you're Mr. Innocent. Alex told me all about how you are. You've got quite the reputation, Loverboy. Let's hope you'll settle down now that you have a baby on the way."

"What? I have no idea what you're talking about. What stories?" he demands.

"You and all those women!" A surge of jealousy races through me.

Tyler could win an Academy award with the look of shock and surprise on his face.

"Karrie," he pleads as he begins to shake his head back and forth, possibly trying to deny the facts.

"I don't care what *you* did, but you dragged Alex down and put him in those situations."

"Is that what you think? Is that the kind of person you think I am?" Each word is articulated and enunciated slowly.

My feet stomp over angrily to where Tyler is sitting up, my face merely inches away from his.

"I don't *think*. I *know*."

Enraged with quiet fury, we stare at one another, eye to eye, until his gaze falls to my lips.

Without warning, Tyler's hands fly up and grab my head, tilting it as his mouth crashes against mine. My body responds immediately as my mind tells me to pull away yet one hand finds its way to the nape of his neck and the other cradles his head. The feel of his warm lips against mine electrifies my core, reminding me that I am a woman. A woman in need.

Slowly yet desperately, he moves his lips against mine, opening his mouth enough to allow his tongue to slip through, inviting my tongue to join in. Exploring the warmth and taste of his kiss, I lose myself completely, forgetting momentarily who I am and of who he is. And despite the repercussions I may face, I relish this once in a lifetime opportunity to kiss Tyler Strong. With each tangle of his tongue against mine, Tyler deepens the kiss, pouring raw and sensual lust into it.

I moan with unexpected pleasure.

Running his hands through my hair, he manages to hold me in place as he continues to kiss me senseless with a long-forgotten passion. I claw my way against his chest, wanting, needing to be closer to him. With our breaths now ragged pants, Tyler brings the kiss to an end, pressing his forehead against mine.

Licking my lips, I savor the taste of forbidden fruit,

"Karrie, I—"

"Oh, sorry!" Stacy's high-pitched voice interrupts his words as she backtracks out of the room. I pull away from his hold without a second thought.

And immediately I feel a sense of regret and great loss.

My hands cover my face as shame washes over me and my chin begins to quiver.

"Oh God. What did I do? I'm sorry! Oh my God! I'm so stupid. What is wrong with me? Oh God!"

Tyler reaches for my hand and gently pulls it away from my face, encouraging me to stop berating myself.

"Look at me."

I close my eyes and shake my head.

"I can't."

The tickle of his lips on my knuckles forces my eyes open. I watch as he continues to kiss each one.

"What are you doing, Tyler? What is happening?"

Ignoring my frantic questions, Tyler continues to press his lips against my skin.

"I don't understand what that just was."

From beneath his eyelashes, he looks up.

"That was the best kiss I've ever had in my entire life."

"But it shouldn't have happened!"

Guilt seeps in for having lost all sense of self-control. I could blame it on a moment of temporary insanity. Perhaps I could claim I kissed him under duress at having recently lost my husband.

But the truth is I wanted to kiss him. I wanted to feel his lips against mine.

I wanted...*him*.

"I have to go," I utter in alarm, pulling my hand from his grasp.

"You don't have to go. Stay here."

Wordlessly, I beg for mercy, hoping he'll have compassion and let me leave with a small amount of dignity.

"Have dinner with me."

"I'm so confused," I sigh heavily.

"So stay and talk to me."

My chest shudders when I lean back against his bed, burying my head in the palm of my hands, wanting to disappear into thin air.

"If you won't talk to me, will you at least listen to me?"

I look over my shoulder and find him waiting for a reply.

"Tyler, this is wrong on so many levels. Alex was your best friend. And you're having a baby."

With a firm shake of his head, he refutes my words before adding, "A friend wouldn't do what he did to me or to you."

"And what about Penny? You're not together anymore?"

"What? God no! I'm not with her!"

"Tyler, you're having a child together. That's got to mean something to you."

"She is not my problem!" Anger seeps through his deepened voice.

The memory of seeing Tyler have sex with her outside the bar rushes forward.

"But I saw you."

"What do you mean 'You saw me?'" he asks.

"I saw you two having sex in the doorway of your truck at The Black Horse."

His expression transforms to one of bewilderment.

"What are you talking about?"

My head bobs continuously, reiterating my statement and what my eyes witnessed.

Tyler blinks rapidly as if he's remembering something important.

A light knock on the door is followed by a hesitant Stacy whose grin quickly gives way to a full-blown smile.

"Hi. Hope I'm… not interrupting." She smiles, casting a quick knowing glance between the two of us.

"You're alright, Ma. We were just talking."

I bite the inside of my cheek to prevent myself from laughing.

"Ah…I see…talking."

Stacy places a large cardboard box on the side table and proceeds to cut the tape.

"I thought you might want something different for dinner. I know the food's not the best here. I would've preferred you to be at the other place."

Tyler nods in appreciation.

"It's fine, Ma. It's not so bad here, and besides, I won't be here much longer anyway."

My head snaps in his direction and my eyebrows rise up. "You're going home?"

"Against my doctor's wishes." Tyler shrugs. "I have to continue physical therapy, but I don't want to stay here. I'm going stir crazy."

Stacy serves his dinner on a flimsy paper plate which gives way, almost spilling the entire plate of spaghetti and marinara sauce on Tyler's lap. Flustered by the near accident, she grabs the serving of food and sets it down.

"These people…they can't even give me real plates to use." She continues mumbling as she rushes out of the room in search of sturdier dinnerware.

"Is she okay?" I ask.

He shrugs.

"She's worried about me going home. She's afraid I won't be able to take care of myself in the apartment or get out if there's a fire."

My expression displays my agreement with her concerns. "You do live above the garage on the second floor," I point out with raised eyebrows and a smirk. "She is kind of right."

"I'll manage."

"Why can't you stay with her?"

"Her place is tiny and Tre spends a lot of time there in the afternoon if his mom has to work late. There's no room.

A million scenarios race around my brain, all competing for what makes the most sense for Tyler's situation.

"You could stay with me. I mean," I force a deep swallow, "You could stay at my house until your leg heals and the cast comes off."

Disbelief spreads across his face.

"Really?"

"For the love of God," Stacy storms back into the room. "A Styrofoam tray. That's what they gave me!"

"Ma, relax. I told you it's fine." Tyler reaches for his dinner and eats every last morsel.

After dinner and another two éclairs, Tyler's eyes grow heavy and sleep beckons him.

"I have to work tomorrow, but I'll call you," I say, standing awkwardly beside his bed. My fingers clench into tight fists and I bite down on my bottom lip, restraining myself from leaning over to kiss him. But God do I want to kiss him.

His hand slips from its place against his flat stomach and brushes against mine. He uncurls my fist and tugs on my loosened fingers.

"Thank you," he whispers.

Keeping his eyes locked with mine, Tyler lifts my hand and brings it to his lips and kisses it gently.

I gnaw on my lower lip once again.

"Good night," I whisper, leaning over to offer a long and lingering kiss on his cheek.

I hug his mother goodbye before I leave.

With my head hung low, I walk down the long narrow hallway, bypassing the other patients varying in ages and ailments. I clutch at my chest hidden beneath my jacket as an ache takes up residence.

*What am I doing?*

There's a vortex of emotions swirling inside of me, the tension continuing to rise and finally spill from my eyes.

"Karrie?"

At the sound of my name, I stop and turn around to face Stacy.

"Sweetheart." She opens her arms and I walk right in. "What's the matter?"

As the floodgates open, I fall apart and sob like a lost child in this woman's arms. I cry for Alex. I cry for the demise of our marriage. I cry for the life we won't ever have. I cry for the beautiful man lying in the bed a few doors back. I cry for the betrayal of Alex's friendship and love. I cry for the feelings deep in my heart. I cry for the guilt which I don't think I can bear. I cry for the desire I can no longer ignore.

I'm falling in love with Tyler Strong.

Stacy offers a cocoon of support along with added words of encouragement.

"I told you that boy doesn't hate you." She pulls back to look at my face which is covered in hot, painful tears.

I pull out of her hold and lean back, letting her hands slowly move along my arm until she clutches my fingertips. ""I'm sorry. I just don't understand what is happening."

"You don't need to apologize to me. You need to listen to your heart."

"But my heart is so confused."

Stacy narrows her eyes with question.

"What's so confusing?"

"How did this happen? How could it happen? My God, I didn't even like Tyler."

"And now?"

Words of conviction emerge.

"And now I think I've fallen in love with him."

Gently, Stacy pats my cheek and wipes away the line of tears.

"Then it'll all work out as it's supposed to. Let destiny take its course."

*"Destiny?" I gasp.* "I'm not meant to be with Tyler."

My lips continue to mumble that I was married to Alex; I loved Alex.

"Sweetheart, destiny always finds its way."

# TWELVE

"It's your decision, Karrie. And like you said, you've looked at the pros and cons."

"I have," I answer confidently.

"Well then if you're sure that's what you want to do, then you have my support."

Nodding eagerly, I confirm Dr. Mancini's statement with a simple, "It is." I rise to my feet, feeling strong and sure. "Thank you for everything." I look into the kind eyes of this man and wonder how fortunate I've been to have had his friendship and guidance for the past several months.

"You're most welcome." He spreads his arms wide, offering an embrace. I step in awkwardly and squeeze tightly, silently offering another gesture of thanks.

I PULL MY CAR around to the front of the building and park in the fire lane despite looks from people passing by. I smile sheepishly and want to tell them not to worry and that this will be a quick visit today.

Knocking quickly, I push open the door to Tyler's room where his bag and the rest of his belongings are packed up, waiting by the hospital bed. His handsome face lights up with a smile when he sees me enter the room before returning his attention to the nurse reviewing his discharge papers.

"If you have any questions, give your doctor a call." She hands him a few pages of paper stapled together then smiles. "Good luck to you. We hope to never see you again."

While Tyler accepts the papers with a laugh, I find myself grinning happily at the pleasant sound I'm becoming quite fond of.

"You take good care of him," the nurse whispers with a wink of her eye as she leaves the room.

"Hi," I stride across the room and lean in to kiss Tyler's cheek. His hair is still damp from a recent shower and the light scent of cologne tickles my nose when I inhale softly.

I step back and hide my eyes, knowing my cheeks are flushed pink.

"Damn! You look good," he remarks, allowing his eyes to travel the length of my body, appraising my tall leather boots paired with skinny jeans and a fitted button down shirt. "You have a date or something?" He fights a smile and loses.

"Something like that. I promised this guy that I'd help him out while he recovers from a broken leg. Apparently he lives on the second floor and can't manage stairs too well."

"Good thing for broken legs then," he chuckles, taking my hand in his. "Seriously," he looks at me. "Thank you."

I fill my lungs with a deep breath, silently wanting to thank him but don't. "I don't mind. That big house is pretty quiet these days."

Open mouth insert foot.

I freeze the moment the words slip from my lips. "Sorry."

"Karrie, are you sure about this?" A look of pity washes over his face.

I smile reassuringly as I cup his jaw. "A hundred and ten percent."

Grabbing the crutches, I offer Tyler some assistance while he adjusts himself. I collect his belongings and walk slowly alongside him. We make our exit from the rehabilitation center that was his home for the past few months.

"Isn't your mom coming?" I ask, glancing at the time on the wall clock.

Tyler clears his throat. "I asked her not to."

"Oh…okay." I nod, catching a glimpse of something resembling desire reflected in his eyes.

Tyler climbs into the passenger seat of the car and waves his hands around, trying to block my view as I use my phone to record the momentous occasion.

"Stop it!" I wrestle his hands down to no avail. "I'm doing this for your mom. Cut it out!" I reprimand playfully until he finally surrenders, looks at the camera and says, "Hi Mom! I'm going home!"

"See! That wasn't so bad now, was it?" I tease, closing the door just before he says, "I'm not a big fan of videos."

I start my car and pull out of the lot, driving cautiously down the side road until I reach the main intersection. Debating which route to take, I signal left then right.

"What's wrong?" Tyler asks when the light turns green.

"I…I was thinking about which way to go," I admit.

The light turns yellow and then red. I glance in the rearview mirror, breathing a sigh of relief that no one is behind me.

As if he could read my mind, Tyler asks if we could drive by the scene of the accident. I grimace with uncertainty, wondering if it's a good idea or if he's even ready to see where it all happened.

"I'm sure," he replies after I've commented several times that I'm not too keen on the idea.

I sign left and proceed through the green light, driving through the town until we reach the destination marked with remnants of a makeshift memorial.

"Can you pull over?"

"Tyler," I whisper pleadingly.

"Please."

Against my better judgment, I maneuver the car onto the side of the road in front of the tree. We sit in silence for a long while staring at the candles, hand-written posters, stuffed animals and deflated Mylar balloons. Each object reopens the wound, causing my heart to pound thunderously.

It pounds with anger.

It pounds with hurt.

It pounds with confusion.

Suppressing the tears, I glance at Tyler and notice his eyes are laser focused on the thick wood. His jaw begins to tick as his eyes narrow before closing. His body shudders with a shiver while his closed eyelids move rapidly and his lips mumble wordlessly.

I reach down and cover his tight fist with my hand, hoping to soothe his pain.

"You okay?"

He loosens the grip of his clenched hand, slowly extending his fingers before entwining them with mine.

"I'm sorry," he utters. "I'm so sorry."

I unbuckle my seatbelt and practically throw myself in his arms, each of us holding the other tightly as if our lives depended on it.

"I'm sorry. I'm sorry you had to go through this. I'm sorry for everything," I whisper against his neck.

"God...in one single second everything changed." His broken voice trails off. "If only I hadn't—"

"This was *not* your fault. You weren't the one driving with a blood alcohol level one and a half times higher than the legal limit. You weren't the one driving nearly a hundred miles an hour that late at night. You weren't the one who lost control."

"No, but—"

"No!" I counter adamantly. "This is not your fault. I won't let you take the blame for this."

Tyler rests his forehead against mine and cups my face, using his thumb to wipe away the few tears that managed to slip through.

"Please don't cry."

I swallow hard and nod my head to appease him.

"I hate what he did to you. I hate it so much." Tyler's voice deepens and his tone darkens. "He didn't deserve you."

His eyes roam over my face as his lips move.

"He didn't deserve you. *He never did.*"

And for the second time, Tyler joins our lips in a tender kiss. He doesn't open his mouth or tease my tongue with his. He kisses me slowly, reverently, lovingly.

Everything in me comes alive at his touch. Every cell is infused with desire. Every breath longs to be graced with his scent.

I wrap my hands around the nape of his neck and kiss him harder, desperate to sate the need for deeper contact. Our mouths move succinctly, creating a beautiful wave, an ebb and flow, of giving and taking. His lips trail down to my neck and shower me with licks and pecks. Sweet nothings are murmured effortlessly. Tyler understands my need and gives me what I want until his hands claw at my jacket in an attempt to remove it.

"Tyler," I pant breathlessly, closing my eyes as I pull away and break our kiss. "What are we doing?"

"We're doing what feels right."

"But is it?" I inquire, wishing the ache in my heart would disappear. "Is it right?"

Taking hold of my face, Tyler encourages me to open my eyes and look at him. "Who is to say what's right or wrong? Who cares about what anyone says? I don't."

I shrug because I have no response. Although I believe he's completely right, I don't know that people would necessarily agree.

"One thing I've learned over the past few months is that life is short and unpredictable. You have to take advantage of every single moment. You would think I would've learned that lesson when my brother died, but it took this accident which claimed Alex's life and almost mine to make me realize this...take chances, live life to the fullest and tell those you love that you love them."

Once again his words draw tears to the surface of my wide and astonished eyes.

"Karrie, I will never let a day go by without telling you how I feel."

A rush of warmth surges through my veins as I kiss his lips gently, silently affirming his feelings.

"Ugh, God. I need to stop crying all the time." I jam my fingertips over my lids and dry the moisture. "What are you doing to me?" I chuckle and shake my head.

Tyler's left eyebrow rises playfully, challenging me. "You really want me to answer that?"

I park my car in the garage when we arrive at my house less than twenty minutes later. The ride through town was unbearably quiet as Tyler stared out the passenger's side window, only commenting on the change of the season as we passed a park with a huge oak tree.

"Where's his tr—"

"Let me get—"

I meet Tyler's eyes and immediately resent the culpability in them.

"It was totaled. There was no point in bringing it home."

He nods his understanding and tightens his lips.

"Let's get you inside, okay?"

Grabbing Tyler's bag, I guide him slowly, climbing the three steps into the house.

Having him here in my home feels strange; I almost expect Alex to walk in the door or around the corner. By looking at Tyler, I know this is awkward for him too just by the way he scans the room, observing everything. Maybe he's expecting Alex to walk in, too.

"So I set you up in the guest room since it's on the first floor. I hope that's okay." I lead him down the hall to the far end of the house. He follows along with a rhythmic *thud, step, thud, step*, keeping pace with me. I open the door wide, step through and set his bag on the bed.

Walking around the room, I point out everything he needs to know and open the door to the half bath. "There's no shower in here. Al— we never got around to finishing it."

"Thanks." Tyler moves slowly into the room and leans against the bed before dragging his eyes up to look at me. "If this is too weird, I can stay at my mom's."

Even before he finishes his statement, my head is already shaking from left to right, determined to set him straight one last time.

"No. You're fine."

He raises his eyebrows at my words.

"I mean," I stammer. "It's fine that you're here. I think Alex would have wanted it this way."

Thoughtless, unpredictable words continue to spill from my lips and my cheeks flush a deep shade of red. The truth of the matter is that Alex would not be "fine" with this. My husband would have blown a gasket at the idea of me being alone with another man especially when he's going to be sleeping here for a few weeks until his leg is completely healed.

Alex Parker was many things, but above all, he was extremely jealous and possessive. I was his. And his alone.

Awkwardly I glance down at the shiny hardwood floor, afraid to either utter another falsehood or make a mad dash to kiss him again.

"Karrie?"

I hum and look up, narrowing my eyes quietly at the peaceful look on his face.

"Thank you."

I smile.

"No worries. Like I said, it's fine."

"I'm not just thanking you for letting me stay here. I'm thanking you for so much more."

Those beautiful bluish-green eyes of his reach into my soul, caressing it gently with compassion and longing intertwined.

"I guess I should thank you then."

"Thank me?" he questions humorously. "For what?"

Inhaling quietly, I muster the courage to confess. "For not being the person I thought you were."

Within seconds, Tyler hobbles across the floor, closing the short distance between us. As he stands there before me, leaning on a single crutch, his free hand slides upward. While scanning my face slowly as his fingers move, Tyler licks his lips as his eyes follow his touch. I could see the restraint written all over his face, the tension radiating in his clenched and ticking jaw. Dragging his eyes upward, he smiles and exhales.

"Thank you for being the person I always knew you were."

I cover his hand with my own as I tilt my face into his palm, allowing my eyes a moment of rest when they close. My mind drifts away to a peaceful place. A place far away from here. A place not wrought by accidents, death, lawyers and wills. Somewhere between the place where the ocean meets the sand, where hills descend and roll into valleys.

A place where pain no longer exists.

Mimicking Tyler's earlier action, I moisten my lips with a slow swipe of my tongue, anticipating the feel of his on mine.

I wait and wait and wait until my eyelids separate, reassuring me that I'm not dreaming. Tyler is standing in front of me with desire in his eyes.

His movements are slow and deliberate as he lifts his

face and presses a long kiss onto my forehead.

The kiss of rejection stings.

After swallowing the jagged lump in my throat, I release the hold of his hand and step back, wanting desperately to rewind time and keep my feelings hidden from him. My heart is still fragile; I don't know how much more it can take.

"I'm going to make something for dinner. Can I get you anything before I go?" My voice, laced with feigned confidence, asks.

"No, but you can *give* me something."

"Sure. What do you need?" I ask, looking around the room, wondering if he needs a few extra pillows or another blanket.

"Give me your word," Tyler says, giving me an intense look that burns into me.

I chuckle lightly.

"My word? For what?"

"I need you to promise that you'll give me a chance." He shakes his head, correcting himself, "Give *us* a chance to see where this goes."

"Ty—"

"I know you feel something, too. I just don't know yet what it is and I don't want you to close the door before we've had a chance to walk through it…together."

I pinch my lips and hold my breath before I scream the words, "Yes! Yes! Yes!"

"I'm not saying it's going to be easy, but I know you deserve so much more than you had. I would never do what

Alex did to you." A wave of anger and animosity spread across his face as he spits out the word.

"*Never.*"

At the mention of my husband's name, my lungs deflate like a balloon.

Confusion and heartbreak struggle for dominance in my heart. Alex and I didn't have a perfect marriage as it might have appeared. We fought. He drank. I worked. Things seemed manageable, fixable even, until the first night he laid a hand on me. He apologized profusely, claiming that he was drunk and would never intentionally hurt me…until it happened a second and third time when he blamed me and said I deserved it.

No one deserves to be hit.

Ever.

I can't imagine why Alex would have told Tyler about his abusive behavior; it went against the image everyone loved. Shame floods me. I'm ashamed and embarrassed that Tyler knows how bad things really were; how I allowed myself to be a victim when I knew better. I knew I should've called the police. I knew I should have told someone. I knew I should have left him. The expression 'blinded by love' was more than an expression; it was my reality.

I have no reason to trust Tyler, but I do. There's something about him. And I want to know more.

"I promise," I murmur softly.

Forcing my feet in the direction of the door, I turn and walk away. I know myself too well. I tend to rush into things without really considering all the options. That's how I ended up at the altar so quickly.

The bed creaks when Tyler collapses onto it. As I close the door, I pause a moment when I hear him release a heavy sigh and the words, "Finally. After all these years."

"Hey," I shriek, glancing over to where Tyler leans against the doorframe. "How long have you been standing there?" I run my hands along my warm face, suddenly aware that I'm in my bathrobe and my wet hair is wrapped in a towel. "I thought you were still asleep."

He simply shakes his head as his eyes travel the length of my body, lingering on my legs. The dark expression I perceive doesn't seem to be one of a man hungry for food.

I bend down carefully to remove the casserole from the oven. A breeze meets my backside and I stand quickly. Even with my tugging at the thin material then tightening the sash, I fail miserably to cover myself.

"I'll be right back." My arm brushes against his as I rush from the kitchen. "I'll be down in five minutes," I call, taking the steps two at a time.

I close my bedroom door and lean against it, my head falling forward in disbelief as the throbbing in my core becomes even more pronounced. While squeezing my thighs together, I attempt to quell the long-forgotten feeling of lust and desire. *Pull yourself together, woman!*

After dressing quickly in a pair of yoga pants and a long-sleeved shirt, I splash cold water on my face and look at myself in the vanity mirror. "What are you doing?" I whisper, questioning the woman's reflection. Staring back at me, she smiles softly and shakes her head.

My slow steps become hurried when I hear voices coming up from the kitchen.

"Oh, hi!" I give my parents a pointed look as they stand there chatting with Tyler.

I lean in and hug my mom, asking quietly why they're at my house. I told her I wanted to do this alone.

"Just here to support you, Kare Bear," she promises, assuring me with a wink.

I roll my eyes then smile in appreciation.

My dad nods and mumbles, "Keep me posted," before following Tyler to the kitchen table and helping him set the crutches off to the side.

"Thanks," Tyler remarks, giving my dad a genuine smile.

"Would you guys like to stay for dinner? I made a casserole and it's just the two of us." I stutter momentarily, trying to clarify that it's just Tyler and me, not an "us."

"We were on our way to grab something to eat, but..." My mom looks over at my dad, silently suggesting they stay.

"That's fine with me." My dad peeks under the aluminum foils then flashes a grin in Tyler's direction. "Have you ever had Karrie's casserole before?"

Tyler's face shifts from looking uncomfortable to passive. "No, I haven't. Is it good?"

Leaning over with mischief etched across his face, my dad faux-whispers, "It's better than my wife's."

"Ha!" my mom laughs, striking my dad's shoulder with a playful swat. "See if you get dessert tonight."

"Mom! Please!" I beg, knowing that "dessert" is code for sex.

My mother laughs it off as she opens the fridge to grab a chilled bottle of wine.

"Is there anything I can do to help?" Tyler asks eagerly. I smirk and tell him that he can sit and relax. "I wouldn't want you to break my dishes."

My parents, Tyler and I settle into a comfortable conversation about their recent trip and the change of the seasons. I shiver at the mention of the farmer almanac's prediction of an early and brutal winter.

"Why don't you like the snow?" Tyler sets his fork down and sits back. He wears the look of well-fed and satisfied.

"It's not so much the snow as it is the cold I don't like."

"Oh man, this kid would be outside from sun up until sun down on snow days. She didn't care about the cold back then," my dad adds, remembering the days of my childhood.

"I was young!" I defend myself. "I didn't know any better."

An awkward moment seeps into the kitchen. Those were the words I said to my dad when I confided in him that my marriage to Alex was in jeopardy. I didn't give him specifics; he would've killed Alex. I made him promise not to tell my mother which he did anyway. I avoided her for a few days afterward because I knew she'd pull the old "I told you so" or "You should have listened to me." While I was free to make my own decisions in life, my mother liked to have a say. My father told me to stick it out and try to make things work. Divorce is a taboo word.

"So, no Tyler, I don't like the snow."

"I bet I can change your mind." Tyler challenges with an air of confidence. Something in his demeanor reminds me of Alex. He had a way of making me do things I didn't always want to do. *Wear this not that. Do this not that. Go here not there.* In the beginning I loved pleasing him, but that faded very quickly.

I respond sharply with contempt. "I doubt it." I stand and excuse myself from the table.

When I return, the table has been cleared, the casserole put away and the dishes loaded and running in the dishwasher. I look around for my dinner companions and find them in the living room where my parents, respectively, sip on what little wine is left.

No one mentions my outburst or sudden exit.

Alex's words ring in my ear. *"You're nothing but a spoiled little bitch."*

The realization that he may have been right sucker punches me in the gut as I sit in the single chair by the window, listening absentmindedly to the conversation around me.

An unfamiliar tone rings from across the room. Tyler picks it up and answers the call, connecting briefly with my eyes as he glances my way.

"Hi, Mom."

I watch intently as Tyler talks with his mother and then his nephew. His whole character changes when he becomes spirited and animated on the phone.

Before I realize what I'm doing, I'm smiling, enjoying the Tyler Strong show.

"We're going to get going home." My mother, followed by my father, rises and leans over to kiss my cheek. My dad thanks me for dinner and then whispers in my ear, "It really is better than your mother's."

I return the loving smile.

"Hey! I heard that!" my mom quips.

"Thanks for coming over." I stand and walk them to the door. "But please call next time."

With a loud booming ruckus, Tyler hobbles into the foyer and extends his hand to my dad. They seem to exchange something more than just a hearty shake.

"Mr. Miller, it was good to see you again."

"You take care and rest that leg. I might take you up on that offer when you're back on your feet."

My mom receives a quick kiss on the cheek along with a cordial salutation. "Thanks for the visit."

"Bye guys! Love you!" I close the door and turn to face Tyler with narrowed, inquisitive eyes. "What was that about?"

He feigns innocence and I laugh.

"You just met my parents for the first time and now you've become best friends with my dad and my mom just about swooned over you!"

Tyler's broad shoulder shrug with amusement. "I have that effect on people."

"You're so full of yourself!" I breeze past him and sit on the couch, curling up with a throw pillow on my lap.

A few moments later, Tyler takes a seat beside me; he's close enough yet still far enough away. He props the crutches on the armrest.

"You realize your parents and I met before, don't you?"

"You did?" He has my full attention. When?"

"At your wedding."

The ghost of my former life slaps me in the face, reminding me that it'll always be there.

"That's right," I sigh sadly. "Sorry. I guess I was in my own little world back then."

Seconds become minutes as we lose ourselves in thought.

"That was a tough day for me."

I burst out in confused laughter.

"What? Why would my wedding day have been a tough day for *you?*"

Tyler looks away, blinking slowly before sweeping his eyes back to mine. "I didn't want to be there—"

"Then you shouldn't have come!" I interject. "No one forced you to go, did they?"

With rounded eyes and raised eyebrows, Tyler's face reveals his complete shock and utter surprise.

"That's not what I was going to say."

"Then what?" I antagonize. The kindling in my belly is

set ablaze; I'm ready to spit fire.

"Forget it." His chest fills with air and he releases the breath. "I don't want to fight with you. That's so far from what I want to do with you."

Humiliation sets in. "I'm sorry." I reach out and touch his forearm, extending an olive branch. "I don't know how to do this. Do we talk about what happened? Or do we act like it all never happened?"

Tyler moves his arm so that his fingers lace with mine.

"Karrie, we *have* to talk about it. All of it, but we don't have to do it all tonight."

"I feel like I'm walking on eggshells. I'm afraid to do or say the wrong thing."

Tyler squints at me, perhaps processing my words. "You can't do or say the wrong thing…not to me. Just be yourself. That's all I ask."

I nod and smile softly. "Okay, but that's easier said than done." I stop myself from revealing that I don't know *who* I am these days. Since the day I met Alex, I slowly transformed into someone else. Someone I didn't even recognize some days.

Reaching for the remote, I click on the television and flip through the channels until I come to a rerun of Dawson's Creek. I always did envy Joey's life and her romantic relationships with Dawson and Pacey. What a lucky girl to have been loved by both; but in the end, only one boy won her heart forever.

"This show was awful!"

"What? This is classic 1998!" I toss the pillow in his direction. "What did you watch then?"

"I didn't. I was always outside playing some sport."

"Even in the winter?" I challenge.

"Ice hockey is one of my favorite sports."

I shiver dramatically and over-exaggerate a look of abhorrence just thinking about the cold.

I compromise and change the channel, bypassing ESPN entirely and wait for his response. When he says nothing, I ask, "Want to watch the sports highlights?"

"No. I'd rather play than watch." He grins. "Besides I already checked the scores on my phone."

I listen intently as Tyler recalls stories upon stories from his youth. He understands the sacrifice his parents, particularly his mother, made for him and his brother.

"How'd you get into racing?" I ask, knowing we're towing the line carefully because it's something he did with Alex.

"My dad was into sports. We had dirt bikes and four-wheelers before we had bicycles."

I sense there's something he's not telling me, but I don't want to push the subject.

"My dad keeps saying he's going to get a Harley cruiser." I laugh heartily. "That'll be the day."

"You're pretty close to your dad, huh?"

I nod. "My mom, too. Perks of being an only child."

"That's good. My dad took off the day after my brother and I turned twelve. The last time I saw him was at Tommy's funeral. He had the nerve to show up after all this time."

The tone in his voice changes and I get the impression he's getting upset.

"Then it's his loss." I offer comfort.

"That's what people say, but we lost, too. We grew up without a father. My brother didn't handle it so well."

I shift my weight to sit closer beside him and lean my head on his shoulder while the show continues. Neither one of us is really paying attention.

"I think that's why Alex and I got so close so fast."

I sit up quickly at the mention of my husband's name.

"You don't have to do this." My words offer an escape.

"Why not? If it weren't for Alex I wouldn't be here right now. We wouldn't be sitting here on your couch watching crap TV."

"Why do you do that?"

He hums in question.

"Make things light-hearted."

"Karrie," Tyler moves to look directly at me. "Life is short. From the day we're born, we already start to die. I don't want to waste a single second being angry. Believe me, I'm furious with Alex, but I can't change it. It is what it is. Life goes on."

"Wow! You really live up to your name, don't you?"

A sheepish smile tugs at his lips.

"It is a great name."

# THIRTEEN

MY EYES FLUTTER OPEN AT the sound of the obnoxious guy screaming on an infomercial. I struggle to make sense of why the television is sideways. Closing my eyes again, I drift back into a deep slumber until the sun shines on my face.

When my eyes open for a final time, Tyler's leg, still bound in a plaster cast, comes into view. I blink quickly as my brain registers that I'm laying across Tyler's chest and my hand is around his neck. I turn my nose inward and inhale the scent of his T-shirt.

I curse myself for having this dream. This *has* to be a dream, but the movement of his chest beneath mine confirms my worst fear. I am awake and I'm in Tyler's arms.

Like a little mouse, I squeak a quick hello when he looks down at me.

"Good morning," he says with a grin. "Did you sleep well?"

I nod before sliding my hands down from his neck and resting them on his chest. Beneath my fingertips, I feel his heart pounding wildly. Overwhelmed by what's happening, I move to stand up, but Tyler tightens his hold on my back and asks me to wait just a minute.

"You have no idea how long I've wanted to do this."

I'm pulled tightly against his warm body and his hand rubs circles on my back.

"I don't understand what you mean."

He kisses the top of my head.

"For so long…from the very beginning…"

I jerk back and look at him cautiously.

"What are you talking about?"

He smiles softly then asks what I'm doing today.

"Don't change the subject!"

He laughs.

"I'm not, I promise. I want to spend the day with you. Can I take you somewhere?"

A tickle of anticipation rumbles in my stomach.

"Sure, but today's my shift at the clinic. I'll only be gone for a few hours."

A wary look flashes on Tyler's face.

"What's wrong? Are you okay?"

Clearing his throat, he nods, ending any further conversation.

"Will you be alright on your own for a few hours?"

"Yeah."

"Are you sure? I can call my mom to come stay with you. Or you can call your mom."

"I'll be fine. I wouldn't want to inconvenience your mom and my mom works third shift so she sleeps most of the day."

"I didn't realize that." I adjust the throw pillows and walk into the kitchen, calling over my shoulder, asking if he'd like coffee or tea.

"Coffee would be great."

I set about brewing a pot of coffee as Tyler stands at the window, overlooking the backyard.

"I remember when Alex had this pool put in. He wanted to go with the bigger one, but you had to convince him to go with this one."

My hand freezes on the refrigerator door when I realize how casually Tyler is talking about Alex. I resume the task of getting things for breakfast as my heart pounds heavily in my chest.

"How can you do it?"

Tyler turns to face me. "Do what?"

"Talk about Alex like nothing happened? He *died*. He's not coming back."

His lips tighten into a thin line. "You think I don't know that. He was my best friend and the closest thing to a brother. I've forgiven him and I hope to God he's forgiven me."

I feel an ache in my heart.

"Every day when I open my eyes I realize I'm alive and he's not. I realize I have another day to live my life. Another day to make things right."

His voice trails off somberly.

"You make it sound like you're this awful person who needs to be redeemed."

Tyler's eyes drift away and look down.

"There are things I need to make right. The most important one starts," he hobbles over on his crutches, "right here with you."

Mere inches create the space between our chests. My eyes scan the thin material of his fitted T-shirt. I moisten my lips quickly, preparing for his kiss.

His fingertips crawl up my arm until they reach my neck and he begins to massage my skin slowly. My entire body goes on high alert.

"Why are you doing this? Months ago we hated each other."

A side grin appears. "You hated me?"

"Loathed immensely," I admit.

He tips my head back, forcing my eyes to meet his straight on.

"And now?" I force myself not to look down at his mouth.

*I'm in love with you.*

My teeth clamp down on my lip as I suppress a smile when my voice becomes breathy and low.

"And now you're here with a broken leg, driving me crazy."

He lowers his mouth to my ear.

"How exactly am I driving you crazy, Karrie?"

I grip his wrist for support as stuttered words emerge.

"I…you…how can this…I want…"

The softest, the most delicate kiss in the history of kisses is placed just below my earlobe followed by a succession of several more.

"Am I wrong to feel this way?" I ask quietly, praying silently he'll say no.

"I don't think so…although others might disagree. But from the first time I saw you, I wanted you."

Shocked by his admission, I gasp and pull back. "What? You did not!"

With gentle yet strong hands, he guides me back to where I was.

"I promise you I did."

His eyes appear more blue than green when he blinks, revealing sincerity and truth. "I've got a lot to tell you."

Dear God, please let me be doing the right thing. You wouldn't have brought Tyler into my life for no reason, right? How did this even happen?

When I arrive back home from my shift at the clinic, I sit in the car for a few minutes to finish my silent conversation before I close the garage door and exit my car. I walk into the house and immediately notice how tidy the kitchen is. I let out an annoyed huff. My mother didn't say anything about coming over today.

The sound of music beckons me to find its source. Following the tempo, I walk down the hall and stop at the guest room.

My eyes aren't prepared for the image before them.

"Seventy-two. Seventy-three."

A shirtless Tyler hisses the numbers as he bends his elbows, lowering his body to the floor and then extending his arms to rise back up. The muscles in his triceps elongate, showing clear definition from hours in the gym.

My tongue betrays me and slips through my lips, licking slowly in anticipation of savoring something delicious.

As if they have a mind of their own, my eyes rake over him, taking in the complete view of his body drenched in a sheen of sweat. Quietly I ogle him as he continues to push himself through the point of exhaustion noted by the trembling of his arms. From this angle, I can see how strong his core is, each layer of muscle reveals itself through his abs. When the last rep is done, Tyler flips over and lays flat against the floor, throwing his arms over his face while keeping his legs propped on the bed where they've always been.

"Ten more," he grunts, sitting up quickly, curling his body.

I step into the room to stop this man from ripping his muscles away.

"Hey! I think you've done enough for today."

Tyler snaps his head in my direction with surprise etched on his face. Quickly, he attempts to get up from the floor, but the awkward position has him stuck.

I drop my purse and rush to help him.

"I've got you."

The conciliatory smile on my face transforms to a look of desire when my hands slide across his back. Bending down, I lean forward, press my chest against his and lift.

He tucks his head down to his chin and huffs, shrugging off my efforts to help.

He mumbles, "I can do it."

Moving forward, he presses his hands to the floor, lifting himself slowly off the floor.

Immediately I miss the contact with his skin. I miss the salty scent of his sweat. I miss him.

Ignoring his words, I slide my arms underneath his and use all of my strength to lift him onto the bed. I grunt and groan, struggling to maintain a solid hold of him.

*Do not let him fall. Do not let go of him.* I silently convince myself as I fight the weight of his body and the pull of gravity. I collapse on top of him when I've finally managed to get him to the middle of the bed, safe and sound. A loud grunt escapes my mouth as my hands land on his chest and my eyes on his. The proximity of our mouths sends a wave of anticipation through me.

"Hi!" I pant, my lips tugging back into a crooked smile.

"Hi yourself."

Tyler lifts his hand to my face now covered in a layer of sweat as tiny beads form at my temple. Using his fingertips, he wipes the line of moisture away as his eyes maintain constant contact.

I freeze at the gesture.

"You're strong," he whispers with a raspy voice.

I inhale his breath and hum, allowing my eyes to close and savor the intimacy of this moment.

"You're a lot stronger than people think."

"*I know you deserve so much more than you had. I would never do what Alex did to you.*" Tyler knows what I've been through. For some reason, Alex confided in him. While Alex would never go to church with me, he did confess his sins to someone.

I have no response. Instead, I do what feels natural. What feels right.

I lower my lips and kiss him softly.

His hand moves to the nape of my neck, angling my head to the side while his tongue sneaks through his warm lips, seeking its lover.

My fingers spread wide across his chest, wanting to feel the heat radiating from within. In small circular motions, my thumb rubs gently until it glides over raised skin. My lips freeze and my eyes open.

Mumbling against my lips, Tyler tells me not to look, but I don't listen. I pull back slightly, creating a small space between our bodies to inspect his scar. The raised seam runs from his breastbone to the top of his abdomen. I slide my index finger along the fading pink line, a painful reminder that his chest was broken open so that his life could be spared. I remember that incident vividly.

John Doe number one and John Doe number two.

Alex Parker and Tyler Strong.

That night I loved one and hated the other.

Today things are the complete opposite.

Tears form in my eyes as I close them, lowering my face to his chest. I place my lips at the top of his scar and gently kiss my way to the end where I'm met with taut skin and the curve of his abs.

First, a kiss for his pain. Next, a kiss for his strength. Then a kiss for his resiliency. And finally, a kiss for his will to live.

I sniffle as a single tear falls and gets lost in the sprinkling of chest hair.

"What are you crying for?" he asks, guiding my eyes back to his.

"I hate that you went through this." My chin quivers as an ache forms in my throat.

"Come here." As if I weigh nothing, Tyler tugs me onto the bed next to him, tucking me beneath his chin while he wraps his arms around me, securing me in place.

With the fingers on one hand, I gently wipe away my tears as the other finds its way back to his scar, moving up and down slowly, tracing the jagged line.

"I hate that Alex was the cause of this. He caused so much pain." My voice cracks, weakening at the end.

"It wasn't all his fault." He clears his throat. "I guess I'm partly to blame."

I look up and silently plead for him to continue.

"We fought that night," he confesses.

I gasp. "You did? Like physically?"

"No, not physically…although he did try to punch me in the face."

For so long I wanted to know what happened the night my husband died. I wanted to find out exactly what happened in the truck and to know why he lost control and hit the tree. I knew he was drunk; the toxicology report indicated that, but I knew there had to be something else. He would never have been driving that fast with the trailer attached to the back. Those motorcycles were priceless to him.

I hold my breath in anticipation.

"He had some issues he was dealing with over the weekend."

*"Issues?"*

"Bikes weren't running right. Other racers were talking trash. He was really agitated."

*Sounds like the man who replaced my husband at the end before he died.*

"There was some other stuff, too. He started drinking about half way home and he didn't stop. He started rambling on and on; most of it didn't make sense. I tried to convince him that we should stay at a hotel or that I should drive, but he wouldn't listen."

Tyler looks at me knowingly.

"You, of all people, know what he was like. You couldn't change his mind about anything. If he thought the sun was purple, it was purple in his mind."

I nod, remembering all the times I tried to convince him to see my perspective when we argued. He never listened.

"And then you came up in conversation."

"Me? Why would my name come up?"

"You were his wife, Karrie."

"Yeah, but I figured he was in the "zone," I air quote, "when he went racing. I mean he could never call or text me because he said he didn't have good cell service down there...at the track."

Tyler swallows nervously as his face transforms to one of anger.

"What?" I prod, wondering what he is withholding.

"There was cell service."

I tuck my hair behind my ear as I sit up.

"What? I don't understand. Why would he lie to me?"

Glaring at me with serious eyes, Tyler reveals through gritted, mumbled words that my husband didn't want to call me.

I roll off the bed and jump to my feet, demanding that he retract his statement, calling him a liar.

"I'm not lying to you. Look at his phone records if you think I'm lying."

No sooner do the words leave his lips, I can tell he regrets them.

"I'm sorry," he says, reaching for my hand and tugging me closer to him. "Karrie, I have no reason to lie to you."

The seriousness in his voice is startling and unexpected, causing an uneasiness in my heart.

I stand silently, blinking slowly, trying to comprehend what Tyler is telling me.

"Was Alex cheating on me?"

Tyler releases a deep, almost painful, sigh as he utters my name.

"Was. Alex. Cheating. On. Me?"

My nostrils flare as the fire in my belly ignites with deep animosity for my deceased spouse.

Rubbing his hands across the scruff of his jaw, Tyler locks eyes with mine and simply nods.

A thousand images of my husband's transgressions appear in my mind and taunt me. His smile. His words. His touch. He shared those with other women.

"And you knew? And you fucking knew?"

I step forward and slap him clear across the face.

Tyler's head falls in shame.

"Why didn't you tell me? Why didn't you tell me?"

I fall to my knees, each word releasing as a ragged cry.

"It killed me! To think that he would do that to you."

Tears rain down from my eyes, staining my face.

Tyler reaches for me and caresses my face softly.

"I would never have done that."

I shove his hand away.

"Who is it?"

Nodding back and forth quickly, Tyler says it's not important anymore.

"It's in the past. Let it go."

"Let it go?" I shriek. "You just told that my husband was

unfaithful and you expect me to *let it go.*"

"I…," he stammers, "I'm sorry."

Hiccups rattle my body.

"If you couldn't tell me then, why now? Why tell me now?"

"I don't want there to be any secrets between us. I want you to trust me completely. I want to be with you more than anything!"

There's no denying the longing in his voice.

"Be with me? You hated me! Every time I saw you, you did all you could to avoid me. How can you all of a sudden, after all these years, want to *be with me?*"

Tyler pushes himself off the bed and stands before me, looking down with a soft expression.

"I have loved you since the very beginning. I think I might've fallen in love with you the very first time I saw you."

Bewilderment forces my eyes to widen as I gasp, "What? What are you talking about?"

Slowly, he lifts a hand to cradle my chin, his gentle touch searing my skin as he tilts my head, leaving me no choice but to look up at him.

"I love you."

I gasp. A breath of air fills my lungs as my face crumbles with confusion and surprise. Only his name manages to slip from my lips before his mouth is on mine. My body melts on the inside from the sensation. He deepens the kiss, pouring undeniable truth into it until my lips ache and my tongue stills.

Pressing his forehead to mine, he whispers, "For so long I watched you. For so long I wanted you. For so long I loved you, but always…always from a distance."

"I don't understand." I search his eyes desperately, hoping to find answers that will only come from his spoken word.

"Let me show you."

A sigh of exasperation seeps out. "Tyler, just tell me." I cover his wrists with my hands and rub gently. "Just tell me."

"I want to show you. I need to show you."

I nod, accepting his terms and the idea that he might have had feelings for me all along. The notion is unimaginable, foreign and suspicious— unnatural even. Could it really be possible that Tyler Strong loved me when I was his best friend's wife?

A shadow of doubt creeps into my mind and casts a seed of suspicion to take up residence. This is about money. After all these years, upon my husband's death when the benefactor of his will was changed, now Tyler tells me about his concealed desires.

"You don't have to do this. You don't have to make up stories. Everything in Alex's will is yours. I don't know what game you're playing."

Even as the words emerge, I regret them instantly because in the pit of my belly I don't believe the deceit. For some inexplicable reason, I believe him…especially as a look passes over his face, transforming it into a mask of sheer pain.

"You don't get it. I don't want anything of Alex's —

except you. I want you."

My mind and my heart engage in a full out battle, each charging forward with swords of truth and knives of doubt. My heart wants to believe him, but my mind challenges his reasons and intentions.

"Do you remember the first time we met?" he asks huskily, a slow release of air sweeps across my face

I wrack my brain, but only come up with the first time I met Alex at the concession stand. I remember looking back and seeing Tyler there, but I didn't talk to him so I wouldn't consider it an actual "meeting."

"You were sitting in the stands reading a book." He laughs. "I thought it was so strange that you would come to one of the loudest places possible and try to read. Someone distracted you, causing the book to slip from your lap and fall through the bleachers."

I remember that day. I was cramming for finals and John had to work overtime so I went along for the day. I couldn't concentrate at all. The sights, the sounds, the smells. I was distracted all day whenever the motorcycles lined up and the announcer's voice blared through the speaker. Every time I tried to read, my eyes wandered over to where the racers stood around their trailers. I followed the cluster of black suits as they inspected their bikes and made last minute adjustments. One man, dressed in all black, stood out; his dress pants and button down shirt weren't exactly appropriate for the race track.

"I was watching you when you scrambled to grab the

book before it fell. I thought for sure you were going to fall too so I rushed over. You mumbled under your breath, cursing like a trooper. I figured you were in a bad mood so I just picked up the book and slid it to you."

"And I grabbed your hand when I reached for the book."

Slowly he nods, confirming my words.

"That was you?" I ask incredulously, remembering seeing the man dressed in all black walk away. "I called out to thank you, but you didn't turn around. Instead you pulled your ball cap lower and covered your face."

Tyler's expression changes, his face displaying a deep sadness. "I was in a really bad place that day. I had just come from my brother's funeral. I needed something quick to relieve the stress of the day. I felt a connection just with that quick graze and I knew if I looked at you, I would've seduced you and probably taken you back to the trailer. Even though I didn't know you, I had seen you before and when I touched your hand… I felt something. There was an instant attraction. And I knew I couldn't do that to you…or rather I didn't want to do that to you."

I immediately consider all the other women he *did* do that to. The stories Alex told me about Tyler and the women at the track rush forward like a tsunami, making my stomach wretch. I'll never forget the explicit and intimate details my husband described as if he had been there himself. It sickened me and when I asked him to stop, he got annoyed and said it was just "guy talk."

"You were attracted to *me*?" I question, my voice rising

an octave higher. "I had no idea. I felt something too, but I didn't realize it was you."

"He noticed me looking in your direction and asked who I was looking at. I ignored him and was on my way back over to you, but he told me not…"

"What? What did he tell you not to do?"

"He told me I didn't need to get involved with anyone. He said I needed to concentrate on racing. I needed to get my head in the right place after having just lost my brother."

"Tyler, that doesn't make sense. Why would you listen to Alex?"

His shoulders raise up quickly as he shrugs. "Honestly," he chuckles dryly, "I don't know, but it was a good thing I did because two weeks later, he turned on the charm and you fell for him." He gives me a pointed look; one I can't deny. I fell hard for Alex the first time I met him.

"I couldn't compete with that," he utters quietly, admitting his abandonment of a pursuit before making any real attempt.

This revelation hurts my heart. Hoping to erase the look of despair on his face, I close my eyes and shake my head, unable to believe that this other option was never even given the chance to be explored.

"*Compete?* You didn't even give me a chance. You didn't give *yourself* a chance!"

"Karrie, you would've chosen him."

"You don't know that!" I argue as the adrenaline races through my body and quickens my heart beat.

"He was Alex Parker. He always won. It's what he did. It's *who* he was."

It's my turn to concede and acknowledge the truth in his words.

Alex Parker was larger than life. He lived life boldly, choosing to live every day to the fullest. That, and the fact that he was sexy and older, was what drew me in. I never stood a chance against him. I loved that he was admired and respected even though he always wanted to be the center of attention. He thrived on it to the point I think he depended on it. I know he felt the heat when Tyler started winning races and everyone's focus shifted to the young, up and coming drag racer. That was the beginning of the end for Alex. That's when he changed. I didn't know then what it was, but now it all makes sense.

"And so you just sat back and let him win."

He nods sadly.

My heart is beating wildly in my chest; it's ready to explode with anger, sorrow and joy. The notion that Tyler had these feelings and kept them hidden for all these years pains me, yet the same idea makes me realize how noble he is. He stepped aside so his best friend could be happy. He obviously didn't pine over me for too long considering all the stories Alex told me.

A million different occasions flit across my mind, remembering all the times I saw Tyler, how much I disliked him because he was standoffish. I search his face, looking for any trace of the bitterness I became accustomed to seeing.

One day above all stands out. My wedding day. As I walked down the aisle, I caught his eyes briefly and what I perceived as animosity on Tyler's face wasn't that at all; it was envy. He wanted what Alex had. He wanted *me*. And each time I tried to talk to him, his responses were always short and curt. I can't imagine how hard it was for him to see me with Alex…especially when Alex was unfaithful.

I stammer through broken words. "I don't know what to say." My teeth clamp down on my bottom lip as my brain struggles to comprehend it all.

"So you see…I never hated you. I just couldn't be near you. I saw the way you looked at me through the window every time we left for a race. I wanted to break the door down and tell you, but how could I?"

His name falls from my lips in breathless whisper.

"I died that night, Karrie."

My head snaps up. "What?"

"The night of the accident. I died on that table, but you brought me back to life." He reaches for my hand and lifts it to his heart. "You made my heart beat. You kept me alive."

"But…how do you know that?" My mouth drops open in surprise and my head shakes from side to side.

He couldn't possibly know that I literally held his heart in my hand. It's impossible!

"You stayed away from me for a month. A lot happened in that time."

Guilt floods my soul at the thought of him alone at the hospital. My emotions were a jumbled mess. Guilt, relief, desire and confusion all fought for prominence because I couldn't believe, I didn't want to believe, that I was falling in love with my husband's best friend.

I shift my body to sit on the bed as exhaustion, physically and emotionally, sets in. Tyler sits beside me, taking my hand in his.

"I know this is new for you...the idea of us, but it's not for me. I've loved you for a very long time."

I smile at his words, wishing I could reciprocate his feelings, but I can't. We have so much to learn about each other and so many obstacles to overcome.

"I don't expect you to say anything in return. At least... not right now." He tips his head and raises his shoulder, those bluish-green eyes holding me still, causing my insides to stir until a crooked grin appears on his face. "Maybe tomorrow though."

"Do you understand now why I didn't come around or talk to you?"

# FOURTEEN

"I PROMISE YOU IT'S JUST OFF the road about a quarter of a mile," Tyler laughs, pointing straight ahead.

I smirk and give him a side eye as my car travels slowly over the dips of the uneven road. I'm sure the front end will need an alignment after this trip.

"What's *that* look for?"

"That's my side eye!" I quip. "I reserve it for special occasions."

Minutes later, Tyler directs me to park in a secluded area before he maneuvers his crutches and gets himself out with little assistance.

"Hang on! I'll help you." I race around the car, but I'm too late.

"Karrie, my leg is broken, but the rest of my body works just fine."

I'm left speechless, remembering how hard he felt last night as his erection pressed into my belly. It was supposed to be a quick kiss goodnight, but our hands had other plans.

"C'mon this way," he motions with his head and my legs take strides behind him, following along closely.

"Are you sure we're supposed to be here? I don't know about this."

Tyler continues trudging on through the overgrown grass until he reaches a dilapidated fence. My eyes scan the view before me. The city cloaked in evening twilight glows a shade of purple with a hint of faded orange.

"It's beautiful."

Never in my life have I seen the place I've always lived from this perspective.

My arm brushes against his as I place my forearms on the fence, mirroring his actions.

Down in the distance, cars rush by and streetlights illuminate, marking the end of another day. Moments slip by as we relish the peace and quiet.

"Why'd you bring me here?"

Tyler ignores my question and leans over, pointing to something far away.

"I don't know what you're pointing to." I squint, trying to see clearly.

"That right there." With one arm, he pulls me close and lines his finger up with my line of sight.

"The clock tower?" I ask, wondering what's so special about it. I've seen it a million times.

"It's been repainted. See how the light reflects off the windows facing west?"

My eyebrows cock upwards. "And?"

"Did you notice it before right now?" he challenges.

My hands rise and twist. "I don't know. I guess not."

"You're that for me."

I palm his forehead, checking for the presence of a fever.

"Sometimes you don't see the beauty in something until you step back and look at it from a distance."

I smile softly as my heart swells. "From a distance," I whisper, repeating his words.

"You're my clock tower."

I bury my face in his chest, inhaling deeply, and wrap my arms around his waist. His hold on me tightens, his lips press a kiss on my hair.

"How are we going to do this?" I ask, wiping the moisture from my eyes.

"One day at a time." He tips my chin and kisses me chastely before adding, "I'm not going anywhere."

"Thank you for this."

TYLER AND I FALL into a routine relatively quickly over the next few weeks. After sleeping in the guest room the nights I work, he greets me in the morning with a light breakfast before I sleep for a few hours.

I wake to the sound of voices. Grabbing my robe, I head

downstairs into the kitchen and find Tyler sitting across from Roger. Both men's eyes flash in my direction and the papers on the table are immediately slid back into a manila folder.

My suspicion and curiosity are awakened, replacing my desire to kiss Tyler good morning.

"What's going on?"

I breeze into the room, neglecting to greet Roger as I take a seat at the table. I have a niggling feeling this conversation is about me.

"How are you, Karrie?"

Roger leans over to offer a kiss, but stops shy when my body tenses. My eyes snap in Tyler's direction by way of habit.

"I'm fine." My tone is softer.

Tyler and Roger speak at the same time.

"It's nothing—"

"We're going over—"

I finish the sentence as I reach for the folder. "Alex's will."

With a quick motion, Tyler's hand covers mine and he looks down, confirming what I know to be true. His touch feels different; it's one of sympathy mingled with pity. I slide my hand out from beneath his and sigh heavily.

The weight of Alex's betrayal feels like a boulder sitting on my chest. Not only is the document a painful reminder of what Alex did, but for Tyler and Roger to review it here, in my own house, is completely wrong, downright rude and disrespectful.

"When do I have to leave by?" I ask, my voice completely devoid of emotion.

"What?" Tyler gasps. "What are you talking about?" His eyes round into balls of disbelief.

My heart cracks at the idea that he's played me for a fool. He never wanted me; he didn't want me to contest the will. I said I wouldn't and I won't. I don't want Alex's money.

"Karrie, nobody said anything about you leaving," Roger intervenes as a look of sincerity spreads across his face. "In fact—"

"Roger, could you give us a minute?" Tyler asks, clenching his jaw tightly, staring at me intensely. I try to decipher what I see, but I can't. My eyes aren't working properly; they're blurred and tainted by the ugly color of lies and betrayal.

When I flatten my palms to push myself up and away from the table, Tyler grabs my wrist firmly.

"Sit down."

I narrow my eyes, slightly offended by his tone.

"Please," he adds, although he's glaring at me in complete anger.

I huff, surrendering the fight and sit down.

"I told you I wouldn't challenge his will."

Leaning closer, bringing his face inches from mine, he growls, "And I told you I don't want anything of his...except you."

I swallow nervously and ask, "Then why is Roger here?"

He blows a puff of air through flared nostrils as his chest rises and falls.

"I contested the will, stating that I do not believe Alex was of sound mind and body when he made these changes."

"What?" I shriek. "Can you do that?"

"I don't know, but I did."

I continue in astonishment. "*Why* would you do that?"

Determination alters his face and his eyes gleam with intensity. "You still don't get it. You're keeping the house, the business, the bikes. Everything. I don't want it…I only want you."

With his hand around the nape of my neck, he pulls me forward, kissing me slowly… perfectly.

Never have I met someone so selfless, so giving, so thoughtful. Never have I loved someone more. My chin quivers as tears of gratitude flood my eyes.

"There is one thing though," he says, wiping his thumb across my cheek, preventing the tear from falling further.

I meet his eyes, assuring him I trust him with whatever he decides.

"I've asked Roger to set aside some money for a college fund."

My forehead wrinkles in confusion and then smooths out, thinking about his nephew Tre.

"I think that's a great idea." I smile, thinking about how much he loves that little boy as I reach for his hand and lace my fingers with his.

"I didn't hear any pots and pans being thrown around so I'm assuming it's safe to come back in." Roger walks in and sits down. His eyes flash to our joined hands before he stares at me, offering a subtle nod and the hint of a smile.

Roger turns his attention to Tyler. "So we're all set?"

"We are," he confirms decisively.

"I'll be in touch," Roger calls from the door as he opens it wide and calls my name. "Hey Karrie?"

My feet stop dead in their tracks and I turn around to face him.

"Take care of each other."

I glance at Tyler and smile.

"Always."

"I'm going to take a shower. I'll be down in a bit," I announce, spinning on my heels and heading for the door before I utter the words and ask him to join me. I know it's an impossibility with his cast and the fact that we've not defined any specific terms to our unexpected relationship, but God I'm desperate for him.

"Don't be too long."

I duck my head with embarrassment, thinking about his comments a few days ago when he teased about how flushed my face was. I'm sure he realized why I took such a long shower after our kissing escalated to touching.

I climb the stairs quietly, suppressing a smile, trying desperately to contain my excitement that he might be able to join me in the shower sooner rather than later.

Hot water rains down on me as I stand there, thinking about Alex as I lather myself with soap. As my hand glides over my breasts, the image of Tyler's hands come to mind. I quietly moan as I pleasure myself. When my heartbeat slows and my breathing returns to normal, I step out of the shower and dry off. I pat my face dry and meet my reflection in the mirror. With each swipe of my hand, I erase the steam and realize that each day Alex is becoming a distant memory. Someone from my past.

"You good?" Tyler asks after he finds me by the front window. It's at this same window where I stood so many times watching him as he waited for Alex.

I sweep a glance at him, freshly showered and looking scrumptious with a hooded sweatshirt and his sweatpants cut above the knee to accommodate the binding.

"How'd you manage to take a shower? I mean," I drag my eyes lower away from his face and motion to his leg, "with that cast and all."

He grins wickedly, piercing me with a meaningful stare. "Wouldn't you like to know?"

"Don't let the door hit you in the ass!" I adjust the oversized bag on my shoulder and walk through the front door, leaving him behind.

Even though I don't turn around, I know he's laughing when he claims he can't close the door.

The drive through the city is fine, but we're faced with incredible traffic due to construction once we hit the highway. Tyler changes the radio station often until he stops and turns the dial.

"You like country music?"

He pretends to tip his hat and feigns a southern accent. "Yes, ma'am, I do."

I roll my eyes in disbelief.

"Oh yeah, who's this?" I nod my chin toward the radio.

"Sam Hunt."

I giggle and hum, storing this little nugget of information.

I park the car and turn off the engine. My fingers comb through my hair and massage my temples.

"What's wrong?"

"I don't know why you made me suffer through that!"

We walk into the building discussing the pros and cons of country music.

After waiting for almost an hour from the time we arrived at the orthopedic surgeon's office, we head over to radiology for Tyler's x-rays.

We wait and wait and then we wait some more until Tyler eventually stands, adjusting his crutches when his name is called by a young medical assistant who's wearing fitted zebra printed scrubs.

"Hey Ty," she draws his name out slowly, smiling seductively. Her red smeared lips pull back into a sly Cheshire cat smile. I suddenly want to gouge her eyeballs out and smack that smile off her face. I might just kill her cat, too.

After acknowledging her quickly, he turns to me. "Come on."

"You want me to go in with you?" I close the magazine in my hand. It's not something I've done before. I usually sit here waiting while I catch up on the Hollywood gossip that fills the pages of People or In Touch weekly.

"It's okay. She doesn't have to come if she doesn't want to," Zebra Girl interjects.

She huffs quietly when Tyler ignores her.

"Do I really have to ask again?" An eyebrow lifts in question.

I suppress a smile as I set the magazine down and proceed to walk alongside him.

"Excuse me," I say, breezing past Zebra Girl who simply smirks at me.

Tyler hops onto the stiff exam table and the crinkling of the paper is deafening. There's an underlying tension in the small room and I don't like it.

"I'm just going to check your vitals real quick."

He nods as she secures the cuff around his bicep.

"Would you mind taking off your sweatshirt?" She giggles nervously then continues, "I need to get a good reading."

Reaching from behind, Tyler pulls the thick material over his head and drops it into his lap. He watches me as I watch her as she removes the stethoscope from around her neck and places it on his chest.

"Good strong heart."

Tyler glances at her.

"I bet you can go for hours."

My eyes widen and my jaw drops open.

"What?" I gasp loudly while Ty exclaims, "Excuse me?"

Zebra Girl glows bright red, almost matching the color of her hair.

"I thought...you're a runner, aren't you?" she stutters, tying to claw her way out of the hole she's dug herself into.

His face transforms into one of disgust. "No! I hate running!"

"Oh, sorry! I must have you confused with someone else." She turns away and types into the small computer sitting on the counter. "What is it that you do again?"

"I race. I'm a drag racer."

"Yes! That's right!" She spins around quickly, facing him with wild excitement on her face.

*Bike bitch.* That's what this one is. *A total and complete bike bitch.* Women like her were the reason I stopped going to the track in the first place. I hated the way they all gathered at the trailers, waiting and hoping to get an ounce of attention from the guys. Especially the guys who always won. Like Alex.

"I'm going to have to come see you race. I'd love to cheer you on."

I want to wave my hand and remind her that I'm still in the room.

"Nah," he shakes his head, "that's okay. I've got my number one cheerleader right here." He smiles at me and my heart soars.

Finally, she receives the message.

He's taken.

He's off the market.

He's mine.

"The doctor will be in to see you soon," she replies,

ignoring the fact that he's just rejected her offer. She closes the door behind her and I blow out a deep breath.

"Can you believe her? My God, I thought she was going to throw herself on top of you."

A light chuckle floats in the air. "Yeah, she was a little much."

"A little?"

"You should see the ones at the tr—"

My countenance falls.

"Sorry. I didn't mean to say that."

"You don't have to apologize to me for what you guys did."

"*You guys?*"

"You don't have to lie to me. I know all about your girls in the trailer." I chuck dryly. "Believe me, Alex didn't spare *any* details."

Tyler inhales sharply, his chest puffing out before he blows the hot air out as his fists clench tightly. "Son of a bitch," he mumbles. "That son of a bitch."

I'm surprised by the ferocity of his voice. I don't understand why he's so upset and angry that Alex told me how he screwed all those women. It didn't matter to me then.

A light knock on the door is followed by the entry of Dr. McLeod, a petite woman with short black hair. Her smile is warm and friendly as she introduces herself to me and then proceeds to wash her hands, turning over her shoulder to ask Tyler how he's feeling. The results of the x-rays reveal the fracture is now healed. She's happy with the progress and results.

"So are you ready to get this thing off?" She balls her small hand into a fist and knocks on the plaster covering.

"Yes," he hisses, failing miserably to disguise irritation in his voice.

Dr. McLeod peeks up at him.

"Everything okay?"

"It will be."

He turns his eyes on me and suddenly I feel as though I'm the perpetrator.

Using some sort of drill, the doctor carefully cuts through the cast, slicing right through the names written colorfully in Sharpie marker. Friends and colleagues, nurses and hospital staff all took a few minutes to decorate the solid mold. I see Penny's name and internally cringe.

The angry expression fades from Tyler's face the moment the cast falls away, setting his bare leg free. The skin is moist and pale, the hair on his leg is matted down. Using his hand, he massages his leg, bringing sensation back.

"How does it feel?"

"Like pizza dough."

The doctor laughs lightly. "Well... that's one I've never heard before."

Tyler grins.

She offers careful assistance, helping him to stand as he applies his full weight. My eyes never stray from his leg; for some reason, I think it might snap in half carrying the mass of muscle that covers his bones.

Cautiously, Tyler bounces up and down, putting more pressure on that side. I anticipate a hiss of pain or a look of distress, but his face simply beams with sheer joy.

"Feels great."

"Are you sure? It was a pretty severe fracture."

Nodding adamantly, he reassures her.

"Well, then. You're good to go. Just take it easy for a few days."

The words fly out of his mouth. "When can I start racing again?"

Dr. McLeod glances at me with raised brows before she addresses him. "That's completely up to you."

She extends her hand and says it was nice to meet me. Her eyes meet his as she offers a warning. "You—please be careful."

Moments later, Tyler and I stand alone in the room. He can't seem to control his elation; he's like a kid in a candy store who's just swallowed tubes and tubes of pure sugar.

I wait for him to speak first.

"Thank you for coming with me today. I'm glad you were here."

I smile and bite my bottom lip, replying, "Me, too" just as my phone buzzes in my purse.

"Aw, damn!"

My eyes snap up, fearing his leg is snapped in half or something. "What's wrong?"

Tyler looks down at his sweatpants. "I can't go outside like this."

Laughter erupts when we realize one pant leg is cut short above the knee while the other one is still long.

"I didn't really think about this."

I unzip my bag and reach in. With my hand extended, I offer the rolled-up jeans.

"I did."

I pray silently they fit. It's been so long since he's worn jeans, but I remember seeing him in jeans and my God, he looked so good.

The look of surprise and disbelief on his face is priceless.

"What the— how did you know?"

"I'm a nurse. Very rarely do patients go home in the same clothes they arrived in."

Looking at me with grateful eyes, Tyler takes them and toes off his boots.

Then he drops his sweatpants.

Only wearing a T-shirt and fitted black boxers, Tyler stands before me, tempting me, teasing me, daring me not to look. His thighs are thick and muscular, not long and lean like a runner's. I slide my tongue across my bottom lip at the sight of his stiffness.

"Do you want to touch it?" he asks huskily.

Yes! Yes! God, yes!

Taking a small step back, Tyler widens his stance, giving me a perfect view of his erection.

"You have to run your hand up and down then go over it a few times." Grinning, he encourages me further. "I don't mind it."

Given the green light, I raise my hand slowly, moving closer to his body. My fingers graze the material of his cotton shirt on my downward journey into unknown, forbidden until now, territory.

A huge hand clamps down over mine and drags it away from its intended target.

"See! Feels like pizza dough."

My eyes attempt to hide my embarrassment as he massages his leg with my hand. Slowly, I draw my eyes open and meet his playful expression.

"You're a jerk!" I grunt, snatching my hand away.

In all the years I've known Tyler, I don't think I've hated him as much as I do right now. That's not true. I don't hate him. In fact, I kind of love him, but after that stunt, it'll be years before I reveal that.

"Me? What did I do?" He raises his hands defensively as laughter pours out of him.

I narrow my eyes, already plotting my revenge.

"Why Karrie...did you want to touch something else?" He steps forward, closing the gap between our bodies, looking down at me with a sexy smirk.

"Hah! You wish! I wouldn't touch that thing with a ten-foot pole!" I turn my head and lift my chin in defiance.

"Okay," he deadpans and steps back, sliding one leg and then the other into his worn jeans. He does a quick bounce, making sure he has a proper fit.

I try not to peek, but I can't help myself. When he turns to grab his hoodie, I take full advantage and check out his backside.

*Oh. Dear. God.*

My core tightens with arousal and I force myself to swallow.

"Ready to go?" he asks, opening the door and gesturing that I walk through.

"After you." I smile.

The office staff says their goodbyes and wish him well. Zebra Girl is nowhere in sight.

"Come on, Loverboy. Time to get you home."

"Loverboy?" he inquires, coming to a quick stop, pinning me with a serious look.

"We all know how much you love the ladies and how much they love you."

"Listen, do me a favor. Stop staying that. I'm not that guy." The sharp tone in his voice reveals his frustration and annoyance. "I never was."

I spin around and come face to face with him. I feel badly that I keep bringing up the past. His past.

"I'm sorry," I sigh, my face slipping into a frown. "I was just teasing you. I won't do it again."

"Understand this...*you* are the only thing I want. You are the only thing I wanted for the past five years. *Five years!* And now...now that I have the chance to have you, if you'll let me, I don't want anyone or anything screwing that up. Got it?"

I nod.

"Got it!"

Wrapping my arms around his waist, I squeeze him hard and inhale the fresh scent. Together with his arm draped over my shoulder and my hand still around his waist, we walk out in the late autumn air.

# FIFTEEN

"Is that okay?"

Blinking sharply, I snap my attention away from the gorgeous woman who's being ignored by her equally gorgeous husband. Her attempts to hold his hand, only to have him reach for his glass of scotch or the way her eyes slide across the room to see who's watching is a familiar story. Their tale is a familiar one and my heart hurts for her.

"What did you say?" I smile apologetically for my inattentiveness.

"Would you mind if we stopped at my apartment after dinner?" Tyler asks, looking at me over the glass.

"Yeah, of course." I pick up the glass of Sauvignon Blanc and take a large gulp.

"You okay? You seem...distracted."

I glance around the elegant restaurant and try to

appreciate his efforts for our first official date. It's make no difference that we live under the same roof; it's still our first date. I loved the hand-written note that accompanied the flowers, asking me to escort him this evening for dinner. Had I known this is the restaurant he selected, I might've suggested another place.

"Alex and I used to come here a lot in the beginning."

A deep sigh full of disappointment escapes as his head drops low.

"I'm sorry. Do you want to go?"

I reach across the table and clasp my fingers with his, squeezing gently.

"Look at me." I squeeze again, encouraging him to lift his head. "You couldn't have known."

"I wanted to do something nice for you. I thought you would like this."

"This?" I motion with my hand, "is not me. You know that."

"And I kind of wanted to make a good impression."

I toss my head back in laughter.

"Good impression? I'm already so impressed with you."

"I'm not successful. I don't have tons of money. I don't even own a house."

I've never seen this self-degrading and insecure side of him until now. And I don't like it.

"You impress me in lots of ways."

He tugs his lips back tightly, forming a sarcastic grin.

"You make me laugh. You know how to make a mean

pot of sauce and you're by far the best kisser."

His cheeks flush red as a genuine smile spreads across his face.

He inhales sharply and asks, "Do you want to go somewhere else?"

I nod slowly.

"I have the perfect spot," I whisper with excitement.

Tyler flags over the waiter who is rounding the corner with our entrees.

"We're going to need this to go."

Walking out of the fancy restaurant, I wipe tears from my eyes.

"Oh my God!" I laugh as I link my arm with his. "Did you see his face? He was so offended that we asked for a 'to go' container."

Through his own laughter, Tyler adds, "He should've given me the whole damn loaf for what they charge!"

He walks me to the passenger side of the car and stares down at me. I slide my hand through his open jacket and smooth down his blue dress shirt and then tug on his tie.

"You looked good tonight dressed like this, but this isn't you."

"Like I said…I was trying to impress."

I turn my eyes upward and shake my head.

"You're sexiest in jeans and a T-shirt. Or in your leathers."

His eyes widen in surprise.

"You have no idea what seeing you on that bike does," I growl in his ear.

He pulls my body flush with his, his erection straining through his dress pants.

"I'm sorry about how things turned out tonight."

Using his tie, I pull him down and bring our lips closer.

"Tonight is definitely not over."

My jaw is nestled into his open hand as he joins our mouths and leans into me, kissing me senseless until my lips swell and my heart beats wildly.

"I love you," I mumble against his lips. My eyes fly open at my admission as do his.

"What did you just say?" He grins.

"I do. I love you."

"One more time. Say it one more time."

I love the humor reflected in his eyes.

"My name is Karrie Parker and I'm in love with Tyler Strong!" I yell at the top of my lungs, drawing odd looks from nicely dressed people entering the restaurant.

I return my gaze to him and find hurt.

"What? Was that not loud enough? I can scream louder."

"*Parker*," he utters sadly. The vulnerable man makes a return.

"Don't do this. Don't do this to us," I plead.

"Alex is always going to come between us, isn't he?"

I huff loudly. "No! Not if we don't let him."

"I won't be able to give you what he gave you."

"God, I hope not! I truly hope not!"

Memories of my drunken husband raising a heavy hand to me send a shiver down my spine.

"I don't ever want you to think that you need to be like him. Look, we can't ignore the fact that he was my husband, but if it also weren't for him, we wouldn't be together right now."

My eyes beg for his understanding.

"You have no idea what it was like for me. Our marriage... it was not as great as everyone thought."

Showboaters—that's what we were. At least *he* was.

"He didn't deserve you."

"Maybe not," I agree, "but he's gone."

"Can you do me a favor? Forget about the past. Let's look forward to the future. Forget that I was Alex's wife, forget that my name is Karrie Parker. Just love me for me. Plain ol' Karrie."

I follow Tyler's eyes as they move across my face slowly, reverently, until eventually they land on my lips.

"Sweetheart, there is nothing plain about you. You are, without a doubt, the most beautiful girl I've ever seen."

I fight a smile but lose. "Thank you," I say, choosing to accept his compliment rather than countering with "I've seen the women at the track."

"It's getting cold out," Tyler says, tucking me beneath his chin as his hands rub my back.

"I thought you liked the cold," I question.

"I do like to be outside, but right now," he murmurs in my ear, causing my breathing to hitch. "I'd really love to be somewhere nice and warm."

"Where's that?" I breathe, tilting my neck to the side.

Goosebumps line my skin.

"In you."

Fastening our seatbelts is a feat within itself as we struggle to keep our hands off each other.

The drive through the city has never *ever* been so torturous.

CLIMBING THE STAIRS with me practically on top of him, Tyler fumbles for the key and shoves it into the lock. My back hits the door, sliding against something which falls to the concrete landing.

"Hurry up!" I laugh as a cold breeze nips at the exposed skin of my thighs; the thin short dress offers little warmth against the frigid air.

"What the hell?" He shuffles his feet over the strewn paper when he manages to open the door.

I slide down his hard body but never break contact with his mouth until my coat hits the floor and I realize his apartment is almost as cold as it is outside.

"Give me two minutes."

Tyler hurries to turn on a lamp as he continues jogging in the opposite direction. I scan the place he calls home. I'd always pictured him living in a run-down apartment since it's above his garage, but this place is anything but. It's warm and comfortable, showing signs of being loved. I spy a blue and green checkered afghan draped over the back of the couch and resist wrapping myself up in it; instead I pull my coat back on and rub my arms.

Vintage yellow Tonka trucks and a bucket of colorful Legos are wedged in the corner near the door. My mind conjures up an image of Tyler playing with his nephew.

Sitting on top of the TV are pictures, many very similar to the ones Stacy brought to the hospital. Tyler and his brother. Tyler on a dirt bike. Tyler skiing.

Then I see Alex and my heart plummets. I hesitate and then pick up the rectangular shaped frame, looking at it carefully. Their entire race team is there, each with a pointed finger in the air while Alex and Tyler hold a trophy up. My finger traces over Alex's face then stills when I see a petite blonde is tucked behind his arm while she leans against him.

Penny.

Betrayal sucker punches me in the gut. My husband was having an affair with Penny and Tyler knew about it.

I gasp and turn quickly when he calls my name. I raise the photograph in question and his eyes widen. He bears the look of a guilty man.

"Penny. He was having an affair with Penny." A mangled, dry chuckle seeps through. "And you knew all along. You fucking knew."

"Karrie, please."

The sound of glass shattering against the wall pierces the cold air.

"You bastards! How could you have done this to me?"

"Me?" he screams, his arms flailing wildly. "I didn't

fucking do anything. I tried to stop him, but he wouldn't listen. Alex was a selfish bastard. All he cared about was himself. Whatever fucking made him happy and he didn't care who he hurt along the way."

I crumble on the spot, falling to my knees, crying out as I curse his name.

Tyler scoops me up and cradles me to his chest.

"Baby, he can't hurt you anymore. I won't let him." His voice cracks with emotion while he wraps his arms around me.

Gently, Tyler lays me on his bed. The blanket is cold, but the heat from the wall mounted fireplace radiates, warming me slightly. The tears continue to fall and I hate that he's broken my heart again. This time from the grave.

"Why? Why did he do those things? Why did he ask me to marry him? Why did he ruin my life?" I stare at the orange glow, silently condemning him to hell where he belongs.

The pendulum of emotion swings from crying softly to full blown screaming until I have nothing left in me. My body shudders as exhaustion overtakes me.

Tyler shifts beside me and props himself up on his elbow. I can feel the weight of his stare.

"Please don't hate me for what he did. I hate myself enough as it is."

I sigh heavily and shake my head in disbelief. "Everything was a lie. My marriage, my life, the past five years...all of it was a lie."

Lies. Everything Alex ever said was a lie.

Realization widens my eyes and I turn to look at the man beside me.

"The stories he told me about you weren't true, were they?"

The blank stare on his face leaves little need for words.

"It was him, wasn't it?" I struggle to get air into my lungs. "My God, he went into so much detail. He screwed all those women and told me it was you. Why would he do that?"

Tyler's throat moves with a hard swallow before he responds. "I don't know."

I howl in anger. "What a bastard!"

My night out with Pam rushes forward.

"That was him at the Black Horse, wasn't it?" Bile rises in my throat. "That was him having sex with Penny, not you."

"I was with Tre that night; it was his birthday." Tyler says as if offering an alibi. He doesn't need one, I already know where my husband was and what he was doing.

I run my fingers through my hair and grip it tightly, thinking hard about the turn my life has taken. I thank God we never had children.

"Penny's baby...is it his?

Tyler's lips tighten into a straight line while his guilt-ridden eyes cast away. Moments later, his eyes sweep upward to look at me and he nods sorrowfully.

"Wow," I snicker. "It's a good thing Alex is dead because I probably would have killed him myself."

Tyler's hands replace mine in my hair, pulling the strands back slowly.

"Is there anything else I need to know?"

I can see the internal war he's raging.

"He knew I was in love with you."

"What?" I gasp. "How would he know that?"

"The night he died...in the truck." He inhales then exhales loudly before continuing, "that's what we fought about. He couldn't understand why I was always defending you. He didn't understand why I was always pissed off when we raced and he disappeared. And then it dawned on him. He said some pretty nasty things about me...and you."

I steady his hand with mine and slide our fingers together, my thumb moves slowly over the calluses on his palm. To think this man, whom I hated for so many years because of my husband's falsehoods and betrayals, defended me. I never knew until now that he defended my honor because he loved me.

"If there's anything else, please tell me now." I beg for mercy as pity stains my voice.

He leans over and presses a slow lingering kiss onto my forehead.

"Because tomorrow, I am done with Alex Parker for good."

I bury my nose in his chest, kissing the spot where his heart is and seal it with two taps before reaching around and running my hand rhythmically over the bare skin of his back.

"Me, too. I'm going to find a new job as soon as I can. Maybe I'll get back into the union and as far as racing, I'll find a new sponsor. I'm done with anything that has to do with Alex Parker."

I never realized how closely intertwined their lives were. Their names were practically synonymous in their circle of the drag racing world.

Sighing loudly, I release a cleansing breath. My life, my world will begin anew. I will move forward and leave the past where it belongs—in the past.

I search the face of the man I love, feeling a connection to him like I've never felt with anyone else. Pushing myself, aligning my body with his, I reach up and caress his face that is now covered with a scruff.

"I love you."

He closes his eyes while my fingers slide over them. They reopen when the tips of my fingers reach his lips.

"Let me show you how much I do."

I lower my mouth to his and begin a slow dance of licking, lapping and tasting. Each movement filled with sensual promises of what is in store for him. For us.

He rolls me over and hovers above me, staring down with a combination of incredible desire and hunger in his eyes.

I smile shyly.

"Why are you smiling?" he asks.

"You look hungry."

I love the devilish twinkle that shines in his playful eyes.

"I'm ravenous," he groans in my ear as his hand moves from my face and travels over the curves of my body, moving the material of my short dress as he continues. His warm hand stills at my core then begins a slow circular motion, teasing... tempting...arousing me incredibly. My core throbs at his touch and my adrenaline races; I need an immediate release. I close my hands around his biceps, securing him in place. A soft moan emerges from my throat and encourages him to move those dexterous fingers, providing me with the highest summit from which I jump, freefalling into complete and utter bliss.

His mouth devours mine.

"I love you," he mumbles against the corner of my mouth.

"Show me." I stare at him with hooded, lust-filled eyes.

I want more.

I want all of him.

Tyler carries me to the bathroom. While the water in the shower heats, he turns me to face the mirror. My cheeks are darkened with smeared mascara and my eyes are still puffy and red, but with him standing behind me, looking at me the way he is, I feel more beautiful than I ever have.

He presses a kiss onto my shoulder as he unzips my dress. Every kiss is matched with the lowering and then removal of the silky material until I stand naked. His hand slides over my nipples which constrict immediately, forming tight pink buds.

"Beautiful," he whispers.

Staring at the oval mirror, my light brown eyes meet his pools of bluish-green, holding him captive. I twist in his arms and face him. I begin the process of undressing him slowly, starting with his blue dress shirt. My lips trail a line of kisses over the long, pink scar etched down the middle of his chest.

I bend at the waist to unbutton and unzip his dress pants, sliding his boxers down over his thighs until they both reach the tiled floor. He steps out of them and stands before me in all his glory.

And what a glorious sight it is!

My hand moves involuntarily, reaching out to touch him. With each stroke, he hisses in pleasure. My eyes never leave his.

I'm guided into the shower and lathered with soapy hands as they skate around, washing me, cleansing not only the exterior, but the interior as well. Tyler Strong expunges the pain and suffering caused by a man I once pledged to love until death do us part.

"I need you," I beg, not caring how desperate I sound.

Tyler swipes a hand across the shower curtain and grabs a towel. After drying me off quickly, he lifts me up and I wrap my legs around his waist. I can feel the heat emanating from his hard body.

Landing on the bed, he wastes no time ravaging me with his mouth.

"Please," I beg again.

Conceding to my demands, Tyler spreads my legs with his and slowly, carefully sinks in to me.

I am a goner, completely lost in him as he consumes me.

Time slips away as we join our bodies, tangling ourselves in a sensual declaration of love and adoration.

His breathing finally regulates after he releases and he collapses on top of me. I rub the planes of his back now covered in a layer of sweat. I smile and savor the moment, realizing how much I love the feel of him on me; I love the feel of him in me.

My heart surges with intense emotion because...

I love Tyler Strong.

# SIXTEEN

I AWAKE ALONE IN TYLER'S BED, sitting up quickly and scanning the room for any sign of him. Everything is still as it was last night except for the vacant spot on the adjacent wall and the pile of folded shirts that were sitting on top of the dresser.

Long after he fell asleep last night, I had lain awake for several hours, reviewing the last five years of my life and vowing to never lose myself as a person or accept abuse in any form from anyone.

The glow from the fireplace had provided enough light for me to see the contents of his room. The usual things, a bed, side table and a dresser, filled the confines of the four walls. A huge photograph framed in black hung prominently on the far wall. It was the same picture I'd smashed last night except Penny wasn't in this one and Alex had his arm draped over Tyler's shoulder. They each wore team shirts, Alex's race team logo displayed boldly on the left side of their chests.

Eventually my eyelids grew weary, falling heavily as I drifted off to sleep next to a man who I was convinced would never hurt me.

From the living room, I hear the door swing open as Tyler complains, grumbling about the lock and the cold weather. The bedroom door is wide open so I pull the blanket up to cover my nakedness, fearing he might not be alone. I glance at the clock. Nine o'clock. I never sleep in this late, but then again, my sleep schedule has been off for years since I started working nights. It's like having jet lag without having traveled.

"Good morning." Tyler walks into the room, carrying two coffees in a cardboard tray and a small white box.

Pushing myself up to a sitting position, I smile and lean over to meet his kiss.

"Good morning yourself," I mumble against his cold lips. "What's all this?" I ask, accepting the cup of coffee.

"Breakfast in bed."

He opens the box, pulls out a pastry and holds it out for me to take a bite. Keeping my eyes laser focused on his, I open my mouth, letting the sweet cream drip on my tongue.

"Thank you," I chew, moaning dramatically as my eyes close before dragging them upward to reopen.

Tyler shoves the rest into his mouth. "This is the best éclair I've ever had."

My eyes widen with disappointment while a frown turns

my mouth.

"What?" he asks only to realize the reason for the expression on my face. "Don't worry. I got half a dozen."

We thoroughly enjoy our breakfast in bed together, leaving only crumbs in the box.

I finally drum up the courage to bring up the topic I've been thinking about all morning.

"So about last night…" My statement wafts, lingering in the air as a question.

Tyler's countenance stills, apprehension is clearly defined all over his handsome face.

"Do you regret it?"

I rise to my knees, the blanket falling to the side as I remove his coffee cup from his hands.

"Actually," I grin wickedly. "I was wondering when we could do that again."

My body flies backwards as Tyler pounces on me, attacking my mouth desperately.

We remain locked behind closed doors, choosing not to leave his apartment for two whole days.

"Karrie," Tyler calls, "why is Roger here?"

I smile to myself, watching from the kitchen as Tyler opens the front door and shakes Roger's hand, motioning for him to come inside.

"Good to see you. How's the leg?" Roger wipes his feet,

removing the brown snow from last week's snowfall.

"Stronger than ever."

I breeze into the foyer and kiss Roger lightly on the cheek and whisper, "Thank you for doing this."

"I'm happy to help."

The two men follow me into the kitchen and sit opposite one another. Roger opens his briefcase and removes a thick manila folder.

Tyler's forehead wrinkles in confusion as he inquires what this is all about.

Inhaling deeply, I pray for courage and take his hand in mine.

"I have a business proposition for you."

"A business proposition?"

"I'd like to sell you half of the business and half of the race team."

"Why?" He shakes his head and I can already hear the excuses he's going to try to give me.

"Because you're a good electrician and an even better racer."

"Yeah, but—"

"I told you I was done with *him* and I am." I haven't uttered my deceased spouse's name since the first night Tyler and I made love.

I said I was done and I meant it.

"I," he swallows hard then clears his throat, "I don't have that kind of money." I know it pains him to admit that; he's a proud man who works so hard.

"I know that. That's why I'm selling each part for one dollar."

"What?" he sighs incredulously. "Why would you do that?"

"For the same reason you gave me back everything in *his* will even though legally it was yours."

Tyler stands abruptly and paces the room.

"I don't know a thing about running a business and I want you to race. It's what you love to do. It's who you are."

Roger spreads the documents out on the table.

"Ty, all you have to do is sign by the Xs."

I smile in appreciation.

"And give me a check for two dollars plus my commission, of course."

With hesitation, Tyler reaches out slowly for the proffered pen that's still wedged between Roger's fingers. The tip of the fine point pen finds its mark on the line by the X, but he swiftly pulls away and sets the pen down on the table. My eyes exude encouragement as my hand lifts the pen again.

"Please," I whisper. "All you have to do is sign right here." I tap the X.

"Can I think about this?"

Rising quickly, I stand and haul Tyler into the living room, needing to talk some sense into him.

"What's the matter?" I spin around and pin him with questioning eyes.

"Why are you doing this?"

"Because I want you to have it. You deserve it."

"I never wanted anything of Al—"

I slap my hand over his mouth and narrow my eyes.

"Don't. Don't you dare say it," I warn angrily.

He slides my hand away from his lips.

"I want to build a life with you, but I don't want to take what *he* left behind. I'm not some charity case."

"No, you're not. You're going to be a smart business owner and sign those papers."

His cheeks round as he blows a huge puff of air out.

"I don't know about this."

"You want to know what I know?" I snap before continuing. "What I know is this… I know you love me and I know that I'm so in love with you more than I've ever been with anyone else in my life. Did you hear me? I love you completely, crazily, wildly!"

He cups my face when emotion swells and my chin quivers.

"Tyler," I pause to gather my thoughts once again. "The way I see it is he screwed us both so let's use this to move forward completely. It might seem drastic, but I'm that serious about you and our future."

After some hesitation from him, I implore him with a whispered plea, "Please. Do this for me. Do this for us."

Nodding slowly, he lowers his mouth close to mine and kisses me softly.

"You have me wrapped around your little finger."

"I'm happy to hear that because I have something else

to tell you."

He rolls his eyes dramatically, anticipating the worst.

"I asked Roger to do something else for me."

"Just tell me." His patience is wearing thin.

"I'm putting the house for sale and," I lick my lips and swallow hard. Grinning widely, I say the words he never expected to hear. "I'm changing my last name back to Miller."

A crane might be needed to pick up his jaw from the hardwood floor.

"Are you serious?"

"Yes! Completely! A hundred percent!"

His silence speaks volumes.

"How many times do I have to tell you I'm done with *him*?" I stand on tip toes to kiss him when I see the emotion in his eyes. "I love *you*."

"Where will you live?"

"Wherever you live. You're not getting rid of me that easily!"

After reviewing and signing all the documents and Tyler writing a check for one hundred and fifty-two dollars, Roger promises that he'll return in a few days with our copies of the legal forms.

Two weeks later, a "For Sale" goes up in the yard, and my name is legally changed back to Karrie Miller.

As if we've been together for years and not just a few months, Tyler and I spend each night that I'm not working snuggled together either watching Homeland or Game of Thrones on Netflix. At the start of every episode, I think about how we began watching the series. Tyler and Pam had debated about the classic rock music era. Tyler was overconfident and Pam won, earning her the title and nickname of Rock Chick. The wager was decided that if he won, she'd have to go with me and get her motorcycle license. If she won, we'd have to watch GOT.

Pam is one of those people who won't bet unless she's a thousand percent positive. Tyler was only a hundred percent. Either way, I came out the winner because Pam loves Tyler and he loves her.

Tyler pops his head in through the doorway and startles me, causing my finger to click and close the browser on my laptop.

"Your parents are here."

"Okay." I reply guiltily as he steps further into the room.

"What are you doing?" he sings songs playfully, coming to stand behind me in the leather desk chair.

"I was studying."

"And?" He cocks an eyebrow and squints.

I confess, "Doing a little online shopping."

"That's just going to be more stuff to pack when we sell the house." He alters his choice of words. "When *you* sell the house."

I ignore the unnecessary correction. "I saw something I really wanted to order."

"Oh hey, Kare Bear." My dad suppresses a smile when he catches Tyler giving me a brief kiss.

"Hi, Dad!"

I stand and walk toward the door, stopping to look back. I reach into my pockets only to come up empty. Turning around, I pat my hand over the pile of papers for what my mom had given me two days ago.

Tyler pauses and glances at me.

"What do you need, babe?"

"Nothing really. I just had a flash drive." I look in the desk drawer and then on the floor, wondering where I could have put it.

"My mom wanted me to look at her new design ideas."

My dad chuckles. "Don't worry about it! Your mother has about a hundred of them lying around the house. Trust me, she won't miss that one."

The table has been set and a bottle of wine chilled.

I thank Tyler with a smile and kiss.

"You're so good to me."

Servings of delicious food are scooped onto our dishes and we enjoy good conversation.

"So Ty, how are the guys adjusting to having you back?" My mom sets her glass of wine down carefully, knowing how sensitive the topic is.

"He's their boss!" I interject. "They have to adjust. It's not like they have a choice. And besides, if they don't like it, they can go find another job!"

Tyler slips his hand over mine, soothing me after my

minor outburst.

"It's okay. They really have done a great job keeping things up and running for all these months now. I think it's going to take some adjusting on all our parts."

A tight smile is sent in my direction.

"You should see some of these houses. They're huge, sprawling sixty-five hundred square foot homes with four or five bathrooms and only two people live in them. It's crazy!"

"Have you had any offers on the house?"

I shake my head as I take a sip of wine.

"No, the realtor said winter is a hard time to sell. We may have to wait until spring."

"I can't wait for spring!" Tyler pats his solid stomach and sighs, implying he's eaten enough and thoroughly enjoyed it.

"I thought you race in the summer," my mom asks with a curious expression.

"I usually race down south in the spring but stay locally in the summer. It all depends on the weather and how I do." He hesitates for a moment. "Last year was the fastest I've ever gone. I'm hoping to get back there soon."

My dad asks a few technical questions and about the progress on the turbo Tyler's decided to rebuild. After buying half of the race team, Tyler sold what bikes were left, sold others for parts and is starting from scratch. He's determined to distance himself from his former sponsor, A.P. Racing, and start fresh on his own.

"You guys go talk swing arms, fuel and forks while we get dessert ready." My mom rubs my dad's shoulder lovingly as my two favorite men head into the living room to catch a football game on TV. The smile on my face is immense when Tyler catches my eyes and mouths "I love you."

"God," my mother sighs, "he is perfect for you."

I open the fridge and grab the container of heavy cream.

"Where was he five years ago?"

*Right there. Right in front of me. Loving me…from a distance.*

I ignore her comment and set about beating the white liquid until it's light and airy.

"Have you thought about where you're going to live? You can always move back home until you find the right house."

Turning the hand beater off, I glance at my mom with appreciation.

"Thanks, but Tyler and I will figure it out. It would be weird living in the same house with you and dad."

"Oh, stop! I'll wear clothes when you're home!"

"Ma!" I flick whipped cream in her direction.

"Don't waste it! I was going to save some for later tonight."

"Oh my God, Mom! Do you realize it's not normal to talk to your child about your sex life?"

"You're almost thirty years old, Karrie. You're not exactly a child."

She may have a point, but I still don't want to hear the details.

"And besides, sex is a natural part of relationships. Don't you have sex with Tyler?"

"Not talking about this with you," I repeat on autopilot.

"Has your endometriosis been bothering you?"

"Ma!" I grit.

My mother rolls her eyes.

"I delivered babies for nearly thirty years. I used words like *vagina, labia* and *clitoris.*"

"Are you sure you're my mother? I must've been switched in the hospital!"

"Sweetheart, you know I'm teasing." She reaches for my forearm. "Seriously though, are you okay?"

My expression softens and I nod when I see the genuine concern in her eyes.

I deliberate on how to be tactful with my mother; she is, after all, my mother.

"Tyler is wonderful. He's much more considerate of my needs than *anyone* has ever been."

"So he makes sure you orgasm first then."

Gone is the gentleness on my face quickly replaced by a flush of embarrassment.

"This conversation is now over. Forever." I flick the beater back on and drown out her laughter.

Tyler follows my dad into the kitchen, laughing about how funny it would be to see me on ice skates.

"Why is that so funny?" I challenge, feeling slightly offended.

Dad offers mock sympathy, "You're not exactly the most athletic person, remember?"

"I can ice skate! As soon as the pond by your house

freezes, I'll prove it!"

"This I can't wait to see," Tyler says, digging into his piece of the sweet potato pie my mom brought over.

"Is this from Susie's?" I ask around my fork.

My mom grins, confessing, "I thought I could pass it off as my own."

"I'd know her desserts anywhere." I shovel another forkful into my mouth.

Tyler's phone rings and he sets his fork down, reaching into his pocket before looking at the screen.

"It's my mom. Do you mind if I take it?"

My eyes widen in surprise that he would even ask me.

"Of course not!"

Tyler is not only considerate in the bedroom, but he's considerate in so many other ways. A few nights before, his phone rang incessantly from an unfamiliar number so he let it go to voice mail. When the person called again, he silenced his phone because we were curled up on the couch watching Game of Thrones. I told him to answer if, but he insisted that spending time with me was more important than a phone call which was probably about work anyway.

He rises from the table and walks into the living room before connecting the call.

"I'm considering a motorcycle," my dad announces, looking from my mother then to me. He knows he's shocked us both.

With narrowed eyes, my mom asks, "What do you mean *considering?*"

"You hate racing!" I add.

"Who said anything about racing?" He lifts the cup of coffee and sips slowly. "I'm thinking about a nice touring Harley…." He glances at my mom, gauging her reaction before continuing. "We could take it out on Sunday afternoons."

"Like an old couple?" The spirited smirk on my mother's face matches the humor in her eyes.

He shrugs nonchalantly. "Well then, I'll just have to stop by the senior center to find some little cutie to hop on the back and ride with me."

My mother snaps her teeth, slaps his arm and laughs along with him, knowing full well he's teasing.

But I stiffen. Thankfully it goes unnoticed.

My thoughts drift to Penny as my parents' conversation fades away.

A million questions swirl around my mind from pre-natal care to college. How will she provide for this child? Will she even keep it?

Tyler walks back into the room and the anxious look on his face has me worried immediately. I rise and meet him in the middle of the kitchen, placing my hand at his waist.

"What's wrong?"

"Tre."

Panic sinks my heart. "What's wrong with Tre? Is he okay?" Unimaginable thoughts creep into my head about losing this little boy or that he might be hurt. He means so much to Tyler; his brother's living legacy.

"He's not hurt. At least not physically."

I don't appreciate the cryptic responses.

"Please tell me what's going on," I demand.

"His mom is getting married and they're moving."

Disappointment, frustration and utter helplessness combine and leave a heavy expression on his face.

"Oh no! I'm so sorry!"

I lean in and snake my arms around his back, rubbing the muscles of his strong back. Beneath my fingertips, I feel him inhale and exhale roughly.

"Where are they going?"

"Georgia."

Listening to Tyler explain how Jill, Tre's mom, is moving because her fiancé was offered a better job is heartbreaking because I can tell he's completely torn by this. Tre will be provided with more opportunities, but he'll also be so far away.

"When are they leaving?"

Tyler's throat constricts. "In two weeks."

"Right after the New Year?"

He looks away thoughtfully, his lips tightening into a hard line before he nods.

"Then we need to make this the best Christmas for him. For you."

"What are you two whispering about over here?" my mom asks with a smile.

I sigh and throw her an exasperated look which thankfully she understands.

"Dad and I are leaving. The kitchen is all set and leftovers put away."

A swell of appreciation rises for my parents; two people who would do or give anything for me.

After hugs and quick kisses goodnight, Tyler and I crawl into bed and create a list of all the things he wants to do with Tre in the next two weeks.

"I really wanted to get him a dirt bike for his birthday in April."

My head lifts from his bare chest where my fingers glide, trailing up and down his scar.

"A dirt bike? He's only five!"

"It's never too soon to learn to ride."

"Yeah, but does Jill *want* him to ride?"

His eyes harden briefly. "My brother would've wanted that."

I nearly draw blood as I clamp down on my tongue. My finger stills on his chest.

Thomas Strong was nothing like his brother. He was a reckless and selfish man who took from people and gave nothing in return. A man who got a woman pregnant and then tried to deny it. He was killed before Tre was born. It wasn't until Stacy saw the newborn that she realized the truth; the baby was indeed Thomas' son. From that day forward she vowed to support him in lieu of her son's absence. I give Jill credit for naming her son after his father and grandfather when neither man was faithful.

"Does it bother you?"

"What?" I hum.

"Does my scar bother you?"

His question draws me away from angry thoughts about his brother and …

I rise to an elbow and look at him as a million questions stand in line, preparing to fall from my lips.

Shock widens my eyes when they meet his.

"God no! Why…why would you think that?"

I swallow the ball of emotions before pressing a long slow kiss directly onto the pink seam dividing his chest.

Tyler stares at me thoughtfully, and I immediately wonder what he's thinking.

"Sometimes I wonder what would've happened if—"

"Tyler," I plead. "Please don't finish that sentence."

"I guess I was thinking about my brother and how his life ended. My mom almost lost both her sons. Tommy wasn't perfect and he did some really stupid things, but when push comes to shove, he was my brother."

I sigh, feeling guilty for having thought badly about Thomas mere moments before.

"I want to do things with Tre that my brother can't do. And now he's leaving. I thought I'd have a lot more time with him."

I crawl closer and cover his body with my own, snuggling into the crook of his neck, breathing him in.

"You'll have to make a point to keep in touch with him."

"It won't be the same. That kid…he's like my son."

An ache cripples my heart.

"Do you want kids?" I ask hesitantly, almost afraid of his response.

"I didn't think I did, but now that I have Tre, I think I'd be a good dad. I definitely wouldn't leave my kids for anything or anyone."

I detect the resentment and disappointment in his voice. His father's leaving still hurts.

"Maybe someday we'll have kids."

"You'd want to have kids with me?"

My eyelashes flutter quickly as my brain struggles to understand his question and suddenly I feel a sense of dejection.

"You don't want to have kids with me?" I ask quietly.

Tyler flips me over and hovers above me.

"Baby, I want a whole sports team with you! Enough boys to field a football team and enough girls to cheer them on!"

"What?" I shriek, pushing his face away, denying him my mouth. "That is the most chauvinistic and misogynistic thing I've ever heard you say!"

"No it's not. Football is a rough sport. I wouldn't want my baby girl getting hurt."

"And what if she wanted to race?" I cock an eyebrow probingly.

Tyler sucks in air, hissing from the side of his mouth. "I don't know."

"I do! My kids, girls or boys, will be able to do anything they want."

He laughs. "Look at you! Going all Momma Bear and you don't even have kids yet."

Gazing into his eyes and searching his face, I caress his cheek slowly as I realize he will someday be my children's father. He is the man I will spend the rest of my life with.

I kiss his lips and thank God for sparing Tyler's life and for giving me the opportunity to love him.

"What's that look for?" he asks.

"This is my 'let's practice making a baby' face."

Tyler rolls his hips, hitting my core, teasing me playfully. "Practice makes perfect."

# SEVENTEEN

"I CAN DO THIS!" I FINALLY STAND on the ice, extending my arms for balance. My knees wobble as Artic air whips against my face.

"Come on, Bambi. You can do it." Tyler skates backwards, playfully creating more distance between us.

"It's freezing out here! I hate this!" I yell as my back arches and my legs end up by my ears.

Within seconds, Tyler comes to an abrupt stop after racing over to me. A spray of snow and ice shoot in every direction.

"Are you ready to give up?" he asks, extending a thick black glove.

I set my hand in his and he pulls me up.

"I *can* skate. It's just been a long time." I pout, hoping a little mercy will be tossed my way. I thought I was off the hook after the first time he mentioned ice skating, but no, Pam had to bring it up last week in front of him. So much for confiding in her!

Tyler wraps his arms around my waist and pulls me flush with his body covered in full winter apparel.

"You don't need to prove anything to me."

I huff. "I'm not trying to prove anything. I just want to enjoy the things you do."

A wry smile spreads across his rosy cheeks.

"There are plenty of things I love to do that you enjoy…" He leans down and whispers in my ear. "And we both get satisfaction."

I shiver.

"You cold?"

I shake my head no.

"That's too bad. I was going to warm you up in our bed."

I howl with laughter as I repeat, "Okay! Okay! I'm freezing!"

Back in his truck, he cranks the heat and snuggles close to me.

"I love that you're willing to try new things."

I stare at him, my cheeks flushing a deep crimson thinking about how comfortable we are with each other's bodies.

"I wasn't referring to *that*, but that's good, too."

I offer a long sensual kiss.

"This summer, I'm going to teach you how to water ski."

"Great," I murmur sarcastically.

"You'll be great and you'll get your tan at the same time."

"I'll get that at the track." I stare pointedly.

He gasps and asks, "You're going to come with me?"

Insecurity and doubt creep in.

For so many years I stayed away from the track. Watching those men, one in particular, transform into arrogant assholes was something I didn't want to witness; I had been living with the transformation on a daily basis.

"Unless you don't want me there."

"Are you kidding? I can't wait!" he yells, his excitement nearly uncontainable.

He smacks my mouth with a hard kiss.

"I want you with me at every race. Every test and tune. Everything. Everywhere. Every time."

A little voice in my head whispers, "This man loves you."

Each day of the following week, we spend it with Tre, making the most of the time before he leaves for Atlanta with his mom and Jack. Stacy joins us for dinner several times that week when she's not working.

"You got him a dirt bike?" Jill queries, turning a shocked expression in Tyler's direction with raised eyebrows.

I smirk and suppress the comment, "I told you so."

A slight moment of panic flashes across Tyler's face.

"Jill, can I talk to you over here?"

Jill looks at her son then nods and follows.

Watching Tre jump on the bike, roaring and pretending to race makes me smile. He looks so much like Tyler with his light brown hair and bluish-green eyes.

"Don't forget this, buddy." Jack, Jill's fiancé, says, fitting the helmet on Tre's head.

I remember laughing out loud the first time I met them. I thought for sure they were joking with names like that.

"Tre, will you come see Uncle T race?"

The little boy glances up to his soon-to-be stepdad with hope in his eyes.

"We'll see, buddy. That's up to your mom."

Tyler and Jill rejoin us and he drapes his arm over my shoulder, adding a kiss to my head.

I toss him a questioning look, but he just smiles.

"Mom, can we go see Uncle T race?"

Jill laughs. "Maybe for April vacation or over the summer."

Tre jumps off the dirt bike and runs over, wrapping his arms around Tyler's legs.

"I'm going to miss you Uncle T!"

I disengage myself from Tyler's hold and give them a moment of privacy, stepping closer to the boy's mom.

"You sure you're not too upset?" I ask Jill. "He couldn't resist. He loves that boy so much."

"Nah, it'll be okay. Jack can teach him after he teaches him to ride his bicycle." She smiles at the man she plans on marrying.

I liked Jill instantly when we met her at Tre's hockey

game. We laughed about the number of injuries kids sustained during the last Field Day she coordinated at her school. She doesn't harbor any ill feelings toward Thomas; they had never been serious and she knew exactly who he was.

"I had wanted to hump a hottie," she said with humor in her voice. "And I did."

I comfort Tyler that night after he offers his nephew the usual mantra of "See you later," rather than a goodbye. I didn't realize how affected he would be until he tells me it hurts almost as much as the day he buried his brother.

WEEKS LATER WITH Valentine's Day just around the corner, an offer is finally made on the house and we eagerly accept it. Although Tyler refuses to give me a specific answer as to why he doesn't want us to move back to his apartment, I know deep down it has something to do with *him*.

Like me, Tyler wants to distance himself, free himself from all things A.P. We've moved forward and everyone else needs to do the same. No one *says* anything, but we notice the snickering and side glances when we go out or I stop by the job site to bring him lunch. We quickly got over the initial awkwardness of it all especially when the guys on the crew looked on and then swiftly turned away.

Part of me is looking forward to race season; part of me is not.

Our search for a new home continues, we rent a three-bedroom home on the other side of town. It's a modest place, but the huge garage was the selling point. The bike Tyler's been rebuilding is almost complete; a few more adjustments and minor changes will hopefully make it one of the fastest grudge bikes on the East Coast.

Sitting on the top step that leads from the garage into the house, I watch with awe as he weaves an intricate web of wires, connecting them to different parts. The stretched cotton T-shirt over the curve of his back, the flexing of his tattooed biceps, the thickness of his thighs all drive me insane.

"What are you thinking about?" Tyler asks knowingly, his eyes matching the lust in mine.

"Nothing," I reply coyly. If I answer honestly, he'll devour me here and now.

"I was just thinking about how smart you are." I smile and continue. "How do you know all this stuff?" I ask, motioning with my hands.

"I don't know." He shrugs, tilting his head sideways to look underneath the motor.

"Come on. You didn't go to school for this so how'd you learn?"

His arms flex again as he tightens a bolt.

"I watched. I listened. I learned."

"So you just walked up to some random guy at the track, stood behind him and took notes with a pen and a paper?" I ask, chuckling at the mental image.

"Actually, I took notes on my phone." He grins playfully.

"Haha. Aren't you a funny guy!"

When his chuckle finally subsides, he looks me at me seriously.

"I paid attention. I observed. I learned what to do and what not to do."

"Ahh…so you were a creepy stalker then."

Oil-slicked hands fly in my direction, mere inches away from my face and I flinch, my head hitting the door as I jump back in defense. My heart nearly stops with the moment of déjà vu, but the quick flash of memory vanishes the instant Tyler reaches out and cups my jaw carefully, pulling my mouth to his.

"Come here. I'll give you a creepy stalker."

He kisses me long and hard, his tongue slips into my mouth and swirls around, dancing, tasting, loving me.

"I watched from afar and then moved closer until I was in the thick of things."

A shiver runs through my body at his words; I know he's not just referring to building motorcycles. My belly flutters as butterflies take flight.

"From a distance." My eyes close as I sigh, understanding his words. "You loved me from a distance for so long."

My chin quivers over the wasted years of loving another man.

His thumbs sweep over my closed eyelids and reopen at his tender words.

"I did and I always will."

One tender kiss is followed by another until we give in to desire and satisfy our desperate need for each other. Whispers of intimacy fall from Tyler's lips and waft into my ears as I climax, followed by his own release.

I press my lips to his neck, leaving a trail of kisses until I reach his chest and turn my ear to listen to his beating heart. It beats hard and strong. My hands slide around his back and find their way beneath his T-shirt where my fingernails scratch lightly.

He hums in response.

"Feels so good."

"You like that?"

Tyler lowers his face to mine, pinning me with those soulful eyes I love so much.

"I love it. I love everything you do."

"Even this?" I lower my hand and squeeze his ass and swirl my hips, feeling him harden.

"If you keep doing that, I'll never get this bike ready. I've only got three weeks to finish."

I sigh dramatically and sing song, drawing out a single word. "Okay."

Tyler pushes up and adjusts his clothing while I do the same. He turns his attention to the sleek motorcycle and continues the task at hand.

"Did you put in those vacation days at work?"

My eyes brighten as I nod eagerly.

"I hope you don't mind, but I actually looked at your schedule for the entire season and requested those days off, too. Hopefully, I'll get them approved. If not, I'll see if someone can switch with me."

A genuine smile stretches across his face.

"Thank you." His face lights up like a Christmas tree. "And why would I mind? I want you to be there so you can give me a good luck kiss."

I bite down on my lip and grin.

"Not that I need luck, but I would love the kiss."

I roll my eyes and toss a dirty rag in his direction.

"Don't be arrogant!"

"I'm not!" He chuckles, adding a quick shrug of his shoulders. "I just know I'm good."

"I believe that's called arrogance."

He smirks and shakes his head.

"In my book, it's called confidence."

"Whatever," I retort.

"You'll see."

Another hour slips by as I sit there, watching him. I text with Pam who's giving me a hard time about spending all my spare time with Tyler. She thinks I'm falling into an old habit of letting a guy dictate what I do and don't do. I think I eventually convince her that Tyler isn't like anyone I've been with. Aside from my father, he's the most considerate and loving man I've ever met.

I stand and stretch, announcing that I'm tired and am going to take a shower and possibly read.

"I won't be much longer."

My face distorts and my stomach rolls when the smell of

race fuel infiltrates my nose.

"Ugh! How can you stand that?" I wave my hand in the air, clearing the air in front of my face.

Closing his eyes momentarily, Tyler inhales deeply as if he were savoring it.

"I love the smell of MR12."

"Why?" I ask incredulously, placing a hand over my mouth.

"It's the scent of victory."

I laugh, moving in to kiss him.

"Hah! Do you know what I just realized?" I raise my eyebrows and wait until I have his full attention. "A doesn't stand for Anthony. It's for Arrogant. Tyler Arrogant Strong."

Turning on my heels, I climb the three steps, enter the house and close the door behind me. With my hand still on the handle, my back sags against the door as a sigh releases.

*I love Tyler Strong.*

# EIGHTEEN

"IT'S NOT MY BIRTHDAY. Not for another two months."
Tyler's eyebrows raise up as he inspects the colorfully wrapped boxes on the kitchen table.

"What?" I squawk. "I thought your birthday was March 7th!"

With narrowed eyes, he smiles playfully.

"Tyler, you're exactly two months older than I am. How could I forget that?"

I wasn't in the mood last year to celebrate my birthday so I didn't care that it slipped by without notice. Neither Susie's sweet éclairs or Pam's promises to find me a hot date could cheer me up. The fog I had been in had only begun to lift; things were still clouded and hazy especially where Tyler was concerned.

"I'm opening it," he sings, slowly peeling off a sliver of

clear tape.

The anticipation is killing me. I do have to give my mother credit for the idea; but the logo and its meaning is all mine.

Bits of paper fly everywhere as Tyler rips into it, leaving the cardboard box naked. He pulls an Army knife from his back pocket and cuts the tape, finally revealing its contents.

"Shirts?"

I can see the gears working in his brain.

"Well, you have to take them out and look at them!"

He grabs a T-shirt and stretches it out on the table, using his hand to flatten the material.

"Superman?"

There's a mask of confusion on his face at the logo printed on the left side of the shirt.

"Now turn it over."

He obliges.

"T.A.S. Racing." Tyler smiles in surprise and awe when he sees the bold printed script.

I can almost feel the excitement seeping through his pores.

"Did you read what it says below?"

"Stronger than ever."

The muscle in his jaw clenches as he bites back the moisture in his eyes.

"I love this! Thank you."

Slipping from his grasp, the soft material falls to the table when he turns to face me, sliding his rough hands over my face.

My heart melts into a pool of emotions.

"You are the most thoughtful person. All the little things you do make me fall more in love with you each and every day. I don't think I could possibly love you more."

"I feel the same way about you." I sweep my lips across his.

Tyler's body crushes against mine, his arms locking me in place...my favorite place in the world.

"Can I ask you a question?" he breathes into my hair as his kisses line my neck.

I hum, unable to locate the words to respond.

He chuckles lightly and asks, "What's up with the Superman logo? I'm not a fan of superheroes."

I pull back to look at him.

"I know that...but you're my superhero. You're my Superman."

Angling my body to free my arms, I turn and guide his attention to the logo.

"S." I swallow the lump in my throat. "While some may see "S" for Superman, I see it as "S" for Strong. You are the strongest person I know. You've overcome so much. You give so much."

"But—"

I cover his mouth.

"I wasn't finished yet." I smirk.

"Like Superman, you want to make the world a better place. Like him, you take care of people. Like him, you flew in, came out of nowhere, and saved the girl."

My eyes meet his and express a deep connection.

"You saved me, Tyler. You saved my life."

This man, this strong and loving man, buries his head in the crook of my neck as the emotion he tries to suppress finally overwhelms him.

"I wish I could've saved you sooner." Broken words are mumbled.

My fingers run along the nape of his neck, gripping tightly as his body shudders against my breasts.

My lips move quietly, whispering, "You're *my* Superman."

Together we release a torrent of moisture, giving and taking what we need from each other until our faces are stained with dried tears and our bodies thoroughly exhausted.

"You made me cry," he declares with a hint of shame and disbelief.

"So what?" I pull back and smile. "I'm sure Clark Kent shed a few tears over Lois Lane."

"I don't cry."

I grimace as a humorous warning emerges. "Don't make me change that logo!"

"Why would you change it?

"Because "S" is also for sweet."

I've embarrassed him based on the red flush on his cheeks and the turning away of his eyes.

"And it's for sexy."

His eyes drag up slowly.

"And solid."

My gaze falls to his hard abdomen and then lowers as my hand follows the trail.

"And sensual."

I graze his groin.

"And satisfying."

My hand moves against him causing his erection to stiffen.

"And surprising."

I pull my hand upward and place it on his chest with my palm splayed flatly. My thumb rubs over the top of his scar slowly.

"But above all, you are strong. Stronger than ever."

The air between us crackles with passion; its blanket envelopes me. I know my expression mirrors that of Tyler's.

"You know I'm going to marry you, don't you?" A rushed question flies from his lips while his hand covers mine on his chest.

"What did you say?" I ask with hesitancy as my mind works in overdrive, struggling for comprehension that he wants to be my husband. The idea of marrying has nudged my brain for some time, but now that I hear them, I'm stunned.

"I'm going to marry you, Karrie."

His words, dripping with longing, reach my ears and take hold of my heart.

"I thought that's what you said." I sigh, releasing the pent-up ball of air.

"I love you and I don't want to spend another day with you as my girlfriend."

Intensity laces his voice.

"I'm your girlfriend," I breathe; the intonation of my statement sounds more like a question.

"You're so much more than that! I'm serious. I can't wait for you to be my wife."

The pounding of my heart rings in my ears.

"Ty—"

His eyebrows furrow and his countenance darkens.

I smile.

"When you *ask*, I'll say yes."

Judging by the open mouth, I believe I've shocked him until his lips give way to a massive grin and his arms lock around me. Tyler lifts me off the ground, spinning me so my legs are left to dangle as I fly around. Joyous laughter floats in the air.

When the room finally comes to a complete stop, my head is left dizzy. I bury it in his chest and hold onto his biceps for support.

"So?"

"So what?" I ask, keeping my head down.

"When do you want to get married?"

I drag my head up and my eyes meet his.

"What? Wait…you didn't actually ask me anything," I laugh before becoming serious. "Here's the thing." I inhale drumming up courage. "I do want to marry you…someday, but I don't want to rush into it. I rushed into a marriage last time with a man I hardly knew and look how that turned out."

"Don't compare me to him! I'm not Alex; I'm nothing like him!"

My eyes close in response to his harsh tone before I eventually take a deep breath, reopen my eyes and look at him with compassion.

"You think I don't know that? You think I don't realize how damn lucky I am to have found you? You don't think I know how special this is?" I motion between our bodies. "I love you so incredibly much and that scares the hell out of me."

"I want you to be mine."

"And I am! A piece of paper isn't going to change that."

I caress his face gently, soothing away the stress I see.

"I am yours in every way possible. You've claimed me. Heart. Body. Soul."

"So you're saying we're not going to get married right away?"

"I'm saying when the time is right…when you actually *propose* after asking my father, of course," I tease, "I will be the luckiest girl in the world and completely honored to become your bride."

When he takes me to bed, it's more than sex; it's a promise of what's to come; a promise of our future as husband and wife.

"Are you sure you have everything?" I quip, looking inside the trailer where his bikes are strapped down and secured for the ride down south. Over the past two weeks, Tyler's excitement grew daily. He's ready to race hard and win big.

"I could do this with a blindfold on."

"Arrogance."

Tyler's smirk is followed by a kiss.

"Confidence."

I climb into his truck and slide next to him, getting comfortable for the six-hour trip.

My eyes flutter open and my belly rumbles with a combination of hunger and anxiety when I spy the state sign.

"We're here?" I yawn, stretch and crack my neck.

"Just about. How'd you sleep?"

"Good, I guess. I didn't realize how tired I was. I haven't been sleeping well the past few nights."

"I noticed." He chuckles.

"Well maybe if you stop waking me up for Midnight Madness, I'll sleep more."

Tyler pulls up to the gate and rolls the window down to talk to the lot attendant.

"Name and sponsor?" a tall, thin man asks, checking over the list attached to a clipboard.

"Strong. TAS Racing."

The man's eyes nearly fall from his face with realization.

"Tyler?"

With his hand extended, Tyler greets him.

"Hey Matt. What's up?"

"Yo, brother. I didn't recognize you or this truck." Matt says as he sweeps a quick glance at the dark truck and trailer. "You look good, man! Real good."

Tyler nods in response.

"Hey man, I'm sorry about Alex. I can't believe he's gone. One day he's here and the next he's gone. I wish I could've made it up for the funeral. I wanted to go, but you how things are down here."

Tyler pulls his eyes away from the gate attendant, ignoring his comment entirely.

I listen as the two men chat about the weather forecast and the other teams coming in for the weekend. Apparently, the return of Tyler Strong has been the talk of the town and all eyes will be on him. Races have been secured and bets placed. There's a lot at stake for him. It's his time to come out from behind the shadows of his former sponsor and show everyone he's still one of the country's top racers.

When we drive through the gate and enter the open lot, I turn and ask him why I wasn't introduced.

"You don't want to know him. He's a dick."

"Oh," I say as my eyes widen.

"A lot of these guys are just like him and I don't want you talking to them. Stay close by me."

I heed the warning in his voice and it raises my suspicion.

"What's going on?"

"You're going to hear Alex's name a lot this weekend. I just want you to be prepared."

"I know. I kind of figured as much." I exhale slowly,

hoping I have the courage to face all these people.

Trucks and trailers of every size and color line the lot. Pop up tents with team logos fill in almost every vacant space.

Curling the bill of my ballcap, I pull it down low, protecting my face from the scorching sun. I step out of the truck. Glancing around, I immediately spot them...scantily clad bike bitches circling around the trailers like piranha.

"You look good."

I look down at my team logo shirt paired with cut off shorts and smile.

"I do, don't I?"

I wave a quick hello to Gabe and Matt, two guys whom I'd met before when they came up to help rebuild the engine with Tyler a few times. They ended up staying for the weekend and I'm almost a hundred percent positive Gabe went home with Pam ...or was it Matt?

"Did you bring the earplugs like I told you?" Gabe asks.

I shake my head, kicking myself for not grabbing a pair when I was at the store last week.

Matt raises his chin in greeting before helping the rest of the crew unload the bikes from the trailer while Tyler gets bombarded by fellow racers and their cronies. Of course, the bike bitches follow and focus all their attention on my man. My attempt to step back is thwarted when Tyler reaches for my hand and keeps me in place right beside him.

I don't understand half the terms they're using; I never had the desire or the need to pay attention before. This time is different. I want to know everything. I listen intently, making mental notes of things I want to ask Tyler about.

After what seems like forever, I excuse myself to find the restroom. The long ride left me feeling queasy and car sick.

I lock the stall door and stand against it, regulating my breathing when a hot flash fires through me. A shadow of doubt tells me I don't belong here; I'm an outsider.

After splashing water on my face, I feel the weight of someone's stare and I catch her eye in the mirror.

I recognize the petite blonde instantly and fight hard to suppress a surge of anger.

"I thought that was you," Penny says, fixing a hard stare at me.

*Breathe, Karrie. Breathe.*

The dilemma I face is whether to address her kindly or as the whore she is for sleeping with my husband.

"Hi, Penny." I take the high road.

"I don't think you've ever been down here before, have you?" Her southern drawl seems more pronounced than I recall.

"No," I answer, moving to the dryer and rubbing my hands together.

"And now you're here with Tyler." She chuckles dryly. "You know about me and Alex, don't you?"

I swallow the lump and look away. I don't want to think about her or him or that part of my life. It's dead just like he is.

Inflicting another wound, she continues. "He was going

to leave you."

My voice vanishes and I am left with nothing to use as my defense or to launch a verbal retaliation so I turn to leave.

"I had his baby. A little girl. Her name is Alexandra, but I call her Alex… after her daddy."

"Alexandra," I breathe, my voice re-emerging weakly as I get sucker punched in the gut at the mention of the name he always said he wanted to name our daughter.

"Want to see pictures?"

I spin on my heels, ready to spew venom. That's when I notice the swell of her belly.

"You're pregnant again?" I don't even try to hide the disdain in my expression.

Her mouth transforms into a smug smile and she straightens her shoulders, exuding an aura of pride.

"Seems these guys can't keep their hands off me. None of them ever could. Not even Tyler."

My lips move slowly, mumbling, whispering words of hate I know will never reach her ears.

"It's hot outside. Make sure you lotion up. God forbid you burn that white trash skin of yours."

The last thing I see is her smile fall from her face and her mouth drop open. I'm pretty sure she calls me some choice words as the bathroom door shuts behind me.

A quick stop at the concession stand does little to settle my stomach. I make a mental note to pack Dramamine next time. I purchase a few fried snacks and meet Tyler back at the trailer where he's getting suited up to make his first pass of the afternoon.

Damn, he looks good! I've suddenly lost my appetite for the food in the tray.

"Don't look at me like that," he whispers in my ear after he kisses me. "Especially when you know I can't do anything about it right now."

# NINETEEN

THE NEXT MORNING, I TRAIL behind Tyler and his crew as they make their way to the track and line up. I can hardly hear myself think over the roar of the engines. Plumes of white smoke hide the lethal looking motorcycles as their back tires spin and heat up.

Getting lost in the commotion, I fall deep into the excitement of the crowd, eventually standing off to the side. I see Tyler's helmet move from right to left as he scans the sea of onlookers. He flips his visor up and calls Gabe over. Gabe nods and is gone. Moments later he finds me and ushers me back to where I was next to Tyler.

The shiny helmet is ripped off his head as he leans over to speak to me.

"I told you." He warns with stern eyes. "I want you by my side. Got it?"

I nod and smile when a warm and fuzzy feeling flows through me.

Noise and chaos settle into silence; a bubble of tenderness and intimacy consume us the instant his lush lips crash against mine.

"Go fast," I mumble against his lips when Matt and the other guys start to heckle.

"That's my plan."

Our eyes lock as I close his visor and silently pray for his safety. Stepping back, I watch as he shifts his bike into gear. It roars loudly when he launches forward to the pre-staging line.

*Who knew racing was so sexy?*

A distant voice booms through the speakers announcing the next race. It's a highly anticipated race after last night's test and tune. Everyone had the chance to see Tyler in action; they got to see the motorcycle called Black Mambo fly down the track. He is better than ever. Faster than ever. Stronger than ever.

I narrow my eyes when yet another plume of white smoke rises in the air, the smell of rubber burning permeates my nose as each racer heats up their back tires.

Like a predator ready to pounce, Tyler bends at the waist and lowers his long hard body over the gas tank. My attention is pinned directly on him, traveling up and down from the black leather suit to the laced-up racing shoes. Hovering over the shiny black metal, his chest barely touches it. The roar of his turbo motorcycle sounds like the warning growl of a vicious bear.

I look for any sign of movement, but he's perfectly still, keeping his eyes laser focused on the top lights as they prepare to descend. The tip of my tongue peeks through, moistening my bottom lip before my teeth clamp down on it. I force a deep swallow in anticipation of the moment his hands shift, releasing the firm grip on the clutch and cracking open the throttle in his other hand. The hammering of my heart is almost as loud as the roar of the aligned motorcycles, two beasts gearing up for an attack on the asphalt as they race to the finish line.

The anticipation is thick and coats my skin. As if no one else exists, I watch him as he watches the tree of lights. One light. Two lights. Seconds later when every light is illuminated, Tyler accelerates, thrusting forward, racing down the straight track at an incredible speed. I stand on my tip toes to see him; the farther he goes, the smaller he seems.

"Go! C'mon, baby!" Quiet, mumbled words of encouragement fly from my mouth.

At the end of the track, a white arrow flashes on the right side, indicating Tyler's win. The crowd returns and erupts into a wave of cheers and hollers. I glance around quickly and notice everyone offering hugs and high fives. Gabe steps close and wraps his arms around me, smiling fiercely.

"Hot damn! Can you believe it?" he yells.

My eyes widen in surprise.

"He's never gone that fast! Never! What are you doing to him?"

We both turn to look at Tyler who is moving slowly back in our direction, traveling a narrow path alongside the track.

I laugh then smile. "That's all him."

The memory of long nights sitting in the garage while he worked on his bike cross my mind. The memory of celebrating when he finally finished rebuilding this motorcycle makes the butterflies in my belly dance. My ovaries are going to explode recalling what we did on that bike when he finally finished rebuilding it.

His whispered words he growled in my ear now ring loudly.

"Time to celebrate, baby."

I felt a chill down my spine when he took me by the hand and led me over to inspect the sleek, sexy turbo bike he'd built with his own hands.

"That's beautiful," I said, running my hand over the polished metal as I admired the intricacy of the highway of wires and pipes.

Tyler's chin rested on my shoulder and he kissed my neck. "You are beautiful."

The moment transformed. His sweet, loving gesture quickly changed to one that had us clawing off each other's clothes before he bent me over the bike and widened my stance, driving hard into me.

The purr of Tyler's bike as he approaches pulls me back to the here and now.

I watch him wave to the crowd as he passes them and I smile at his earned arrogance.

The throng of gathered people part like the Red Sea when Tyler slowly maneuvers through the dense crowd. Cheers of appreciation and respect are tossed his way. He nods and smiles confidently until he reaches me. Even before he removes his helmet, he slides his arms around my waist and pulls me to him. I could feel the heat from the engine tickling my skin so I lean in, careful to avoid a burn.

I flip open his visor and catch his eyes; they're beaming with happiness, pride and love and yet I detect a hint of insecurity and vulnerability.

"That was amazing!"

The helmet is removed, leaving his short hair matted down. I run my fingers through his hair and cup his jaw as I bring his face closer to mine. I tilt slowly and meet his lips, offering a congratulatory kiss and celebratory promise of what's to come.

"I'm so proud of you!"

I kiss him again, completely oblivious to the stares until Gabe clears his throat.

"Take it to the trailer, bro! We've got other races lined up."

Tyler smiles against my lips. "Get on."

I pull back in question.

He moves forward on the bike, creating a sliver of a space for me.

"Baby, I can't fit there. You know I have a big ass!"

"Karrie, get on. Now."

The command in his voice supersedes my doubt as I

straddle the bike and snake my arms around his waist.

Together, we ride slowly through the crowds who wait for the next race to begin.

Race after race, Tyler wins, destroying Alex's old records and setting new ones.

His confidence is palpable; his arrogance deserved.

The day has been nothing short of amazing.

The sun falls below the horizon, worn and weary after having worked hard all day providing light and heat.

I gather my hair in a messy bun at the nape of my neck and wipe the sweat from my brow. A shower and the hotel bed beckon me, inviting me in as if I were a wanderer seeking refuge.

After the last ratchet strap is secured, holding the motorcycles in place, Tyler stands there in jeans and a T-shirt, moving slowly in my direction.

"Thank you for being here today."

I smile and step into his arms, forgetting how hot and sweaty I am,

"I'm glad I was here with you. It's where I belong."

Strong arms envelope me and I am kissed senselessly. His hands travel from my face to my neck before finally resting at my bun. When I'm with him, I feel as though the outside world no longer exists.

"I love you," he whispers in my ear.

My eyes close briefly and slowly reopen as the words "I love you more" tumble from my lips in response.

"But I've loved you longer." He smirks and cocks his

eyebrow, proving his point.

I smile because I can't argue back. I hate to think of the years I wasted, the years he watched me from afar, loving me even though I belonged to someone else.

"You know I would do anything for you. I would give up racing for you."

I gasp. Disbelief and shock mar my face before I nod and smile.

"I would never ask you to do that."

"I know you wouldn't, but what I'm saying is I would *if* you asked. *You* are the most important thing in my life."

His loving words send warmth through my body.

"Can you do something for me?" he asks, dropping his hands. The look in his eyes suddenly serious.

I slide my hand over the scruff of his jaw.

"Of course. Whatever you need. You know that!"

Searching my face, Tyler kisses me lightly before taking a small step back and dropping to one knee, sliding my hands in his.

My heart stops.

"Karrie Ann Miller, I need to ask you something important, but I need to tell you something first." He swallows nervously, forcing down his emotions as he stares at me with love etched on his face.

"From the first time I saw you, I knew you were special. From the first time I touched your skin, I knew we had a connection. From then, I knew I wanted to get to know you, but when I lost that chance, I stood in the background and watched you. I watched you struggle and I watched you soar. At times, I saw the happiness in your eyes, but more often I saw the sadness. Karrie, the only thing I ever wanted to do was to take you away, to protect you and to love you. Now that I have the chance to do those things, I don't ever want to lose it."

The hammering of my heart thumps loudly in my ears, the blood is racing wildly through my veins.

"So…" He reaches into a small pocket to retrieve something then uncurls his palm, revealing a diamond ring. Cast upon me are eyes filled with absolute and complete joy.

"I'd like to ask you something. I'm asking you to be my wife, to spend every day and every night with me, to be by my side at every race for the rest of my life. Your life. Will you marry me?"

Through expectant eyes, I realize he identifies the expression on my face as one of shock and surprise. But my hand reaches down to touch his face, my thumb sliding across his bottom lip.

In a matter of seconds, a thousand questions surface; all opportunities for me to reject his offer.

But I don't.

I can't.

I am completely, irrevocably and madly in love with Tyler Strong.

My knees buckle from the excess weight of happiness resting on my shoulders and I lower myself, mirroring his position. Pools of water fill my eyes as my vision blurs and I wipe them away desperately, not wanting to miss a moment of this with him.

"There are so many reasons why I should say no..."

Hurt flickers across his face.

"But I don't care. I don't care about the past. I don't care about what people might say, I don't care that I used to hate you."

At my words, a small smile tugs on his mouth.

"But here's the thing. I *want* you. I *need* you. I *love* you."

Tyler kisses me chastely and asks, "Is that a yes?"

"Absolutely! Yes! For all the reasons I should say no, I'm saying yes!"

Taking my left hand in his, Tyler guides the beautiful ring in place and seals it with a kiss.

"You've just made me the happiest man alive."

My lips tease his, touching lightly before pulling back until he crushes his mouth against mine.

"I'm going to love you forever."

A heavy knock and the jiggling of the trailer door forces us to separate from our embrace.

Tyler rises and unlocks it, pushing the door wide open.

"What do you want?" he asks someone who remains hidden behind the door and is out of my line of sight.

"I need to talk to you," a woman's voice demands.

"Now's not a good time."

"Really? Why? Because your girlfriend—"

Tyler glances back at me sympathetically then steps out, quickly closing the door behind him.

Curiosity and apprehension flood me as I sit back on my heels. Feeling as though the enormous wave of emotions is crashing, leaving me buried in the sand, I sigh and look around the trailer at the motorcycles and equipment. I can't believe how much my life has changed in a year. My gaze falls to my ring, admiring its beauty and simplicity. The solid square of diamond nestled in platinum sparkles, demands my attention. I'm lost in imaginary thoughts of Tyler going to the jewelry store and picking out this ring when I'm suddenly startled and sent running at the sound of voices shouting.

The door swings open and I step out just in time to see Penny's hand connect with Tyler's cheek.

"What the hell? What are you doing?" I screech as my feet come to a full stop before them.

Tyler remains unmoving, accepting the barrage of small balled fists to his chest.

"Penny, stop! What are you doing?" I shout.

I turn to Tyler, trying to understand what's happening, but the look in his eyes makes my heart plummet.

"What's wrong?"

"Go back inside."

"No!" I refuse his command. My stern face and tight lips reveal my steadfast decision.

"Karrie, I said go back inside."

Standing my ground against ever being told what to do again, I bellow a single word.

"No!"

"She's upset. Let me talk to her."

"Clearly she's upset," I motion with my hands at the woman who is now crying against his T-shirt. "Why? Why is she upset? What happened?"

"Please trust me."

A plead for mercy and compassion is imprinted on his face as he speaks with a gentle voice.

*Trust him?* I've just agreed to marry him and he's consoling another woman. The woman who had an affair and a child with my husband. Images fill my mind. All the race trips they took down here. The muffled voices in the background. The lies he told. The deceit he lived. The plan he hatched.

Rage bubbles to the surface.

"You know what? Fuck you!" I turn and head in the opposite direction. My legs carry me fast and far away before my heart explodes.

"Karrie!"

I can hear Tyler footstep's behind me until he stops me in my tracks.

"Stop, Karrie!"

Desperately trying to avoid him, I sidestep right and then left. Each step is matched by one of his own.

His hands reach for my arms.

"I'm not letting you go."

Hot heavy tears spill from my eyes when I finally look at him.

"Why are you doing this? Why would you do this?"

He caresses my face.

"Baby, it's not what you think. She needs help."

I narrow my eyes and scowl.

"I don't give a shit what she needs!"

"She needs money. For the baby."

"I. Don't. Care!"

Tyler glances quickly over my shoulder and then looks back to me.

"I have to help her. I owe that to her."

"What?" I snarl. "You don't owe that woman anything."

A flash of comprehension races through my mind.

"It's your kid, isn't it?"

My stomach opposes and lunch threatens to rise.

"Hell no!"

"Don't lie to me."

Tyler meets me at eye level.

"I swear to God I never touched her. Never!"

"Then why do you owe her? Why is she your responsibility?"

His chest rises and falls in defeat.

"I should've warned her." He shakes his head sadly and blows out a puff of air. "I should've protected her from *him*."

I swallow the bitter, venom-filled words, keeping them locked away. I don't want to hurt him even though my heart is shredding.

"It's not your job to protect her. Or me for that matter."

The hard expression on his face indicates his disagreement.

"I love you so I will protect you."

"And what about her? Did you love her?"

Tyler closes the space between our bodies and brings his face centimeters away from mine. I can feel the heat radiating from his skin.

"Listen to me and listen good because I have two things to tell you. One, I have never in my life touched that woman." His eyes tighten momentarily. "Ever."

Softness and love replace the hardness of his countenance.

"I love you. I love you so much I can hardly see straight sometimes. I love you so much and the thought of ever losing you chokes me and I feel like I can't breathe.

My chin quivers as my emotions burst at the seams. I throw my arms around his neck, burying my face into his chest and sob quietly. His hands rub circles on my back as he consoles me with loving words.

I wipe my nose with the back of my hand and look up at this incredible man.

"You smell like her." I smile sadly.

"Want me to roll in the dirt? You know I'll do it just to get rid of the smell."

I slap his chest playfully, stilling my hand over his heart then tapping it twice.

"You're a good man, Tyler Strong."

"You are the better half of me. You make me feel strong. You make me feel like I can do anything in the world."

I absorb his words and embrace him once again.

"She's not as nice as you think she is."

"I never said she was nice. I've seen first-hand how vicious she can be."

In agreement, I nod and tell him about the bathroom incident the day before. "She's not worth it. I actually feel sorry for her daughter and the new one on the way."

"Me too."

Something in Tyler's voice raises questions in my mind.

"Are you giving her money? Are you supporting her?"

Gone is the sun-kissed glow when Tyler's face pales. Blinking rapidly, I can almost see his thought process working.

"Yes and no." He releases a deep exhale.

My body, from the hair on my head to the tips of my toes, tenses.

"Let's go inside," he says, glancing at the few people meandering around, all within earshot of us.

"I want you to tell me everything, Tyler. Everything."

He holds my gaze before nodding once.

TYLER LEADS ME BY the hand to the truck before opening the door.

"Give me two minutes," he says when Penny walks over.

If her goal was to drive a wedge between us, she failed miserably. Our bond is stronger than ever.

I suppress a chuckle when she leans in for a hug and Tyler steps back out of her reach.

He climbs into the truck and starts the engine, briefly checking for any other vehicles as we pull out of the nearly empty parking lot. Tapping the dial on the radio, Tyler finds a country station. Tim McGraw sings about being humble and kind.

I smile, thinking about how the song describes Tyler perfectly.

"Tell me everything."

Tyler's hand turns palm up, seeking its mate.

I lace my fingers with his and squeeze, reassuring him that I'm ready to hear why he's supporting my ex-husband's lover and baby mama.

"I knew what *he* was like better than anyone. I knew what *his* plan was."

I feel an ache in my heart.

"The day I brought her in to the clinic, she was terrified. She knew he didn't want kids and would force her to have an abortion. She saw him as a way out of her life. She thought if she could give him something you couldn't, he would stay. I felt sorry for her."

"But…" I start but then say nothing, choosing to listen instead.

"What?"

"It's not that I couldn't have kids, he never wanted them and… we didn't have sex often."

Tyler looks upward as if seeking help from God.

"When he found out she was pregnant, he went berserk and beat the crap out of her."

I cringe, a cold shiver running through my veins.

"She threatened to tell you. She even called your phone once, but I snatched it away. I could hear you on the other end and I wanted so much to tell you to leave him. I wanted to tell you to run as far away as you could."

"Why are we talking about this? Alex is dead. He doesn't mean anything to me anymore. Nothing."

"Before he died, he changed his mind and promised he would take care of her and the baby. I knew then that he was going to leave you. I tried so hard to wrap my mind around the fact he was leaving *you for her*. You were perfect and he was willing to walk away."

Hearing Tyler recall the story fills me with sorrow, but produces a renewed sense of strength.

"When he left everything in his will to me, I didn't want it. None of it. Not a single dime. The only thing of his that I ever wanted was you."

He brings our linked hands to his mouth and places a soft kiss.

"Because he said he would take care of her and the baby, I wanted to honor that. It's not that little girl's fault her father was an asshole. I asked Roger to set up a college fund for her. I wanted to give her the opportunities her mother never had."

"Why was she yelling at you tonight?"

"Because she's flat broke with another kid on the way. She wants the money now not when the kid goes off to college."

"So what are you going to do?"

"I'm going to ask Roger for advice, but I'll probably have him cut her a check for the lump sum. Then I'll be done with her." He turns to me. "What do you think?"

I chuckle darkly. "I think you're a much better person than I am."

After a quick stop at a local BBQ restaurant, we trek back home, talking about anything and everything, never once again mentioning Penny and Alex. During the middle of the night, the stifled emotions emerge and I end up bent over the toilet, purging my dinner and my hatred for Alex Parker.

# TWENTY

"OH MY GOD, PAM!" I laugh as Tyler pokes his head through the open window of my car, his crossed arms resting high on the top of the door frame. His bare chest fills the open space.

"Call me on your lunch break."

I click my seat belt in place after sending an emoji in reply to Pam's inappropriate text and drop my phone in my purse before looking at him.

"Babe, that's not until two o'clock in the morning and you'll be sleeping."

"I'll be up working on my bike. They need to drain the gas and change the plugs."

My nose wrinkles with curiosity as I lean over for another kiss, the hold of the restraint limits my reach.

"But last week I thought your bike went faster than it's

ever gone and you set the new track record."

"It did," he confirms confidently.

"So why are you changing things on your bike then?"

"Because records are meant to be broken."

I raise my eyebrows and widen my eyes. "Yeah... just as long as *you* don't get broken!"

"WHAT A BUSY NIGHT!" Odessa grumbles, throwing herself onto the vinyl-covered seat, stretching her legs out on the table. I look over my shoulder and eye her black Crocs, commenting that she needs to buy new ones based on the worn sole.

"Oh shut it!"

"You make enough money, don't you?" I tease, knowing she's still paying off her medical school bills. One of the perks to being an only child was having parents who paid for everything, including my education.

"I make ends meet. I cut corners when I need to."

The counter is covered with a smorgasbord of ethnic foods for our monthly pot luck dinner. I reach for the ladle and scoop some of Odessa's Guyanese stew over yellow rice.

"Take that dish you're about to eat, for example."

After combining the gravy and rice, I look at her while shoving yet another forkful into my mouth. I hum my appreciation for the savory meal.

"Mmm...so good."

"It's goat liver."

My stomach immediately revolts and I gag, spitting the food back onto the paper plate. I gargle half a bottle of water and rinse my mouth out over the sink. Turning to face her, I wipe my mouth and give her a horrible side eye.

"Why would you do that?"

Clutching her stomach, Odessa laughs.

"It was on sale."

I dry heave and press my hand against my stomach.

"That's disgusting!"

"But you said it was so good."

"Yeah, but that was before I knew it was goat liver. Who the hell eats that crap anyway?"

"My people."

She rises and stands next to me as she jabs her palms over her eyes, wiping away tears of laughter.

"Oh God, that was funny!"

Perusing the dessert table, she reaches for an Italian cookie with white icing, but I slap it out of her hand.

"No dessert for you!"

"Don't be such a baby! I've made this before and you loved it."

"I hate you!" I walk over and toss my dinner into the garbage.

"You love me."

Hours later, my stomach reminds me that I ate goat liver and rises once again in opposition, sending me sprinting to the nearest bathroom.

"I think you poisoned me," I bark at Odessa as we walk side by side to the waiting ambulance.

"Good Lord, woman, you're fine." She rolls her eyes dramatically.

"Says the goat liver eater from Guyana."

"Maybe you're pregnant."

The EMTs unload a man in his early thirties, his neck fastened securely by a brace. His moans emerge as he cries out in apology. It's reported that he is the cause of a motor vehicle accident involving alcohol. He is the drunk driver who crossed the road and slammed into a tree.

The scene is familiar and still heartbreaking.

Thirty-three minutes later, he is pronounced dead.

Overwhelmed by the death of a stranger, I find a storage closet and sob. I cry for the man whose life ended. I cry for the family now left behind. I cry for missed opportunities and chances not taken.

In this moment, I need Tyler. I need to hear his voice. I need to know he is alive and well.

"Hey babe. I was just going to text you." The quiet tone of his voice indicates his fatigue.

I open my mouth to speak, but only silence emerges.

"Karrie, you okay?"

I quickly nod my head, not realizing he can't see me so I muster the strength and release a squeaked "yes." My single word resembles that of a small mouse.

"Are you crying? Are you hurt?"

I swallow hard and reply, "No."

The shuffling sound on the other end of the phone makes me think he's getting dressed.

"Where are you? I'm on my way."

"No, it's okay," I say quietly, sighing into the phone. "I just needed to talk to you. I needed to hear your voice."

"What happened?"

I desperately long to step into his arms and be comforted by him.

"A man died tonight. It reminded me of—"

He exhales and murmurs, "I understand. I don't think you'll ever get over seeing Alex die."

"Alex?" I gasp. "This isn't about *Alex*. This is about *you*."

I slide down against the door and pull my knees to my chest.

"Tyler, that night when you were brought in, I worked on you. I held your heart in my hands and prayed so hard that you'd live. I didn't understand why I needed you to live. I didn't know then that you were the other half of me."

Tears flow freely down my face and I hear Tyler sniff then clear his throat.

The door knob jiggles and I hear my name being called.

"I have to get back to work."

I stand and wipe my face with my hands.

"I'll be up for a while so call me back if you can."

"Okay," I agree.

"I love you, Karrie."

"I love you more."

"Impossible."

I picture his grin as he says the word.

Odessa stands before me when I open the door.

"What's wrong?"

Choosing not to answer, I smile and shake my head.

"Are you sure you're not pregnant?" she sneers. "You've been all emotional and shit."

I laugh but then freeze in my tracks. Blinking rapidly, I mentally consider her words.

"Actually...I don't think it's the goat liver that's bothering my stomach. I think I might have morning sickness."

Her dark arm links with mine and she drags me down the hall to an empty bathroom.

"Here." She hands me a small empty container. "Go pee."

I DRIVE HOME IN a fog while the rising sun burns off the early morning dew. My sense of awareness is acute, everything I see looks different. I glance at the trees in full bloom and think about the never-ending cycle of life, knowing a baby grows in me. Tyler's child. *Our* child.

After kicking off my shoes, I crawl into bed beside him and watch him sleep. The gentle rise and fall of his chest signals his serenity. My fingers itch to caress his face as my mind wonders about what this child will look like.

Will she have his bluish-green eyes? Will he have darker hair like mine?

Tyler's eyes flutter open when I finally slide my arms over

his bare chest, my thumb strumming as usual over his scar.

He kisses my forehead and offers a "Good morning, beautiful." The arms I love so much wrap around me and press me flush against his warm skin. "Are you okay? I was worried about you."

I reply with a tight smile.

"I'm okay. It was a rough night and my emotions were running high."

He brushes the hair away from my face.

"I felt so bad. I was ready to get in my truck and come see you."

I smile.

"I know you were. But I'm okay," I inhale quietly, "I'm just... a little pregnant."

Tyler shoots up into a sitting position as I tumble to his pillow.

"What did you say?" he asks, looking down at me.

"I'm pregnant." I announce casually now that the initial shock of seeing a plus sign on the plastic stick has worn off.

He pounces on me, wedging himself between my legs and bearing his weight on his elbows.

"You're having a baby? My baby?"

I grin at his disbelief.

"No, actually it's Mr. Magoo's."

He narrows his eyes humorously.

"Yes. We're having a baby."

"I'm going to be a father? I'm going to be someone's dad?"

"You are. And you're going to be an incredible daddy."

A rapid succession of blinking makes me think he's overwhelmed, simply running on autopilot.

"Tyler, are you okay with this? I mean…we've talked about starting a family after we got married. The timing is a little off, but…"

He snaps out of the trance.

"Am I okay? I've never been happier in my life. Karrie, we did this. We —"

His words fall silent as he buries his face in my neck, the torrent of emotion breaking through the stoic damn.

Moments later with his head hung low, he moves down my body, removing the article of clothing away from my belly.

His lips graze my skin before he places what feels like a thousand gentle kisses.

"I love you," he murmurs.

I don't know if he's talking to me or our unborn child, but either way my heart fills with unimaginable happiness.

# TWENTY-ONE

FOR THE NEXT SEVERAL WEEKS, I rearrange my work schedule to accompany Tyler to races. His name is quickly becoming synonymous with victory and he's enjoying the perks of being on top.

"Would you ever sell the business to race full-time?" my dad asks, eyeing Tyler carefully over a steak dinner.

"No, sir. As much as I love racing, I know it's going to end someday and I have a family to support."

"A family?" my mom interjects suspiciously, setting her glass of wine down on the patio table.

Tyler and I share a quick glance and a smile.

"Congratulations, Gramma and Grampa."

My mother jumps to her feet and accidently knocks the glass to the ground, wine splattering everywhere.

"You're pregnant?! How did this happen?"

A loud guffaw rips through me. "Do I really need to explain how it works? You are a doctor after all."

"Get over here!"

My body is wrapped in her arms as she whispers in my ear.

"I'm so happy for you."

While still in her embrace, I dart my eyes to Tyler who is shaking my father's hand, offering an apology for the sequence of events.

"I'm sure you would've liked for us to have been married already, but..."

My dad rejects his apology, telling him instead to take care of me and our baby. "You asked my permission before hand *and* you got down on one knee. At least that's what Karrie said you did. I'm still waiting to see the video."

"I keep meaning to pull it from the surveillance tape."

After a quick switch, Tyler's face turns bright red when my mother makes a sexual reference and is immediately shushed by my dad.

"Behave yourself, woman!"

"That's not what you said last night, dear."

"C'mon here, Kare Bear." My father lifts me from the ground, leaving my feet dangling. "If you need anything, you know I'm always here for you."

"Thanks, Daddy."

I'm set back on my feet gently.

"And lay off the sweets. You're getting heavy."

"Dad!" My jaw drops open.

"Oh, you know I'm just kidding! But you are getting a little wide right here." He slides his hands down his own hips, slapping twice before smiling.

I narrow my eyes in response.

"I'm always wide right there! I have mom's genes!"

Tyler tosses his arm around my shoulder and announces that we're leaving after thanking my parents for dinner and praising my mother for her scrumptious dessert."

"You're such a flirt."

He feigns innocence. "Me? What did I do?"

"The way you charm my mother."

"What can I say? I have a way with the Miller ladies."

Our short commute back to our house is interrupted by a phone call from Tre. Tyler taps the Bluetooth device, filling the cab of his truck with his nephew's sweet and very excited voice.

"Hi, Uncle T! Hi, Aunt Karrie!"

"Hey, buddy! How are you?"

Tre rambles on for a solid ten minutes about his new school in Georgia, the house they bought, his baseball team and how Jack is teaching him how to ride the dirt bike.

"Can you come visit me when grandma comes?"

I see the struggle on Tyler's face.

"We'll see, buddy. It's race season, remember?"

Tre sighs dejectedly. "Can you come after that?"

"I'll try my best."

"Okay."

"Guess what, Tre! You're going to have a cousin!"

"I hope it's a boy. I don't really like girls."

I laugh and comment that girls are just as good as boys.

"When I find out, I'll tell you."

We say our goodbyes as we arrive at the house.

"Don't forget we have an appointment on Thursday."

Tyler smirks. "Like I'd forget that."

I don't think I've ever seen a man so excited to have a child.

"You forgot about the appointment for the wedding venue."

"I didn't forget. I got caught in traffic and besides, I didn't like that place."

Confusion appears on my face. "Why didn't you like it?"

"I just didn't." He adds a quick shrug of his shoulders.

"Well, since you're already taking the day off, I figured we could go to lunch and look at another place. I hate that I'm going to be a pregnant bride."

"What? That's ridiculous! You're going to be a stunning bride. Especially because you're my bride."

By Thursday morning, I'm anxious to hear the baby's heart beat again and find out the sex. From all the tossing and turning, I'd say Tyler's just as excited.

The technician, a woman I used to work with, squirts a cold jelly on my belly and proceeds to search for our baby's heartbeat.

"I can't believe you're this far along and you didn't know you were pregnant."

I detect the skepticism in her tone.

"I got a period every month. Why would I think anything?" I retort.

"I guess you were lucky. I swear I knew the second the egg was fertilized. I was a roaring bitch for nine months. My poor husband!"

I glance at Tyler and smile, feeling thankful that my hormones haven't caused any major catastrophes except for some late night runs to Susie's for an éclair or two.

"Are you going to breastfeed?"

I drop my chin to my chest, eyeing my boobs, which are quickly becoming the size of cantaloupes.

"I plan on it. I hope I don't choke the poor kid with an overabundance of milk."

When I look at Tyler, he's practically salivating at the sight of my boobs.

We watch as she moves the wand around my belly with one hand, clicking the keyboard and mouse with the other.

"There. See that?"

I nod eagerly before I turn to Tyler whose eyes are squinted while trying to decipher the blurry image on the screen.

"Unless this baby has a third leg, I'm pretty sure it's a boy."

"What?" Tyler shrieks. "*That's* my kid's di—"

"Penis!" The technician and I interject simultaneously.

"That's my kid's *penis?*" he asks, overexaggerating the last word.

I grin and nod as laughter erupts.

"Yep! Like father like son."

Tyler's hands move away from his mouth and reach up, encasing his head in disbelief.

"You okay?" I pull my hand out from behind my head and tug at his T-shirt, drawing him closer. "I'm sure he'll grow into it."

"It's not that," he breathes. "That's my son. Our son."

The blue color of his eyes dominates as the tears well up.

"Can we listen to his heart again?"

The room stills as the sound of our child's heart beats. The loud thumping and pumping indicates its health.

"It's so loud. So strong."

I pucker my lips in hopes of a kiss.

"Just like his daddy's." I run my fingers over his heart, remembering how I held it in my hand.

"I love you," Tyler murmurs against my lips.

The technician clears her throat and hands us printed copies of the ultrasound.

"In just a few months, you'll get to meet this little boy," she says with a smile. "The doctor will be right in."

After a quick visit with the doctor, Tyler and I stop for lunch at a quaint, seaside restaurant and choose to sit outside on the patio. The ocean breeze offers a respite from the summer's brutal temperature.

"This place is really beautiful." I look out at the ocean where sailboats move easily on the water. "This might be a really nice place for a wedding. Small, intimate, on the water."

I turn my attention to the man sitting across from me

when I get no response. I smile, realizing he's not heard a word I've said because he's lost in the black and white image.

"What are you thinking about?" I ask, curious to know what's behind his expression.

He slides his hand across the table and takes my ring finger between his, twisting my diamond from left to right before he sets it in its original position.

"I never would've believed this could happen to me. To be marrying the girl of my dreams and for her to carry my child at the same time. I can't believe I get to have this life with you."

"This is going to sound crazy so please don't take it the wrong way."

He cocks an eyebrow.

"I'm glad we didn't have a relationship when we first met."

His eyes widen then fall with hurt.

"Let me finish." I smile. "Yes, it would've saved us both a lot of heartache and sorrow, but this is our time. Now is our time. I think going through what I did, what we did, made us so much stronger than we possibly could ever have been. There isn't anything we can't face."

The waiter brings our food and I stare at his entrée longingly, wishing I could have a bite of the fresh white fish.

"Have a bite." He offers a forkful.

I lean over and open my mouth.

"Why didn't you order this instead of a salad?"

"Two reasons. If I eat any more fish, I'm going to grow

gills and… I need to watch my weight."

After giving me a stern look, Tyler switches our entrées and orders me to eat.

# TWENTY-TWO

"WHAT ARE YOU DOING?" I ask cautiously, glancing over to find Odessa with her legs propped up on the arm rest of the sofa and an intense look on her face. Her eyes are laser focused on her phone.

"Researching something."

I read Tyler's text and sigh. A shy smile tickles my lips and warmth spreads through me at my carefully crafted words of response.

"What are *you* doing?" she asks, rising from her position and walking in my direction.

I drag my eyes away from my phone.

"Talking to the man I'm going to marry."

"Remember when you used to hate him?"

I roll my eyes, snap my teeth and hiss, "Please don't remind me."

"Here." Odessa sets her phone down and taps the screen.

The V in my forehead tightens in confusion as I look at the list of names.

"What's this?" I pick up her phone.

"Nirmala. That's a great name! It was my great grandmother's name. You should name your kid that."

I burst out laughing at her suggestion.

"I'm not naming my kid after your goat-eating grandmother."

I see the whites of her teeth when her full lips pull back and she howls with amusement.

"Her nickname could be Mala."

"That means 'bad,' doesn't it?"

She nods firmly and releases a devious grin.

"My great-grandmother was notorious in Guyana."

"Yeah, for killing goats maybe. Besides, I'm having a boy."

"Code Pink to NICU. Code Pink to NICU," a monotone voice declares for several moments.

My hand involuntarily reaches down and caresses my belly, protecting my unborn child. My heart races for the parents of the child whose life is in danger. I close my eyes and offer up a quick prayer for the tiny life who may have been born prematurely. Then I murmur one for my own baby.

"Hey!" Odessa interrupts my quiet thoughts, causing me to open my eyes and look at her. "C'mon Teletubby! Break's over."

I place a quick kiss on my fingertips and pat my belly

twice.

"Hɪ!" I PRACTICALLY throw myself onto Tyler when I see him standing at the registration desk. He returns the embrace with one arm. "What are you doing here?"

"I missed you."

I smile and kiss his lips before realization hits me.

"What's wrong with your arm?"

From behind his back, he reveals a small bouquet of hand-picked lilacs.

"For you," he says with a smile.

I exhale, nearly melting on the spot... as do the other triage nurses.

Bringing the flowers to my nose, I close my eyes and breathe in, enjoying the scent of the purple flowers. It reminds me of early evenings sitting outside by the lilac bush, tangled up in Tyler's arms as we make plans for our future.

Our future.

My eyes flutter open and I notice the white gauze around his bicep.

"What happened?"

Reaching out gently, my fingers graze his arm.

He shrugs.

"I got some new ink. Just a little something."

Based on the size of the bandage, it appears to be much

larger than 'just a little something.'

"What is it?" I ask, taking him by the hand and leading him down a quiet hall to an empty room, away from prying eyes.

"Words."

"I bet I can guess." I laugh as his lips meet mine. "How many words?"

"Three."

"I know!"

I raise my index finger to accommodate the word "I."

A second goes up. "Love."

Then a third. "Karrie."

A delicious grin stretches across his face.

"Not quite…although those three words are absolutely true."

"Let me try again."

He nods slowly as he smashes his mouth against mine, sliding his tongue in to silence me. My body kicks into overdrive as my hormones awaken. My nipples tighten and my core contracts. My need for this man has been insatiable these last few weeks. If I could lock him away in our bedroom, I would.

"Karrie Ann Miller?" I ask, mumbling against his lips.

He chuckles and again shakes his head.

I love the twinkle in his eyes when he says "no."

"I'll show you when you get home."

I huff playfully then add, "I have an appointment at eleven."

Nodding, he says he knows and he'll meet me there.

"Go get some sleep. I'm going to need you to have lots of energy and stamina later."

"Pfft! I can keep up. Trust me!"

I link my arm with his and walk him to the sliding doors.

"I'll see you in a few hours."

Tyler leans down to kiss me before bending at the waist. His hands cup my belly as he places a soft kiss followed by two light taps.

My fingers run through the short hair at the back of his head and the close shave tickles my palm.

"I love you both so much." He presses his chest against mine on his rise to his full height. His breath rises and he whispers in my ear.

I watch him stride to his truck parked in the lower lot.

My hand finds its spot over my heart, knowing he's taken it with him.

The sound of someone whistling makes me turn around. I roll my eyes when I see Odessa mocking me.

"Girl, you've got it bad!"

"Shut up!" I say, breezing past her.

"I was going to knock on the door and interrupt you."

"We were talking."

She pinches her lips and rolls her eyes. "Is that what you call it now?"

"Ummm…have you seen that man?"

"I know. He's hot! I told you that a long time ago," she counters with a smirk.

I suppress a smile, remembering how much I hated him. I had to give him one thing…he was always nice to look at.

"TAKE THIS SLIP down the hall. They'll send the results back here. You should be there for about an hour or so."

"Thanks." I fold the white paper in half and walk through the door as Tyler follows closely behind.

"What's wrong? Are you feeling okay?"

I chew on my bottom lip and cast my eyes on his. He knows I'm withholding something.

"Tell me."

"I had a dream about *him* again."

His attempt to keep his countenance unaffected fails when I see his eyes tighten.

"It was different this time. He kept showing up everywhere I went, saying that no matter where I go, he'll be there. He said we'll always be connected somehow."

Tyler reaches for my face, his rough hands cupping my jaw. His eyes are full of promise.

"He's gone. He can never hurt you again. He has no hold on you. I won't let him."

I wrap my arms around his waist and rest my cheek against his chest. I can feel his heart pounding erratically.

I'm still amazed that I held his heart in my hands.

"I must've eaten something a little too acidic last night," I joke, making light of the situation for his sake. "I'm fine. I know it was just a dream."

"Or maybe I need to pay more attention to you," he counters, raising an eyebrow suggestively.

"Oh, you pay me plenty of attention!"

He kisses my lips softly.

"Seriously, stop worrying about it."

I nod and slide through the open door, thanking him along the way.

After sitting for ten minutes, my name is called and I proceed to drink the glucose solution to check for gestational diabetes.

I gag and dry heave.

"God this is disgusting!"

"It can't be that bad."

Tyler receives a terrible side eye.

"Believe me, it's bad." I take a small sip, forcing myself to swallow.

"As bad as the first time you tried—"

I nearly spit the orange liquid on the floor.

"Ty!"

"What?"

I glance around to see who might be listening.

"I can't believe you were going to say what you were going to say!"

He grins. "I was going to say…the first time you tried a hot dog with mustard and relish."

I narrow my eyes and smirk. "Yeah, that's totally what you were going to say!"

He laughs and pulls out his phone, responding to his mom's text.

"And for the record, ketchup is much better on hot dogs!"

# TWENTY-THREE

"PLEASE BE CAREFUL," I WHISPER in Tyler's ear before he secures his race helmet and pulls up to the pre-staging area, revving the engine as he goes.

Everyone and their mother is in attendance for this race. It's the semi-finals and Tyler's opponent is proving to be quite the competitor.

I move away from the crowd and lean against the fence with my hands steepled around my nose as I pray for his safely *and* block out the fumes from the motorcycles' exhausts. I know our son will spend endless hours here, but I'm going to protect him from all these pollutants and chemicals while he's still in me.

"Why are you so nervous? Afraid he's going to lose?"

I ignore Penny's snide questions and keep my eyes focused on the man clad in black leather.

"He's not as good as Alex was. Not on the race track and certainly not in bed."

I force myself to remain calm, keeping my thoughts on the innocent little boy in my womb.

White smoke fills the air as Tyler heats up the rear tire. Gabe does a final check and gives his approval, sending Tyler up to the line.

The sound of his engine revs loudly indicating the growling bear is back, angrier than ever. One by one, starting from the top, the descending lights illuminate until they flash one solid color and Tyler launches like a bat out of hell. Flying down the straight track at an unbelievable speed, he becomes a tiny speck by the time he reaches the finish line with his opponent hot on his trail.

"Ladies and gentleman, Tyler Strong has done it again!" The announcement bellows through the speaker.

I release the breath I was holding and cheer along with the rest of the crowd.

"Don't jump around too much. You don't want to hurt that kid. Is it even Tyler's? I know mine is."

My heart sinks momentarily before my head snaps in her direction. Gone is the calm woman when the protective mother in me emerges and I verbally attack her.

"Go fuck yourself. You're nothing but trailer park trash! Tyler would never touch you! He thinks you're disgusting!"

She stands there with a scornful grin on her face, accepting my bombardment.

"Whoa! Look at you! Who knew you could be so…" she

looks up, appearing to search her stupid brain for a word, "feisty? Clearly, your husband didn't. Why do you think he came looking for me?"

I drag my eyes up and down her swollen belly. "Because you're a nasty whore who spreads her legs for any man. And to think I actually felt sorry for you once."

"Don't pity me. I gave Alex what you couldn't."

"Didn't!" I clarify. "I didn't give him kids by my own choice, not that I need to explain that to you!"

"Karrie!" Tyler rushes to my side then moves in front of me, blocking my path to her. "What's going on?"

My breathing becomes labored and deep as I force myself to calm down.

"I tried to keep quiet, but I lost my shit when she said she was having your baby."

He spins on his heels, pinning Penny with a reproachful glare. "You're a pathetic liar! Why the fuck would you say that?"

She returns the glare but says nothing in response.

"Find your kid and go home."

Turning back to me, Tyler pulls me into a hug.

"I'm sorry. I don't know why she gets like that with you."

It feels as though steam is shooting from my ears as I spit, "She's mean and vindictive and if I weren't pregnant, I'd kick her scrawny little ass!"

His hands wrap around me, calming and soothing me. His hushed words relax me. "Think about our boy."

Feeling guilty for losing my cool, I nod in agreement and

apologize for my outburst.

When he's assured of my calm state, he asks, "Did you see me win?"

"I did! It was amazing. I think you're amazing!"

"Don't let her or anyone else distract you from watching me race," he teases.

I smash my lips against his, kissing him quickly.

"You know I wouldn't miss it for the world!"

As we walk back to the trailer, a young boy comes up and asks Tyler for an autograph. He holds out a black permanent marker and a napkin from the concession stand.

"What's your name, buddy?"

"Chathe," the little boy replies with a lisp because he's missing two front teeth.

"How old are you?"

"Thix."

"Well, Chase. Today's your lucky day."

Tyler reaches up and pulls off his ball cap with his new team logo, signs the brim and sets it on the boy's head. It falls and covers his brown eyes and freckled face.

Chase removes the hat and looks at it with wide eyes.

"Are you Thuperman?"

Tyler and I laugh at the question and he raises his eyebrow proving me wrong that people wouldn't understand the "S" logo.

"He's kind of like Superman but even better," I say.

With his eyes wide and filled with excitement, Chase looks at Tyler's script, but then grimaces.

Tyler squats to his level and points to the hashtag before reading, "Tyler Strong. Stronger than ever."

"Cool!"

Chase runs off without another word.

I smile and squeeze Tyler's bicep where the same three words are etched with thick black ink.

*"Are you sure you can take the bandage off?"*

*"I'm sure," Tyler pulled at the white gauze and revealed his new tattoo.*

*I read the words over and over.*

*"STRONGER THAN EVER."*

*Wiping the tears from my eyes, I looked at him, understanding the meaning.*

*His words confirmed my thoughts.*

*"Karrie, with you by my side, I can do anything because I'm… stronger than ever."*

A kiss lands on top of my head, effectively snapping me out of my reverie.

I look up.

"You are going to be an absolutely amazing father. Our little boy is going to be so lucky!"

Thankfully, the rest of the day goes off without incident and we decide to drive home rather than stay in a hotel. While Tyler drives, I try to read, but end up falling asleep.

Arriving home late that night, Tyler finds yet another flash drive on the kitchen table from my mother along with a note asking me to look over her newest designs.

"Why doesn't she email these?"

I toss him an exasperated look, after having had this conversation a million times.

"She's a nut. She has something against email. I think she watched that movie *Snowden*."

"She could use Google Drive."

"She thinks," I air quote, "the *government* is watching."

"Don't take this the wrong way. I love your mom, but she is a little weird sometimes."

BETWEEN MY MOM, Pam, Odessa and the other girls from work, I don't know who's more excited about the baby shower.

I sit in the oversized chair and enjoy my day as the guest of honor. The girls went overboard with boy-themed decorations, including baseballs and motorcycles in honor of Tyler.

"Have you decided on names?"

I nod but keep my lips sealed, tossing Odessa a peculiar look.

"We're thinking we'd like to go with a family name."

"Oh, good!" she squeals with excitement.

"Not *your* family's name!"

Her excitement deflates with a huff.

"You're not going to tell us, are you?" Pam asks.

I shake my head adamantly.

"Nope!"

Baby Strong is constantly moving, keeping me up half the night and during the day after I work.

"Why don't you stay home for a while?" Tyler asks as I step out of the shower.

"Stay home? Like an early maternity leave?"

I wrap the oversized towel around my body, my belly protrudes through the soft cotton. After running a comb through my wet hair, I look at myself in the mirror and notice how red my face is and how tired I look.

"I'm exhausted and I look awful," I sigh as Tyler moves in behind me, wrapping his arms around me, resting his chin on my shoulder.

"You look beautiful."

His loving eyes hold mine in the mirror.

My arm reaches back and rub the nape of his neck as he lines my jawline with tender kisses. The tenderness transforms into heated passion when his hands sneak into the opening of my towel.

Right there, standing against the bathroom vanity, Tyler brings me to utter and complete bliss until my legs weaken and buckle. Strong arms carry me to our bed where I cuddle with his hard body and fall into a sated sleep.

Unfortunately, our little boy has other plans and wakes me up hours before the sun rises. Since I'm up early, I fire up my laptop, deciding to look at my mother's newest designs.

Her business is increasing weekly; her creativity is well-appreciated by consumers.

I insert the flash drive and open the files, perusing each one, admiring some while critiquing my mother's original work. She certainly has an eye for design. I'm thankful she accepted my request to design the nursery.

Shuffling into the kitchen, I put on a pot of coffee and drop two slices of bread into the toaster. The ringing of Tyler's alarm and the sound of the shower tells me that it's almost seven.

I pour two cups of coffee, carry them upstairs before I cuddle on his side of the bed. Reaching over, I pick up his phone when it rings. The only people who call this early are the general contractors on the job site or one of the guys, usually Michael, to say he's going to be late.

"Hello?"

No response.

"Hello?" I sing song playfully.

"Where's Tyler?"

I sit up and jump to my feet as Tyler steps out of the bathroom with a towel wrapped low around his waist. I bite my lip at the sight of him as the woman on the phone asks again where he is. My hand flies to my abdomen as a searing pain shoots through me.

"Who's that?" he asks, running his fingers through his wet hair.

I hold the phone out and he takes it, greeting the person with a quick hello before his face contorts to one of confusion. "There's no one there."

Hissing through the pain, I sit and massage the underside of my belly.

"Who called?"

I hold my index finger up, silently indicating that he should wait as I breathe slowly.

Tyler drops down, squatting before me, giving me his full attention.

His eyes roam over me.

"Baby, what hurts?"

I exhale slowly, grateful the pain has subsided.

"I think I just got up too fast."

"Baby, you've got to take it easy."

I nod, agreeing and then ask why Penny is calling him.

"Penny?"

My patience is wearing thin at his feigned surprise. My face transforms into a stern look.

"I know it's her. Why is she calling you?" I don't hide the accusation in my question.

"I don't know why." The quick darting away of his eyes fuels my suspicion.

"Tyler, what aren't you telling me?" I ask slowly, fearful of his response.

He pinches his lips and reaches for his phone, dialing a number quickly then tapping the speaker button.

Voicemail after voicemail, Penny's messages range from pleas to demands that he return her call. We both flinch when she tearfully mentions Alex's name.

"I don't answer her calls and I certainly don't call her back."

"Why is she still in our lives?"

"I honestly have no idea. Roger had the money transferred into her account. She has no reason to contact me."

My expression softens momentarily before something occurs to me.

"Why...why does she even have your number?"

Tyler drops his phone on the bed and returns to his low position before me. I can see the guilt clear as day etched on his face.

"He gave it to her a long time ago. In case she needed him when he was—"

"With me."

Moisture pools in my eyes.

"I was such a fool."

Tyler cups my jaw, forcing me to look at him.

"No, baby. It wasn't your fault. He was a selfish, egotistical man. He didn't deserve you."

Pressing my fingers into my tear ducts, I block the flow of tears. I promised myself I would never cry about Alex Parker ever again.

"I'm so sorry I was a part of that. I'm sorry I let him hurt you."

I wrap my hands around Tyler's neck as he rests his cheek on my belly.

"I'm stronger now. I know who I am. I know what I

want."

Circles of bluish-green look up at me.

"I want you. I want our baby. I want our life together."

"Do you want me to change my number so she can't call me anymore?"

"No." *Yes.* "She's not important."

His phone chirps and we both look at it before he reads the text message.

"Mike's running late."

He rises and walks to the tall chest of drawers then drops his towel. Peeking over his shoulder, he catches me staring at his backside.

"Why do you love torturing me?"

He pulls his jeans on and slips on a T-shirt before sauntering over to me for a kiss.

"Now you know how *I* feel." He grins playfully. "Are you still meeting me for lunch?"

I nod eagerly.

My eyes fall heavy even before the diesel truck pulls out of the driveway.

A sweet little boy stars in my dreams. He looks just like his daddy with the same shade of brown hair and those beautiful eyes. Running through the open grassy field, he looks happy and healthy and completely care-free.

"Not too far honey," I call as he continues in the distance. Panic grips me; my adrenaline on high alert when I can no longer see him.

"Baby? Come back!" I call as my feet drag through now

thick mud.

A figure emerges in the shadows and calls to my son.

"No, baby. Come here!"

The tall man bends down and picks up my son, cradling him close.

"Don't touch him! Put him down!" My voice shrieks with unbelievable fear.

Sprinting as if my life depended on it, I close the gap between the stranger and me.

Through a red haze, I see the man looking at my son with curiosity in his eyes.

"Is he ours, Karrie? Is this my son?" The familiar voice asks softly.

I shake my head fiercely and reach for my boy.

"No, Alex," I whimper, "He's not your son."

As if shielding my son, Alex turns and places his hand on the child's face and trails his fingers down over his shoulder until he comes to stop at his chest. He taps twice.

"Hello, little boy. I'm Alex. I'm your dad."

"No!" I cry out. "You're nothing to him."

Alex's eyes glaze over as he looks at me. "I'll always be a part of your life, Karrie. We'll always be connected."

My son is gently set on his feet and urged to step into my waiting arms. I lock my son in my arms and protect him with all that I have as my eyes remain fixed on my deceased husband.

He reaches out again and caresses my child's face before smiling at me.

345 | L.M. CARR

"We will always be connected. I will always be a part of your life. You need me. You'll always need me." The threatening words repeat until Alex fades back into the shadows.

I startle awake. A thick coating of sweat blankets my forehead and my neck. I reach for my chest, my palm spreading across my heart to keep it from pounding out of my body. I am filled with absolute and sheer terror.

"Fuck you, Alex!" I scream repeatedly until my voice becomes hoarse and scratchy. "I don't need you. You're dead! You're nothing to me!"

# TWENTY-FOUR

With the final race of the season just days away, Tyler spends every spare second tweaking and perfecting his motorcycle. Air shifter. Nitrous bottle. Tire pressure. He leaves nothing to chance as this is one opportunity to prove he's the best grudge drag racer in the country.

Each night, he fires up the laptop and reviews videos, statistics and times of his previous races and those of his opponent.

He wants to win. He wants to be the best of the best.

"So other than that one time, you haven't experienced other symptoms?" my doctor asks after completing an exam.

"No." I shake my head. "Just that once."

"I think she was getting sick. That's the day you cancelled lunch, isn't it?"

I swallow, feeling agitated. "Yeah, I had a headache or something."

After a series of questions, my doctor is convinced that I'm fine. Our baby is showing signs of perfect health and growth. I just wish he'd let me sleep at night.

"Do you think I'll be fine to travel down south for the weekend?" I ask, knowing despite what the doctor recommends, I'll be right beside Tyler.

"You should be fine. Stay hydrated. It's pretty hot down there."

"Have you stepped outside this morning? This heat and humidity is killing me! Look at my feet!"

Tyler suppresses a smile at my cankles then shakes the doctor's hand, thanking her before she steps out of the room.

"Guess you're going to be wearing flipflops to our wedding."

I sigh in exasperation.

"We should've waited until after I had this baby to get married. I don't know why I thought this was a good idea."

"Because you said you couldn't wait to marry me!" He leans in for a kiss, tickling my lips with his.

I smirk. "I think it was the other way around, mister."

He nods slowly, eyeing me with desire. "You're right. I have waited a long time for you."

With our September wedding around the corner, the

venue has been paid for and secured. The seaside restaurant patio is the perfect setting for us to exchange our vows. Only those closest to us, important people who have been there from the start of *us*, will be in attendance.

Tyler and I don't need to put on a show for anyone.

LITTLE MAN CONTINUES to keep me awake at night; only the sound of Tyler's voice settles him.

Exhaustion from sleep deprivation is clear with each passing day. My mother insists on taking me for a pregnancy massage. I grab my bag and waddle outside when I hear her car pull into the driveway. If I sit, I won't be able to get up again. If I blink too long, I'll fall asleep.

"Oh, Karrie! You look so tired."

After struggling with my seatbelt, I break down into a fit of tears. I'm a hot mess.

My mother wraps her arms around and encourages me to release the emotion.

"What's wrong? Are you having second thoughts?" She eyes me knowingly.

I shake my head and wipe my eyes.

"No. Not at all. I'm a thousand percent sure about Tyler. It's just…look at me! I'm fat and swollen and he hasn't touched me all week."

My mother chuckles.

"He's a typical man! You know he's probably afraid to

hurt the baby, but let me tell you something…no man is *that* big!'

Laughter erupts and fills the air.

"You have such a way with words, Mom!"

"What else is bothering you?" she asks using a tone laced with her motherly concern.

After an internal battle with my insecurity, I confess the truth.

"This woman Penny has been calling him." I quickly defend him. "But he never takes her call."

"Who is she?" My mom asks as we pull out onto the street and drive on the main road.

Clearing my throat, I inhale sharply. "Alex's lover."

My body thrusts forward when my mother slams her foot down on the brake.

"Alex was having an affair?" Her eyes grow wide and wild with shock.

I cast my eyes down to my belly and nod solemnly. "He wasn't very faithful to me or our marriage."

"That son of a bitch! It's no secret that I never liked him, but I never suspected infidelity."

"He changed so much throughout our marriage. He wasn't the same man when he died that night." I stare out the window in remembrance as sadness overwhelms me.

"Did…did he ever… hit you?"

My heart cracks and my eyes fill with pent up anger and pain.

"Karrie?"

My eyes meet hers. Wordlessly I confirm her worst nightmare.

Devastation drags her mouth down into a hard frown. Her head shakes in disbelief and her chin quivers violently as her grip on the steering wheel tightens.

"Don't tell your father."

I swallow the lump in my throat. "I won't. I never planned on telling you either."

"That bastard!"

We pull into the parking lot of the day spa; the two of us agitated and upset.

"This is the last thing I will say about Alex Parker," my mother hisses vehemently, slamming her index finger into the ignition button and turning off the car's engine. "The only good thing that came from knowing him was meeting Tyler." Her voice cracks before she clears her throat. "That man is crazy about you. I know he would never hurt you, Karrie."

I nod in agreement, adding "I know. He's a really good man."

For the next ninety minutes, I forget about my former life, suppressing any lingering thoughts as I lose myself in an incredible pampering from head to toe. I return home later that afternoon calm, cool and collected. Every muscle has been worked, the tension in my back now gone, my mind restored fully on my upcoming nuptials in less than a month.

My mother has enjoyed herself immensely planning the big day after not having had much of a say the first time around. The wedding planner I was essentially *told* to hire had ideas of her own. With Alex footing the bill for the huge and spectacular occasion, she aimed to please him not me.

"What are you thinking about?" Tyler asks, coming behind me and kissing my neck.

I stare at the newest round of creative logos designed by my mom, my hand resting on the mouse.

Craning my neck to the side, I close my eyes and enjoy the deluge of affection.

"Our wedding," I mumble, relishing the feel of his lips on me. "Thank you for letting our moms have such a big part in it."

"It's not like we've done this before," he whispers in my ear and then freezes, realizing his error.

"We've not done this *together*. None of this." My hand drops and caresses my big round belly. His chin rests on my shoulder as his hands cover mine.

I turn to face him and run my palm over his two-day old scruff.

"I can't wait to meet him." His excitement is shaded with a hint of apprehension.

"Me, too." I smile.

"I remember when Tre was a baby. I wanted nothing more than to protect him since my brother wasn't there to do it. It's insane how much I love this little man and I haven't even seen him yet."

"Are you going to cut the cord?"

"Absolutely! I wouldn't miss it for the world!"

"Good!" I seal my word with a kiss.

AGAIN, I AWAKEN IN the wee hours of the morning, but this time it's a sharp stabbing sensation in my lower abdomen that forces me up. I howl in pain and inadvertently wake Tyler.

With wide, panicked eyes, Tyler inquires about my state, kneeling quickly before me.

"Shit!" I hiss, blowing out a slow breath. My face contorts as my eyes scrunch into tight slits.

"Karrie! What can I do?"

"Get me to the bathroom. I think I peed on myself."

Tyler hops off the bed and tosses the comforter back. Shrieking in horror, he tells me there's blood everywhere.

Dread immobilizes me. Doom threatens me.

"Call my mother."

Seconds later my mother advises me to go directly to the emergency room and promises to meet us there.

"Ty, I'm scared," I cry as I scramble to get unsoiled clothes on.

"Don't be scared, baby. We're okay. He's okay."

I want to believe him, but distress steals his confidence and assurance.

All the way to the hospital, I cry quietly and pray for my baby boy.

Thankful for my mother's forethought to call her friends

in the department, I'm rushed into a waiting room as Dr. Stephens comes in followed by Lisa, one of the other nurses I normally work with.

"Hi, Karrie. What's the matter? You couldn't stay away from us?" He smiles, trying to ease the tension radiating from me.

I smile weakly at Dr. Stephens and confess, "I'm really scared."

"I know you are, but we're going to do everything we can for you and this little one of yours."

While my mother steps out of the room, Tyler remains by my side during my exam.

"Placenta previa."

"Placenta what?" Tyler ask with great concern.

Dr. Stephens provides a detailed explanation of the complication which affects women in their last trimester.

I nod. "Okay. So now that we know what it is, what can we do about it?"

"You'll need to be on bedrest for a few days. No intercourse. No traveling."

I glance at Tyler.

"What about the baby? Is he going to be okay?"

"We're going to start you on steroids to make sure his lungs mature normally."

"That's it?"

"Rest. I can't stress that enough. Think of it as an early vacation before the sleepless nights."

Dr. Stephens accepts Tyler's extended hand of thanks

and shakes it firmly.

"Good and strong. I'm glad to see you're doing so well, young man."

Captivated, I watch as the two men share a silent private moment.

Before I arrive back at home, my mother has cleaned the blood stain and changed the sheets. I finally settle in and fall asleep in Tyler's arm.

I dream of the open grassy field once again.

"ABSOLUTELY NOT! YOU are not going to miss the finals! Are you out of your mind?"

The argument is now going on ten minutes with my insistence that he continues to race while I stay home and rest. Although I hate to miss it, I need to follow the doctor's orders and keep our little boy safe.

"I don't care about the goddamn race! I can't leave you! And besides, it won't mean anything if I win and you're not there."

"Losing your confidence, I see."

"What?" he snaps.

"You said *if* you win not *when* you win."

"I'm not going."

His voice fades as he rounds the corner and leaves the room.

I huff with exasperation, contemplating a plan to get

him to go.

Carrying his laptop, he walks back into the room and props himself up in bed.

"What are you doing?"

"I have a couple of bids to finish," he answers without looking at me which proves he's more upset than he's letting on.

"Do you love me?"

His fingers freeze on the keyboard as his eyes meet mine. "You know I do."

"And you'd do anything for me?"

"You know that, too."

"Then please race. I want you to. It's important that you do."

"But—"

"But nothing. I'll be right here, probably still in bed when you get back."

His eyes light up, shining briefly with happiness, but then the struggle ensues.

"Please…for me."

"I'll come right home. I won't even spend the night!"

"That's crazy! I don't want you driving home that late. I'll be right here. I promise."

His mouth crashes against mine.

"I love you! Do you know that?"

I shrug nonchalantly. "Yeah, you might've said it once or twice."

Suddenly Tyler reaches for his laptop and types

feverishly.

"Here!" He points the screen. "They live stream everything so you can watch."

A smile spreads across my face and my heart races with excitement.

"Just be careful!" I caress his face then slide my hand to my belly, rubbing in small circles.

"Our baby boy needs his daddy."

# TWENTY-FIVE

WADDLING DOWN THE STAIRS, I use a firm grasp and slide my hand along the handrail carefully. After falling asleep quickly, I woke up a few hours later and spent the rest of the night restlessly, thinking about how I am going to miss Tyler's final race of the season.

I click the remote, looking for something to watch on TV but end up dozing until the scent of a freshly showered Tyler wakes me with a kiss. My eyes roam over his black T-shirt with his race team's Superman logo. He looks delicious.

"Why aren't you in our bed?" His fingers slide over my cheek.

I struggle to sit up. He quickly offers a hand as an odd look appears on his face.

"What?" I ask.

"Were you crying?" he asks tenderly.

I shake my head. "No. I don't think so. Why?"

"You have mascara and dried tears on your face."

I touch my face. "I do?" My brain works in overdrive trying to remember what happened last night.

"I had a dream, I think."

The lack of sleep over the past few weeks has apparently caught up to me.

"A dream? About what?"

"I don't really remember. It's all a little fuzzy. I think Penny was in it though."

"Oh man! That would be a nightmare!" He laughs. "Well, you better stay put these next two days. Your mom is coming to stay here."

I reply with a smile. "She's so good to me."

"She's going to talk your ear off about designs, isn't she?"

"Probably. She's already got more designs for me to look at. I don't know why she asks my opinion. I don't have an eye for details and color schemes like she does."

"She values your opinion," he says, licking his lips and moving closer to kiss me. "And you have great taste."

The word "taste" sends a throb to my core and I groan.

"You know what the worst part about having placenta previa is?"

With his mouth against mine, he grins. "I think I know."

"It's killing me!"

"Me, too."

꩜

"Please be careful." My pitiful attempt to mask the worry in my voice fails.

"I'll be fine. You're the one who needs to be careful."

His arms wrap around me firmly, pulling me flush against the flat hard surface of his stomach.

"Um, hello…belly!" I laugh.

He ignores my comment and kisses his way down my neck until he steps back and comes to a stop at my round belly.

"Take care of your mom, little man."

With his palms flat, he taps twice ever so gently.

"I'll call you as soon as I get there."

"Okay," I reply, remembering how differently this conversation used to go with someone else.

After another round of exchanged words of love and affection, I wave goodbye as he maneuvers the truck and trailer into the street.

As if he knows his daddy is leaving, our baby kicks in opposition.

"I know, buddy. I know." I rub my belly. "He'll be back soon."

I step out of the shower, dress in my comfy pajamas and waddle my way downstairs to find my mother lounging on the couch with her laptop open.

"Hi." I lean in for a kiss. "Where's Dad?"

"Out for a ride on his bike."

"Dad's riding a bicycle?" I glance outside, twilight now darkening the sky.

"I told you he got a Harley."

"No, you didn't!"

"I did," she sings.

"You did?" I question skeptically. My pregnancy brain is now also affecting my memory.

"Tyler went with him to pick it out."

"He did?" I ask again, but this time my voice is laced with even more disbelief. "Ty hates Harleys."

"Apparently, your father tried to convince him to get one." She smiles warmly.

"He doesn't think they're fast enough."

Looking at the clock on the mantle, I grab my laptop and settle in next to my mom.

"Did you have a chance to look at the logos?"

"Which ones?" I ask sarcastically. "You've given me a thousand different flash drives over the past few weeks."

"You know how I feel about email."

I roll my eyes as I click on the race track's website to watch the live stream of test and tune.

"Look at that! I see his jacket." My mother shrieks and points to the bold-lettered name of STRONG across his back.

It amazes me how she can be so intelligent yet technologically challenged.

Pass after pass, Tyler flies down the track, testing his

motorcycle's velocity in preparation for tomorrow's big race. Each time he drives past one of the cameras, he lifts his right hand to his heart and taps twice.

*Yes, Tyler. I'm in your heart and you're in mine. Always.*

Late that night, I fall asleep on the phone talking to him.

I wake to several text messages.

Good night, baby.

I miss you.

I love you with all my heart.

Pulling his pillow close to my nose, I inhale his scent slowly. He's been gone for less than a day and I miss him terribly.

My mother has a full breakfast ready for me when I finally make an appearance after breathing through some pretty intense Braxton Hicks contractions.

"How'd you sleep?"

I stretch and yawn. "Good."

My mother knows me almost better than I know myself.

"Karrie?"

"I had contractions again. The last few were pretty painful."

"Why didn't you say something?"

"Because they're Braxton Hicks! I'm fine," I lie.

She eyes me knowingly and releases a huff.

"What time is Ty's race?"

I peer at the time on the microwave and nearly jump to my feet.

"In eight minutes."

"Slow down! You'll hurt yourself!"

My mother chases after me as I hobble to the living room to grab my laptop from the coffee table. I sit down and fire up my device, tapping my finger impatiently as it suddenly decides to restart.

"C'mon. C'mon," I beg, watching the small white dots go around and around in a circle.

"Ma, log in! Hurry."

"I'm trying to save this new design. It'll only take a minute."

Finally, my device loads and Tyler appears on the screen. There may be other things in sight, but I only see him.

"Oh God! This one is full. Can I borrow one of the thousands I've given you over the past few weeks?"

"Yeah, they're in the spare room."

The adrenaline running through my body makes me feel slightly dizzy as the announcer bellows through the speaker, exciting the crowd for the final event in the Nitrous turbo class.

"Ladies and gentleman, before we begin our final race of the day. We'd like to dedicate this race to Alex Parker and ask for a moment of silence."

The crowd settles and men remove their hats. It finally registers how many people are there. The stands are packed with people all interested in the sport.

"Rest in peace, brother. Rest in peace."

The camera focuses on Tyler as he makes his way through the throng of people.

"This race today is only for the best of the best."

Gabe leans in and talks to Tyler. He nods and closes his visor.

"Can Tyler Strong prove he's the best once and for all or will the rookie from Maryland steal his thunder?"

Tyler heats the rear tire, creating a wall of white until he surges forward, pulling up to the pre-staging line. I see Gabe make some final adjustments and then pat Tyler's back firmly.

His right hand, clad in black leather, rises to his chest and taps twice. I wipe my eyes quickly, not wanting to miss a single second.

When the racer next to him does the same, it's go time.

My mom sits beside me and from my peripheral vision, I see her wave something in her hand.

"Found this one. Can I use it?"

I peek over quickly. "Yeah, whatever." I chomp down on my bottom lip as my nerves take center stage.

"Are you s—"

"Yes!" I hiss then quickly offer an apology for my harsh tone.

My eyes are glued to the screen.

"Oh, why won't it go in?"

"What's the matter?"

"It won't go in."

I huff. "Why aren't you watching?"

"I can't. It makes me too nervous. I've seen more than my fair share of mangled bodies during medical school, thank you very much."

"Mom! He's not going to get mangled!"

"I'm just saying—"

"Please stop talking. I *need* to watch this!"

The camera scans the length of the quarter mile track before zooming in on Tyler whose eyes are focused on the lights. There's a determination and an intensity that I've never seen before. A second camera captures the two men from another angle.

Both are ready.

Tyler's feet planted securely, his body low against the machine while the racer beside him taps his foot, a telltale sign of nerves. His gloved hand grips the throttle in anticipation.

Tyler is frozen like a statue, completely immobile until the light changes color; his reaction time is one of the best. He opens the throttle, the engine screeching obnoxiously as if it were a wild caged animal. He lowers his torso, hovering over the gas tank. He is a warrior ready for battle.

Seconds later, the lights illuminate amber then immediately flash to green.

Like a bullet, Tyler surges forward, distancing himself quickly from his opponent on the left. My hands quickly cover my nose, my fingers pressing into the bridge of my nose as I watch the man I love race down the narrow stretch of pavement at two hundred miles an hour. The seconds feel like an eternity. The image of him shrinks in size the closer he gets to crossing the finish line.

The arrow on his side of the track flashes white, indicating his victory.

"He won! Ma, he won! Omigod, he won!"

Tyler shoots his arm up into the air, a single finger pointing to the bright blue sky.

Happy tears pour from my eyes as I celebrate his accomplishment.

Tyler Strong is the best of the best.

I throw my arms around my mother's body, but I'm met with resistance. Loosening my grip, I pull back and look at her.

"Ma, what's wrong?"

Her countenance is ghostly white, her eyes wide with horror, her voice muted silent.

Panic sets in.

"Mom, what's going on?" I ask, tapping her cheek lightly. She appears to be shell-shocked by what she's just witnessed. "He's fine! He won!"

"Oh, Karrie. I'm so sorry."

I follow her eyes down to her laptop.

"What is that?" I squint through my tears and blink rapidly to clear the fuzziness.

A blond woman is bent over a motorcycle as a man drives into her from behind. Although his face is shielded by the angle, I can see his large rough hands yank on her hair, claiming her violently before striking her head. Those same hands, like venomous snakes, slither around to her neck, constricting to restrict her airway.

He hisses in her ear. "Is this what you want? You think you can flirt with that motherfucker and get away with it? You are mine."

I know that voice.

My tears of joy quickly turn sour.

"Please," she whimpers, gasping for air.

His face, one I once considered handsome, contorts as he climaxes.

The trailer door opens and Tyler appears; his expression hard and shocked at the situation in front of him.

"Yo, what the hell? What are you doing?"

My heart thunders in my chest when Alex pushes the woman to the floor, mumbling about what a whore she is. I see the rage in his eyes now.

I've seen it firsthand.

I've experienced it.

After pulling up his pants, he strides over to confront Tyler, jabbing his finger close to Tyler's face.

"Mind your fucking business, Strong. Take this piece of shit out of here with you."

Tyler helps the battered woman up and carefully ushers her through the door.

"You're sick, man! You need help!"

"Fuck you, Strong! I'm Alex Parker. You'd be nothing without me."

Tyler's eyes narrow as he clenches his jaw. Hate is smeared across his face.

Alex turns to look at the camera and smiles deviously,

his eyes are that of a stranger.

"I'm Alex Parker. Nobody fucks with me."

"Karrie..."

It vaguely registers that my mother is speaking to me.

My eyes are transfixed on the screen as yet another clip detailing my ex-husband's infidelities begins. With every one after that, the face that smiles at the camera is eerie, that of a madman. The eyes that once looked at me with love are filled with animosity and rage.

My mother's hand moves to click the X, shielding me from further hurt and humiliation.

A conversation ensues between Alex and Tyler.

"What about your wife?"

"What about her?"

"She's not stupid. She's going to find out and when she does she's going to leave."

"That spoiled bitch isn't going anywhere. She's mine, too."

Tyler shakes his head solemnly and mumbles, "If I had a girl like that, I would nev—"

He's interrupted by Penny.

"Hi Ty," she smiles before asking Alex if he's ready.

Left alone in the trailer, he finishes his statement. "I would never do her wrong."

As if passing a horrible car wreck, I continue to watch.

Tyler appears, dressed in his dark leathers, his helmet goes airborne across the trailer, barely missing a bike.

He yells a string of profanities as he paces back and

forth before a woman's soft southern drawl calls his name. Turning quickly to face the petite blonde, he steps and closes the space between their bodies. Penny wraps her arms around his neck and kisses him hard as she claws away at his pants. The lower half of both their bodies are exposed as he lifts her up and wedges himself between her legs. My mind conjures up the memory of watching a similar scene at The Black Horse the night I went out with Pam.

Tyler lied to me. He swore he never touched her. He lied.

The realization makes my stomach revolt as rancid bile rises into my mouth. I struggle to stand, suddenly needing to purge the food in me.

My mother drops the laptop and jumps to her feet to help me up.

The room spins and I feel faint.

I hear my phone ring with Tyler's tone.

"Ma, I don't fe—"

I remember nothing after my legs give out and my head smashes into the coffee table.

# TWENTY-SIX

THE FEELING OF WEIGHTLESSNESS from being lifted and secured onto a gurney causes my eyes to flutter open in a panic. I glance around at the inside of the ambulance until I hear the door slam shut and one EMT climbs in next to me.

"How are you feeling, ma'am?"

I reach for my pounding head and yelp in pain when my fingers connect with the huge welt.

"What happened? I ask.

"Seems you fainted and hit your head."

"I did?"

The recollection of watching Tyler win the race and then seeing the video of him having sex with Penny hits me like a ton of bricks.

"Tyler," I whisper. "Why would you lie to me?"

"Is that your husband?"

I shake my head slowly and bite back the tears from pooling in my eyes.

After answering a series of questions and being poked and prodded, we arrive at the hospital and are quickly ushered in.

My mother walks alongside the gurney and assures me that I'm going to be okay.

"Where's my phone?"

"I have it. It's in my purse." Her eyes constrict momentarily.

"What's that look for?"

"He's calling relentlessly."

An ache pierces my heart.

"Did you talk to him?"

"No. I figure he's just calling to tell you about the race. It can wait."

Odessa storms into the room and proceeds to lecture me about not taking care of myself as the nurse hooks me up to a stress monitor to make sure our baby is fine.

"I told you to stop eating all those sweets! That's probably what toppled you over, you fat cow!"

I roar in laughter despite her words of insult.

"Just give me some ice and send me home."

The nurse asks to speak privately, whispering and eyeing the machine.

Again, the dizziness returns and my fingers tingle.

"Odes—"

"Roll her onto her left side."

I immediately know what's happening.

My baby's heart rate is dropping rapidly, a sign of distress; his life is in imminent danger.

I see my mother's eyes widen and fill with moisture from worry and fear.

"Mom?"

I need her to say the words. I need her to say my son will be alright.

"Karrie, we need to get him out now. Prep the OR!"

I hate the gravity in Odessa's voice.

"Please save my boy," I cry. "Please save my boy."

"Ma, call Tyler."

I'm not ready for this.

I'm not prepared to give birth.

Tyler isn't here.

This isn't how we planned on bringing our little boy into the world.

WITH TEARS STREAMING down my face, a beautiful baby boy is placed in my waiting arms. The tightness in my lips gives way to a small smile as I try to suppress a full-blown sob when I look at the phone in my mother's hand as she records the momentous occasion.

"He's here, Ty! He's really here."

Broken words emerge as I attempt to lift and show Tyler

his child, a tiny baby with a head full of dark hair and round chubby cheeks. I slide my nose against his soft skin before I kiss his lips, his eyes, and his head repeatedly, trying to convince myself that he's really in my arms.

"Ty, he's beautiful!" I cry.

"Congratulations, Karrie!" Odessa says from behind the sheet covering my lower half.

My mother uses the back of her hand to caress the baby's head before she comments about his coloring. Now that I *really* look at him, I notice the bluish-tinted pallor.

"Odessa? Come here."

"I'm a little busy at the moment," she jokes, but I don't laugh.

"I'm serious. He's turning blue. Something's wrong!"

In a flash, Odessa is at my side and in the next moment, she's ripping my boy away from me.

My world is collapsing before my very eyes.

Somewhere in the chaos, my phone rings with the tone set for Tyler. My mother answers it, handing it to me as she speaks. "Oh God! Hold on, Tyler. Here she is."

The phone rubs against my cheek, hitting the speaker button, when it's shoved up to my ear.

"Tyler," my mother barks.

"Ty," I cry into the phone. "Something's wrong. Something's wrong. He's turning blue."

"What?" he yells helplessly, his voice booming through the phone.

"I can't lose him."

"Baby, I'm so sorry! I can't believe I'm not there with you. He's going to be okay." His anxious voice fills the room.

Shaking my head from side to side, I deny his words.

I know something is wrong.

"Please come home."

There's a hesitation in his response. "Baby, I'm leaving right now. I'll be there as soon as I can."

In his haste, he neglects to end the call. I hear him speak to someone, saying something about how she's going to be okay. Then I hear a woman's soft voice thank him.

I call his name repeatedly but get no response.

Seconds later I hear his truck start and the line goes dead.

My mother and I share a look of bewilderment and disbelief.

"Stay focused on your son, Karrie. Just focus on him."

I nod and clutch the phone to my chest before dropping the phone onto the bed.

*Focus on him.*

"Karrie," Odessa explains when she comes back, "we're going to run a few tests. His Apgar numbers were low."

"He's going to be okay, right?"

Compassion beams from her eyes when she utters, "I hope so."

I slam my palms against my face and wail powerlessly as my mother comforts me.

ODESSA ORDERS THE nurse to start morphine through my IV and although it assists with the pain of my incision, it does little for my heart.

"Where is he?"

"He's in the NICU."

My chin quivers. "He's all alone. He must be scared."

My mother swipes a soft hand across my forehead.

"He's in the best hands. They're taking good care of him."

"I have the best hands for him! He's my baby!" I struggle to get up, but my body simply refuses to cooperate.

"You need to rest. You can see him in a few more hours."

"Hours?"

Darkness pulls me under once again.

"KARRIE, TYLER'S ON the phone. Do you want to talk to him?"

I drag my attention from the pin hole in the hall, the same spot I've been staring at for the last forty-five minutes.

I nod and turn my palm upward.

"Hi," I mumble. "Are you almost here?"

"I'm about another hour away," he replies, his voice raspy and deep.

"How is he?"

I cry, "He's in intensive care."

"Oh God!" The slamming of his fist against the steering wheel and the truck accelerating display his deep fear and anxiety.

"What's taking so long? I thought you were going to leave right after the race."

He sighs into the phone. "I was, but then…"

"What? What happened?"

"Something happened to Penny and she needed my help."

The image of them having sex flashes before my eyes.

"Penny?! What?" I sob, my ears burning from his words of betrayal. "Why? Why are you with her?"

"I couldn't just leave her there on the side of the road."

"I need you. Your son needs you!"

"Baby, I'm sorry. I'm going as fast as I can to get there."

I imagine her naked against him. I imagine them laughing at me, ridiculing my stupidity. I imagine them playing house with her children.

A rush of air escapes.

"You're no different than he was." I shake my head as a sardonic chuckle filled with anger emerges. "You're just like Alex."

"What? Don't say that! You know I'm nothing like that bastard!"

"I hate you!"

Infidelity and deceit puncture then shred my heart.

"Baby, listen to me! She was drunk. Her daughter was in the car."

"I don't care! I don't care about her or her daughter!"

"Apparently, the kid took a pretty hard spill at the track."

"I don't care! You know what, Tyler...stay there! Stay with her! I can take care of my son on my own." I hurl seething words in his direction.

"Our son! He's *our* son!"

My chest heaves as I continue to wail.

My mother grabs the phone and ends the call, silencing Tyler's pleas.

Thirty minutes later, my father arrives and paces the floor after having seen the baby in the NICU.

"You need your boy and your boy needs you."

Two minutes later, a nurse strolls in with a wheelchair.

"Are you ready to go see your son?"

"Thank you," I mouth to my dad.

"Any answers yet?"

"No, we're still waiting for the test results."

Carefully and very slowly, I am situated in the narrow seat and brought to see my child.

I am given the standard attire to wear and my hands disinfected ten times over.

Encased in a small clear plastic incubator, my sweet boy sleeps. He looks so peaceful. I reach my hand through the small opening and touch his tiny fingers, causing him to stir momentarily.

"Hi, buddy. It's me, your mom—"

I break into a fit of uncontrollable tears, but I never

break the connection of our fingers. I will never let him go. I won't do it.

When the tears subside, I stare at him and admire his perfection. His little body is bare except for the tiny diaper and the blue cap which covers his head. He looks like a poster child for a beautiful, healthy newborn, but he's not.

My mother taps on the window and waves her phone at me.

I shake my head. I don't want to talk to Tyler right now.

After my brief visit, I return to bed, fatigued, broken-hearted and dizzy.

There's a brief knock on the door. A team of medical students follows in behind Dr. Baldoni, a pediatric cardiologist. Although a handsome man, his expression is serious and grave.

"Mrs. Miller," he greets me.

"Ms., but please call me Karrie."

With that, Dr. Baldoni delves into an incredibly detailed explanation of my son's severe congenital heart condition. My heart shatters at the grim prognosis.

My phone rings and my father takes the call. I glance over at him and notice his hard expression.

"I'll tell her."

I pull my eyes away from my father and address the doctor.

"How soon do I need to decide?"

"By tomorrow morning at the very latest. We'll need to get him on the list as soon as possible."

I nod my understanding as emotion overwhelms me and steals my voice.

Closing my eyes, I ask God what I've done to deserve this. What has my son done to deserve this?

I hear my mother sniffle.

"You're a doctor. Make him better, Ma. You've always made things better," I beg as I reach for her hand.

A tear slips from her eye.

"I wish I could."

My father steps in and looks on over my mom's shoulder.

"You did good, Kare Bear. He's going to be just fine."

I want to believe my father's words, but I can't.

LESS THAN AN hour later, Tyler bursts through the door and rushes to my side, taking my face in his hands, kissing me softly. His tanned face now pale and his eyes red-rimmed and swollen.

"I'm so sorry, baby. Please forgive me for not being here."

My lips remain still, unaffected by his apology.

"Where is he? Where's our boy?" He looks around the vacant room before turning wide, horror-filled eyes back to me.

I ignore him completely.

"Where is he?" He enunciates slowly, fearfully.

The soft spot in my heart speaks for me.

"They're running more tests, but—"

"But what?" he asks as his hands encase his head and his chest puffs from a deep and loud gasp.

"But he's still in the NICU. It doesn't look good, Ty."

"What does that mean?"

"His heart...he needs a new heart."

"What?" he shrieks. "Why?"

I feel nothing in my heart except his betrayal.

"If you had been here instead of with your girlfriend, you would've heard the doctor's explanation."

Tyler looks utterly confused as he steps closer.

"What are you talking about?"

"You and Penny."

He narrows his eyes.

"What about her? You think I'm cheating on you because I drove her to the hospital? Her kid was hurt. What did you expect me to do?"

"I asked if were ever involved with her and you lied. You told me you never touched her."

"And I didn't!"

I reach out to strike his face, but he grabs my wrist, keeping a firm hold on it.

Our faces are inches apart.

"Don't fucking lie to me." My chin quivers, but I remain steadfast.

"I never touched her. I never kissed her and I certainly never fucked her."

"I saw the video, Tyler. I saw what you two did in the trailer. Granted, it was before we were even together, but you still lied to me."

"Video? What video?"

"The one in Alex's race trailer," I sneer.

I can see the moment of comprehension as his face falls.

"Karrie," he sighs sympathetically. "Baby, you were never supposed to see that. Any of it."

I turn hard eyes on him.

"Well I did. And you know what I think? I think you're no different than he was."

His face morphs as if he is in physical pain.

"Do not compare me to that animal. I am nothing like him. I never was and I never will be."

"Save it for someone who cares."

"You care! You fucking care and you love me!" He grabs my face and smashes his mouth against mine, kissing me hard.

"Stop!" I shove him away. "You lied to me!"

"I didn't lie to you. The girl in the video…that wasn't Penny. It was her sister, Rachel. They're identical twins."

"Twins?" I cry in disbelief.

"Yes. I messed with her that one time and that was only because I lost a race and…"

"And what?"

"I was so angry."

"Why?" A niggling feeling in the pit of my stomach tells me there's more to the story.

"Alex had just told me he was going to leave you."

Overwhelmed by what I'm hearing, I feel like a lost little

child, helpless and vulnerable.

"I don't know why I did it. I just did."

I see regret spread across his face.

Tyler drags the hospital chair over and sits in it. He drops his head onto my covered legs as his hands wrap around my feet.

"I'm sorry for hurting you."

Slowly I lift my hand, my fingers itching to run through his hair.

He continues. "I'm sorry I wasn't here for you. I'm so sorry I missed the birth of our baby. I'm sorry I wasn't holding your hand when you talked to the doctor. I'm so sorry for it all."

The damn breaks open, allowing the deluge of emotion to pour out of me.

"He has a congenital heart defect."

Glancing up at me, a torrent of tears drips from his eyes. He quickly shields his face, burying it into the palms of his hands and his body shudders with quiet, painful sobs. He murmurs, rubbing his chest.

"He can't die. He can't. I'll give him my heart so that he can live."

My own heart is ready to explode, the ache completely unbearable.

"Come here." I tug at his T-shirt and guide him into my arms, carefully avoiding my C-section.

He comes willingly.

Tyler and I cry in each other's arms, vowing to do

whatever we need to do to save our newborn son's life.

"This is crazy," he says, touching our foreheads together. "I haven't even seen him yet and I love him so much."

"He's beautiful and he looks just like you."

His phone chirps with a text alert and I see Penny's name on the screen. Anger and hurt whisper in my ear, telling me to shove him away, but love and trust tell me to hold on. I inhale slowly as he reads the message. He types back quickly and slides the phone back into his pocket.

I glance at him, expecting an answer.

"There's no change."

My expression falls and I sigh heavily.

"I want to see him. I need to see him."

Before I can even say another word, Tyler is out the door.

I stare at the crucifix on the far wall, again asking the question, "Why?"

Bowing my head, I pray the unthinkable, the unimaginable, the most selfish thing I could ever pray for.

When Tyler comes back into the room, his eyes are once again watery and red.

"Did you touch him?"

Shaking his head quickly from side to side, he replies, "I didn't go in. I'm all dirty and sweaty."

I appreciate the thoughtfulness to our son's safety.

"Help me get in the wheelchair. We need to see our boy."

Back in the NICU, the nurse encourages my son's father to wash his hands and slide on proper attire so he can hold the baby.

Tyler sits in the chair and our child is placed gently in his arms. The nurse offers assistance and suggests he support the infant's neck.

He smiles and says, "I know how to hold a baby. I have a nephew."

The nurse returns the smile and proceeds to check on other babies.

My eyes remain fixated on the interaction of Tyler and his son. Genuine love and affection pour out of him as he whispers sweet nothings.

"He doesn't have a name yet."

Tyler's eyes roam over the sweet face of our little boy before he reaches for his phone.

"What are you doing? Hold him with two hands!" I demand.

"He's fine. I've got him. I'd never let anything happen to him."

My anxiety speeds in my veins as he continues to use his phone.

I reach for the baby. "Give him to me. Finish your text and then you can have him back." Even as I beg for the baby, Tyler does not relinquish control of our son.

"I'm not texting. I'm looking for something."

I roll my eyes dramatically and huff angrily.

He looks down at our son thoughtfully; the baby's head fitting perfectly in his father's palm.

"Ethan. His name is Ethan."

"Ethan?"

"It means strong in Hebrew. He's going to need to be strong and brave so he can get through this."

Like father, like son.

"Ethan Tyler Strong," I murmur as a smile creeps onto my face. "It's perfect."

My parents waltz into the room, carrying a large bag of takeout food. My father and mother both give Tyler a stern glance and a frigid greeting.

"It's not what you think," I whisper in my mom's ear when she leans in to kiss me. "We're good. I promise. He feels bad enough. Don't make this worse, please."

She nods and walks over, offering a kinder salutation in the form of a kiss on his cheek followed by, "Congratulations."

Once again, Tyler's phone chirps and I suppress the annoyance when he rises to take the call.

On his way out, my dad grabs him by the shoulder and mutters something inaudible. Tyler nods and responds, "Yes, sir. You know I would never hurt her."

Later that night as we weigh our options about the course of action for our son, Tyler caresses my face and speaks softly. I can see he's troubled.

"I have to tell you something about Penny and I need you to just listen before you flip out."

I stiffen.

"Please."

"Her little girl, Alex, is in really bad shape."

I stare at him as a lump in my throat forms. As much as I hate Penny for what she did, I don't hate her child and I certainly wouldn't want to see her hurt.

"What happened?"

"Penny was drunk and high on something—"

"High on something? She can't be on drugs—she's pregnant."

He shakes his head sadly before mumbling, "Not anymore."

My hand slides across my belly where my son was less than twelve hours before.

"She wasn't paying attention to her kid; she was more interested in getting every guy's attention."

I encourage him to go on.

"Alex slipped and fell from the top of the bleachers, landed flat on her back."

"How do you know all this? Did you see it?"

The image of a toddler falling nearly twenty feet onto the hard concrete horrifies me. Why didn't anyone call the waiting ambulance? Why wasn't she rushed to the hospital?

He releases a deep exhale and again shakes his head.

"Rachel told me…at the hospital."

"Rachel from the video," I affirm quietly.

"Baby, that was a long time ago."

My lips tighten and I pull my eyes away from his.

"Penny rushed over and picked her up. She thought Alex was okay, but apparently, she wasn't because when they left the track to drive home, the kid started bleeding from her nose."

"And that's when you stopped."

His pointed stare suggests that I'm correct.

"Why are you telling me all this?"

"Because she's on life support."

My eyes widen and I clutch my chest, gasping, "Oh God!"

"I can't believe I'm even saying this, but if that little girl dies, Ethan might get a new heart."

My face crumbles in pain. The idea that someone else's child must die so that mine can live is unbearable. I can't fathom the pain of losing a child. The shadow of Death slices my heart open and it feels as though my soul has been ripped away.

"I don't know what to say," I cry broken words. "I don't want her to die, but I don't want my son to die either."

Tyler's voice cracks. "I know. It's so hard…but this is my son, *our son*."

My eyes close, needing a moment away from this unbelievable and unbearable reality.

Haunting words whisper in my ear.

"*We will always be connected. I will always be a part of your life. You need me. You'll always need me.*"

Dr. Baldoni is informed of our decision to put Ethan on the list to receive a new heart. Again, he reviews the plan of action, the procedure and now the wait.

Time is not on our side.

Tyler and I spend every moment in the NICU, touching our boy, loving him, talking to him and praying for him. I want to cherish every single second; I don't know how many more I'll have with him.

My mother taps on the window and holds up a small gift bag. Tyler rises to retrieve it and thanks her with a kiss to her cheek.

Reaching into the white bag, he pulls out a blue onesie with an "S" on the chest.

"Superman," he breathes, smiling back at my mom who is wiping away tears.

"Strong," I correct.

After begging the nurse, she relents and agrees to let me put the onesie on our baby boy. Tyler snaps a picture on his phone and sends it to his mom who is traveling home from a visit with Tre in Georgia.

"Oh, Ty, he's beautiful! He looks just like you and your brother," Stacy smiles before wiping her eyes. "I can't believe how much he looks like Tre, too. All you boys looked so much alike."

"It's all in those handsome genes," I suggest.

Tyler grins at my words and leans down to kiss me as I sit in the wheelchair.

"I can't wait for Tre to see him.," Stacy adds. "He said he wants to show him that he can ride his bike now."

"Excuse me," Tyler says, giving me a look as he holds his phone up, getting an update on Alexandra. He kisses me quickly and walks down the hall.

# TWENTY-SEVEN

Nine days later Ethan is airlifted and transferred to Blakely Children's Hospital.

Our prayers have been answered.

A new heart is on the way.

The idea that someone else's child, this particular child, had to die so that mine could live is excruciatingly painful and nearly unbearable.

Waiting for hours while the team of medical experts gives our son new life is gut-wrenching, my heart stammers in my chest and my tears flow ceaselessly. My arms never leave their place around my husband's back as he stares at the images of Tre on his phone.

I have never seen a man in more agony.

The memory of Stacy bursting through the door, screaming that Tre had been hit by a car while riding his bicycle was shockingly horrific. No one would have expected his life to end that moment. No one would have expected he would be the donor we prayed for. No one would have expected he would be a perfect match for his cousin.

It rocked me to my core and caused Tyler's knees to buckle, sending him to the linoleum floor with a hard crash.

His body shuddered when he cried out a single word and buried his face in his palms. I wanted to reach down and gather the millions of pieces of his broken heart.

Those words will forever be etched in my mind.

Tyler didn't speak. He didn't eat. He didn't move. He simply sat in the NICU and stared at Ethan.

It wasn't until he heard Jill's voice on the phone that he come back to me. Back to us.

I held the phone to his ear while he listened. Jill's insistence that Tre's heart be immediately tested as a match was an incredible testament to her faith in God. Everything she believes in was tested and proven strong as ever as she made the decision no parent should ever have to make.

"Thank y—," he whimpered before emotion robbed him of speech.

I sobbed uncontrollably when she told me she had made the decision to donate all her son's organs so he could save other children's lives.

"It's what he would've wanted."

That conversation plays over and over as we continue to wait.

"Mom, it's taking so long," I say as I hiccup. "Something has to be wrong."

"Sweetheart, that baby is in the best hands possible."

I meet Stacy's sad eyes and silently apologize, wishing there had been another way.

Tyler still has not uttered a single word. I know his heart is completely and irrevocably broken.

Through the window, I see the sun descend and the sky darken.

My eyes fall heavily, my body weary and restless.

My father offers a cup of coffee, but I shake my head and decline it.

As we approach the fifth hour, a tall figure appears in the distance and I blink through the haziness.

"Tyler. Karrie."

My husband jumps to his feet and stands before the door.

The pediatric cardiologist sighs and then smiles warmly. "Your little boy did beautifully. Ethan's new heart is beating loud and strong."

Throwing his arms around the doctor's shoulders, Tyler sobs and thanks him profusely. I rise slowly and join Tyler as my hand rubs circles on his back when he refuses to let the

doctor go,

With a clearing of his throat, the doctor says, "The road ahead won't be easy, but I think he's going to be just fine. He seems like a fighter."

"Did you hear that?" Stacy cries, running her hands through Tyler's hair. "Tre's heart is strong. He gave Ethan his strong heart."

SINCE ETHAN IS IN critical condition, I insist that Tyler accompany his mother to Georgia for Tre's memorial service. I, on the other hand, refuse to leave my son's side.

"I'll be back tomorrow night." Tyler kisses me chastely and tells me that he loves me. He reaches up and taps his heart twice.

*I'm right there with you.*

"I'll be right here waiting for you." I smile at him, the man who I once hated and now love beyond measure.

Tyler looks down at his phone before sliding it into his pocket.

"Rachel."

I nod, accepting his explanation.

"Please tell her I'm still praying for Alexandra."

Penny's little girl, the child she conceived with my husband, is making small improvements every day. The Department of Child Services stepped in and temporarily revoked Penny's parental rights, taking over custody of the toddler.

Alex Parker would be mortified for his child.

"Come here," Tyler insists.

The air in my lungs expels as his arms wrap tightly around me joining our bodies—our souls — together as one.

"I don't know if I can do this without you," he pleads as his eyes fill with moisture.

"You can. You can do this." I caress his wet face.

"I don't understand why it had to be this way," he mumbles into my neck.

"I know. I don't understand either."

"How do I say goodbye to him?"

"You don't." I shake my head. "Tell him you'll see him later...just like you always did."

With a quiet, broken voice, he whispers, "You're incredible." He looks down at my wedding ring and lifts my hand to his lips. A slow reverent kiss is placed on each knuckle.

I pull my hand away and gently cup his face. "And you..." I wipe away the tears, "you are *stronger than ever.*"

I STAND OVER THE hard, clear plastic protecting my baby boy from germs and infection and smile at him. Glancing at the heart monitor, I watch the line spike up and drop down, a sign of his healthy heartbeat.

"Hi, baby! You're doing great, buddy. Before you know it, you'll be crawling around and making a mess."

In his sleep, his chubby cheeks pull back in a smile. I wonder what he's dreaming about.

I pull my eyes away from his face and look down to the line on his tiny chest.

"You and Daddy match." My voice cracks, but I try to stay strong.

"You are such a special little boy! Do you know that?" I reach into the hole and touch his long fingers. "You've got racing hands, don't you?"

Overcome with the realization of how much my life has changed, I swallow the boulder in my throat. I thank God for His precious gifts.

"I love you and your daddy so much. You boys make my life complete. And now," I smile, "I am stronger than ever."

# EPILOGUE

*Five years later...*

"**H**APPY BIRTHDAY, SUPERMAN!"

Ethan roars with laughter, shooting his arms out in front of him while I support him with one hand under his chest and the other beneath his straightened legs.

"I can fly, Dad! I can fly!"

Joy fills my heart at my firstborn's words.

"That's right, buddy. You can do anything!"

The happiness on Ethan's face grows every day as he becomes an energetic little boy and less of a toddler.

It's been five years since he was born. Five years since my nephew's life was taken and my son spared. Five years since Tre's heart was donated and now beats hard and strong in Ethan's chest.

"Put me down, Dad."

I set my boy down on the freshly mowed grass and follow him as he runs over to the tire swing that hangs from the large oak tree in the middle of our backyard. He pokes his head through the opening and pushes off with his feet, calling for me to push him faster.

He looks so much like Tre. One might think they were siblings instead of cousins.

"Go faster, Daddy. I wanna go fast like you do."

The late summer heat beats down on us and the warm breeze offers no relief.

"Who's coming to my party?"

The question is *who isn't*.

"Everybody."

"Who's everybody?"

I go through the list of all the people my wife invited who will be in attendance for his special day.

"Mommy's got the list. There might be a special surprise, too."

As if she heard me mention her name, Karrie calls us in.

"C'mon, buddy. Time to get ready!"

I prop Ethan on my shoulders and run in circles as we make our way up the stairs onto the back porch where the two women I love most in the world stand.

I kiss my mother's cheek as she takes Ethan from me.

"Hello, beautiful." I turn to my wife whose face is sun-kissed by long days at the track.

She looks gorgeous in a short pink sundress, her round

belly protruding through the thin material.

"I'm not beautiful. I'm hugely pregnant and I have cankles."

"Don't make me do it right here," I warn with a raised brow.

She slaps my shoulder playfully. "You better not! We have company."

Worshipping my wife's body, including her cankles, is my all-time favorite pastime; I love it more than racing and I don't care who's around to see how much I love her. This woman is my life.

I take her face in my hands and kiss her gently before slipping my tongue into her mouth. She reacts immediately and clutches the back of my T-shirt as if she needs more.

I'd give this woman everything she wants and more.

The moment of tenderness turns into one of passion as we stand on the porch and practically claw at each other. I pull my lips from hers and slide down her neck until I whisper, "We have company."

"Tyler Strong, what am I going to do with you?" she growls with exasperation.

I waggle my eyebrows suggestively.

"That," she points at my face, "that is why we have three kids running around and a fourth on the way!"

"You love me." I slide back into her arms and lift her off her feet.

"Forever," she adds.

My mother-in-law steps through the sliding door.

"Is Dad going to the airport, or are you?" she asks, addressing me.

I set Karrie down and tell her that I'll go.

I kiss my wife once again then offer one to her mother.

"I'll be back in an hour."

JILL STANDS ON the pavement just outside of the arrival sign. Her hair is piled high on her head as she fans herself with a folded magazine.

I hop out of Karrie's SUV and greet her with a hug and kiss.

"Where's Jack?"

"Hi! He's getting the luggage."

"How are you feeling?" I eye the swell of her belly which looks like she's hiding a basketball underneath her shirt.

"Great! But I think I'd die from this humidity if I lived here."

I stiffen at her choice of words.

Either she doesn't notice or she ignores it.

Once the luggage is stowed in the trunk and Jack wedged in between two car seats, I pull out and hit the highway, eager to return to my family.

"Ethan's going to be really excited that you're here."

"We haven't missed a birthday yet!" Jill announces proudly.

I must admit the first year was the hardest.

Celebrating the year of the boy who lived while commemorating the life of the one who passed wasn't easy for any of us, but Jill, through her faith, told us to believe in God's plan.

Keeping Tre's memory alive is a top priority.

Every morning and each night, we remember to thank Tre for his incredible gift of life.

"How's Karrie feeling? She's getting close to her due date, isn't she?"

I nod, remembering the birth of the twins. Our kids have a thing for terrible timing, always wanting to make an appearance when I'm away racing.

Thankfully I was only two hours away. I made it back in time to be with her and see our boys, Thomas and Benjamin, come into the world.

When we arrive back home, my father-in-law helps Jack with the luggage.

"Hey, Ben!" I slap him heartily on the back. "Good to see you, man. Long time no see."

"Watch it, Strong! My wife is still talking about buying the house across the street so we don't have to drive over here every day."

I smile at him as we walk up the stairs. He knows they are welcome anytime and they are the best babysitters.

Ethan's Superman-themed birthday party is a huge hit with his friends from school, his grandparents and his favorite "Auntie Jill."

My brother's son will never be forgotten; Tre's memory

and his heart will forever live on in my son.

BY THE TIME our guests have left and we settle into bed that night, Karrie is exhausted and her feet swollen. The hot shower we enjoy leaves her cheeks flushed pink and her body wanting more. Her every wish is still my command even after all these years. There isn't anything I wouldn't do for her. I'd give her the world if I could.

I roll onto my side, admiring her.

"What are you thinking about?" I ask, smoothing her wet hair away from her face.

"You." She turns and looks at me, tears fill the corner of her eyes. "Our kids."

"What about us?"

A fat tear falls.

"Don't cry." I pull her close, wrapping my arms around her shoulder as she palms my bare chest.

"I just can't believe how far we've come. That first day I met you… well, the day you handed me my textbook," she laughs lightly, "who knew this would be our life."

Because her words are like kryptonite, weakening me, disabling me from forming a response, I press my lips onto her forehead instead. The pain we've endured and overcome will never be erased. Each and every trial woven into the fabric of who we are and have strengthened us over the years.

"I love you." Her thumb traces the faint scar on my chest

until she reaches the tattoo with my nephew's name. "You and the boys are everything to me."

"Don't forget about the daughter who's on the way."

"Poor girl won't have a chance with three older brothers, her dad *and* a grandpa."

"Can you imagine what her wedding is going to be like?"

"Hey!" I slap her backside lightly. "She's not even born yet and you have her getting married already! No one will ever be good enough for my little girl."

"Are you going to follow her on her first date?"

"Hell yeah! It might be from a distance, but I'll be there."

We settle into a quiet lull.

"Do you ever regret not having a real wedding?"

She pierces me with hard eyes which quickly soften.

"I've told you a million times before and I'll tell you a million times again. It was perfect." She snuggles into my neck. "Absolutely perfect."

I pinch my lips and roll my eyes in exasperation.

"Getting married at the hospital by the same priest who moments before had read our son his last rites wasn't exactly picture perfect."

"It was to me. Tyler, it didn't matter where I married you…because I was marrying *you*. That's all I cared about."

I nod thoughtfully, trying to suppress the rise of emotion.

"Do you remember what you said to me?"

"I do."

I had been in such a haze of devastation; I couldn't believe that my nephew had just been killed. I was so angry yet grateful. I felt so guilty.

Karrie squeezes me and breathes into my neck.

My hands spread across her back, my fingers tugging gently at her hair, forcing her to look up at me as I ask, "How'd I get so lucky to get you?"

"Your creepy stalking skills finally paid off."

I tickle her ribs and tease her playfully.

"What?"

"You always said you watched me from a distance."

"I did," I admit unashamedly. I didn't know how, but I always knew Karrie would be mine.

A noise coming from beneath her pillow forces my hand to retrieve it.

"What's this?"

"A birthday card for Ethan."

My face wrinkles in confusion. "Why didn't you give it to him?"

"It's from Alexandra."

I pull the card from the envelope and read it, my eyes sliding across the childish handwriting.

"She's a good kid. I'm glad she's with Rachel now."

"Me, too." Karrie smiles sadly. "At least her scholarship can't be touched now."

After Alexandra's accident, Penny realized she couldn't take care of her daughter and gave up all parental rights to her sister.

"Does it bother you that Rachel wanted to keep in touch?"

My wife shrugs her shoulders and looks away.

"What's that look for?" I ask quietly.

"Alexandra looks so much like Alex did."

I nod, confirming her observation as my body stiffens. I hate the mention of that bastard.

"Stop. Don't do that." She smooths a hand over my face. "Let it go. I did...a long time ago."

"I'll never forgive him for what he did to you."

"He led me to you."

I search her eyes and detect a deep love.

"I would have found you anyway."

She presses her lips against mine, mouthing the word "Arrogant."

"Confident," I reply.

"You ALWAYS WEAR a helmet, got it?" I offer a firm word as I stand before my son.

"Ok, Dad. I will."

He tosses his leg over the seat of his dirt bike.

"Remember...clutch, throttle, kill switch."

He repeats my words as he touches each one.

"Any problems, you pull the clutch."

"Will I go fast like you? I wanna fly down the track like Superman."

I smile at my boy before I reach down to his chest. Beneath my fingertips, I feel his heart beating hard and fast as adrenaline kicks in. I tap twice.

"You'll be even better than Superman."

Ethan eyes the logo on my T-shirt.

"But you're like Superman!"

I shake my head and follow his eyes to the dirt path.

Leaning down, I whisper in his ear.

"No, buddy. I'm just a man...a man who is stronger than ever."

THE END

39414612R00241

Made in the USA
Middletown, DE
14 January 2017